SHATTERED TRUTH

Off The Grid: FBI Series #15

BARBARA FREETHY

Fog City Publishing

PRAISE FOR BARBARA FREETHY

"Barbara Freethy's first book PERILOUS TRUST in her OFF THE GRID series is an emotional, action packed, crime drama that keeps you on the edge of your seat...I'm exhausted after reading this but in a good way. 5 Stars!" — *Booklovers Anonymous*

"A fabulous, page-turning combination of romance and intrigue. Fans of Nora Roberts and Elizabeth Lowell will love this book." — *NYT Bestselling Author Kristin Hannah on Golden Lies*

"PERILOUS TRUST is a non-stop thriller that seamlessly melds jaw-dropping suspense with sizzling romance. Readers will be breathless in anticipation as this fast-paced and enthralling love story goes in unforeseeable directions." — *USA Today HEA Blog*

"Powerful and absorbing...sheer hold-your-breath suspense." — *NYT Bestselling Author Karen Robards on Don't Say A Word*

"I loved this story from start to finish. Right from the start of PERILOUS TRUST, the tension sets in. Goodness, my heart was starting to beat a little fast by the end of the prologue! I found myself staying up late finishing this book, and that is something I don't normally do." — *My Book Filled Life Blog*

"Freethy hits the ground running as she kicks off another winning romantic suspense series...Freethy is at her prime with a superb combo of engaging characters and gripping plot." — *Publishers' Weekly on Silent Run*

PRAISE FOR BARBARA FREETHY

"Grab a drink, find a comfortable reading nook, and get immersed in this fast paced, realistic, romantic thriller! 5 STARS!" *Perrin – Goodreads on Elusive Promise*

"Words cannot explain how phenomenal this book was. The characters are so believable and relatable. The twists and turns keep you on the edge of your seat and flying through the pages. This is one book you should be desperate to read." *Caroline - Goodreads on Ruthless Cross*

"Barbara Freethy is a master storyteller with a gift for spinning tales about ordinary people in extraordinary situations and drawing readers into their lives." — *Romance Reviews Today*

"Freethy (Silent Fall) has a gift for creating complex, appealing characters and emotionally involving, often suspenseful, sometimes magical stories." — *Library Journal on Suddenly One Summer*

Freethy hits the ground running as she kicks off another winning romantic suspense series...Freethy is at her prime with a superb combo of engaging characters and gripping plot." — *Publishers' Weekly on Silent Run*

"If you love nail-biting suspense and heartbreaking emotion, Silent Run belongs on the top of your to-be-bought list. I could not turn the pages fast enough." — *NYT Bestselling Author Mariah Stewart*

ALSO BY BARBARA FREETHY

OFF THE GRID: FBI SERIES

PERILOUS TRUST

RECKLESS WHISPER

DESPERATE PLAY

ELUSIVE PROMISE

DANGEROUS CHOICE

RUTHLESS CROSS

CRITICAL DOUBT

FEARLESS PURSUIT

DARING DECEPTION

RISKY BARGAIN

PERFECT TARGET

FATAL BETRAYAL

DEADLY TRAP

LETHAL GAME

SHATTERED TRUTH

Have you read the Lightning Strikes Series?

Lightning Strikes Trilogy

BEAUTIFUL STORM

LIGHTNING LINGERS

SUMMER RAIN

For a complete list of books, visit Barbara's Website!

SHATTERED TRUTH

He's sworn to uphold the law. She's willing to break every rule to expose the truth. But what they uncover could destroy everything—including each other.

When a whistleblower is murdered just moments before a secret meeting, Haley Kenton is caught on surveillance near the scene —making her the FBI's top suspect in a case that's far more dangerous than it appears.

FBI Special Agent Matt Lawson doesn't know what to make of the journalist. Haley is secretive and clearly hiding something. But as their paths keep colliding and bodies start to fall, Matt realizes she may be the only one who knows where the truth is buried.

Drawn together by escalating danger and undeniable chemistry, Haley and Matt are forced into an uneasy alliance. But trust comes hard when every secret could be lethal—and someone will do anything to keep the past from coming to light.

Romantic suspense at its most powerful—shocking secrets, a relentless pace, and unforgettable emotion from #1 New York Times Bestselling Author Barbara Freethy.

CHAPTER ONE

She'd been here before. Not this park, but another one just like it—a place where shadows gathered between the trees and secrets died in the dark.

A shiver ran down her spine as Haley Kenton parked her Honda Civic in a nearly empty lot at Griffith Park, a large, wide-sweeping park in the middle of Los Angeles. It was after six on a Thursday evening in April, and the sun was sinking lower in the sky. It would be completely dark within the hour. She needed this meeting to be quick.

When she turned off the engine, the silence felt heavy and foreboding. There was one other car in the lot, a small white electric vehicle, probably belonging to the woman who'd contacted her. She would have preferred to talk here, or somewhere with lights and people, but she'd been told by a woman named Sabrina Lin to take the trail into the woods to the old bridge. It definitely felt wrong, maybe a little stupid, but she had no choice, not if she wanted information, and she did.

As she got out of the car, she took a deep breath to calm her nerves, but as she looked at the trailhead disappearing into the thick trees, she felt herself going back six years...

She was twenty-five and standing at the edge of a different

wood, a campus security officer telling her they'd found her younger brother's body in the pond behind the fraternity house. *It looked like an accident,* they'd said. Landon had probably been drunk or high and had stumbled into the pond, completely disoriented. There was no evidence of foul play.

Angry tears pressed at her eyes now, but she couldn't get emotional. She needed to stay in the present; to find out why some stranger had asked her to come here tonight so she could share information about Landon's death. It seemed doubtful that there was anything new to learn. But she'd always chased every lead, every whispered rumor, every false hope, believing someday she would find the truth. Maybe that day would be today.

As a journalist, she was used to people not always wanting to speak in public or to come forward about something they'd seen, so this type of situation was one she had faced before, but never had it been this personal.

Moving toward the trailhead, a gust of wind lifted her dark-brown hair off her neck, sending goosebumps down her arms. She zipped up her bomber jacket, grateful that she'd changed into jeans after leaving her office. It had been an unusually cool day with the temperature only reaching the high sixties, and it was much colder than that now.

As she left the parking area, her stress level increased. She told herself to breathe. Landon needed her to be here. He needed her to fight for him, and she'd always fought for him. She wasn't going to stop now.

The trail curved again, and she caught sight of the wooden bridge ahead. A figure stood at its center—a woman with straight black hair, wearing a gray business suit that looked out of place in the wilderness setting.

Sabrina Lin? It had to be.

Haley's pulse quickened; every instinct, honed by years of chasing dangerous stories, screamed something was wrong. The woman stood too still, like a deer that sensed a predator. She had a phone in her hand and a black bag over her shoulder.

When Haley reached the bridge, she was still twenty feet away from Sabrina, but she could see the tension in her stance, in her expression.

"Sabrina Lin?" she called out.

Sabrina's gaze met hers. Her mouth opened, but it wasn't a word that came out of her mouth; it was a piercing scream, and then she crumpled to the ground.

Haley froze in shock as Sabrina's body jerked violently before suddenly going still again. And she had the terrible feeling that whatever Sabrina had wanted to tell her would never be said.

"No, no, no!" She ran toward Sabrina, her low-heeled boots pounding against the wood. She dropped to her knees beside the fallen woman, her hands hovering over Sabrina's still form, unsure where to touch, how to help.

Sabrina's eyes were open but unseeing, her pupils dilated. A thin trickle of blood ran from a tiny puncture wound on the left side of her neck, so small she almost missed it. But there—embedded in the flesh just below her jawline—was something that looked like a needle or a dart. Avoiding the needle, she pressed two fingers to Sabrina's throat, searching for a pulse she knew she wouldn't find. The woman's skin was still warm, but there was nothing. No breath, no heartbeat, no flicker of life.

A branch snapped somewhere in the trees.

Her head jerked up, adrenaline flooding her system. The woods had fallen completely silent—no birds, no insects. Even the wind seemed to have stopped. *Someone was out there. Someone who had just killed Sabrina Lin with what looked like a poisoned dart. Someone who might be about to take their next shot.*

Without thinking, she grabbed Sabrina's phone from where it had fallen next to her body and jumped to her feet, sprinting down the bridge.

She hit the dirt trail at a dead run, branches whipping at her face as she crashed through the undergrowth. Behind her, she could hear movement—footsteps, or maybe just her imagination transforming the sound of her own panicked breathing into something more sinister.

She didn't stop running until she reached the parking lot, where there were still only two cars, hers and maybe Sabrina's. Her hand shook as she jumped behind the wheel, locked the door, and then fastened her seat belt. She reversed as quickly as she could, the tires of her car spinning on loose gravel. She didn't take a full breath until she reached the main road, until the normalcy of traffic lights and strip malls eased her panic and allowed her to think clearly.

As she came to a stop at a red light, she drew in her first full breath and tried to make sense of what had happened: *Sabrina Lin was dead. Murdered. With something that left barely a mark.* If she hadn't seen it happen, if she hadn't been standing right there when the woman collapsed, it might have looked like a heart attack or stroke. The attack had been professional, skilled, a killing that suggested resources, planning.

Sabrina had wanted to talk to her about her brother. *Had she been killed to silence her?*

It seemed unbelievable. But she couldn't come up with another conclusion. She glanced down at Sabrina's phone lying on the seat next to hers. Maybe there was a clue on her phone. She was about to reach for it when an impatient horn told her that the light had turned green. She drove several more blocks, then pulled into the parking lot of a fast-food restaurant and picked up Sabrina's phone.

A text message was on the screen: *Stop digging. You don't want to lose your job over this, do you? Let it go.* The message was from someone with the initial, *A.*

What had Sabrina been digging into? Her brother's death? But why?

She hadn't had time to look into Sabrina beyond doing a brief internet search to discover that Sabrina was a lawyer with a renowned Los Angeles law firm, Adler and Briggs. Sabrina was a corporate attorney and had been hired by the firm two years earlier.

None of that information tied Sabrina to her brother, but there had to be a connection, and she needed to find it, especially now.

She shuddered as the image of Sabrina's shocked gaze ran through her head. One minute she'd been alive, a young, vibrant woman, and now she was dead.

She needed to call the police, report the murder. She should have done it before she left the park, but she'd needed to get out of there. Picking up her own phone, she hesitated. If she came forward as a witness, she'd be painting a target on her back. If she stayed silent, Sabrina's killer would go free, and whatever she'd died trying to expose would stay buried. She needed to be careful.

Reaching into her bag, she pulled out a prepaid phone she sometimes used on her job when talking to people she didn't want to have her real number.

After connecting to 911, she said, "There's been a death at Griffith Park, the remote trail entrance off Crystal Springs Drive. It's a female. She's on the wooden bridge about a quarter mile up the trail."

"Ma'am, can I get your name and—"

She ended the call, knowing that even if the police traced her number, they wouldn't get to her. And they didn't need to get to her, because she didn't know anything.

That wasn't exactly true. She did know why Sabrina had been in the woods at that location, but she certainly hadn't seen who had shot her with that dart. The police would have to figure that out. In the meantime, she'd do her own investigation into Sabrina and what possible tie she might have had to her brother.

As she drove home, another question nagged at her mind: *Why hadn't the shooter gone after her?* If Sabrina's death was tied to her brother, then why hadn't the murderer shot her, too? She'd been an easy target, not thinking clearly when she'd run toward Sabrina. Maybe the shooter hadn't known who she was. They might have thought she was just a jogger in the park. They might have left as soon as Sabrina hit the ground.

But it bothered her that the unknown killer might know she'd been there. Even if they didn't know who she was, they might still worry that she'd seen something, that she could be a potential witness, a loose end. They could be following her right now.

Maybe the danger wasn't over. It might be just beginning...

———

FBI Special Agent Matt Lawson's phone buzzed as he pulled into the parking garage of his apartment building in Santa Monica Thursday evening. He was surprised to see Flynn MacKenzie's name on the screen. He was scheduled to start work for Flynn's elite FBI unit on Monday, and he hadn't expected to hear from anyone before then. In fact, he'd turned off his phone for the last three days, taking a break from life, because he'd been exhausted after working a futile case for the LA field office's white-collar crime division that had yielded nothing close to the results he'd wanted, and had been preemptively shut down by the new director. That frustration was the reason he'd joined Flynn's team. He'd heard from Jason Colter, one of his former coworkers, that the unit was fast, agile, and worked without layers of bureaucracy.

"Flynn?" he asked.

"Sorry to cut into your time off, Matt, but something has come up. Are you in town?" Flynn's voice carried a familiar edge of controlled urgency that meant his quiet Thursday evening was about to become a long night.

"Just pulled into my parking garage. Why?"

"We've got a body in Griffith Park, and this one's got your name on it. Literally."

He tensed. "What do you mean—*literally*?"

"Victim had your name and number written on a piece of

paper in her pocket. Her name is Sabrina Lin, attorney at Adler and Briggs. You know her?"

Matt's mind raced through recent contacts, cases, and interviews. "No. I've never heard of her."

"We need to figure out why she had your contact information and why she's dead. How long until you can get to the scene?"

Matt checked his GPS. "Twenty-five minutes."

"Make it twenty."

As the call ended, he reversed out of his parking space and exited the garage, his mind turning to the deceased woman who'd had his contact information—Sabrina Lin. He couldn't place the name. Nor could he remember having any dealings with her law firm. It was possible she was tied to one of his cases and he just didn't remember her, but he was still rolling her name around in his head when he arrived at the park.

The crime scene was in a remote area, poorly lit, and swarming with police. Matt badged his way past the perimeter tape and found Flynn standing on a wooden bridge next to a body bag.

Flynn MacKenzie looked like he should be teaching surf lessons in Malibu instead of running one of the FBI's most elite units. He wore jeans and a brown jacket, his blond hair on the longer side, his skin tan, his laid-back stance deceptively casual.

Flynn gave him a nod, then unzipped the bag, revealing the face of Sabrina Lin. She was young, probably early thirties, attractive, wearing business attire, with no visible sign of an injury.

"What do we know?" he asked as Flynn zipped up the bag.

"She's a thirty-year-old attorney with Adler and Briggs. Time of death appears to be around seven. A 911 call came in at 7:15. Police found her at 7:26." Flynn paused, then handed him an evidence bag containing what looked like a small dart or needle, no bigger than a toothpick. "This was embedded in her neck, barely visible. My guess is that she was injected with a lethal dose of something."

Matt studied the dart through the clear plastic. "Someone wanted this to look natural—heart attack, stroke, maybe an overdose, if it left a trace of drugs in her system. Clean, quiet, and designed to avoid the attention we're giving it now."

"Exactly. We'll have to wait for the autopsy and tox screen to get the full results, but this was definitely a homicide."

"Any witnesses? You said there was a 911 call."

Flynn's expression tightened. "That's where it gets interesting. Park security cameras caught a woman running into the parking lot around the estimated time of death. Dark hair, medium build, driving a silver Honda Civic. We've got a partial on the license plate, but she was moving fast."

"Was she fleeing the scene or running for help?"

"Who knows? But she could be our 911 caller. That woman hung up before dispatch could get any information."

Matt nodded, his mind already working through the possibilities. "She could be a witness or the killer. But if she was the killer, why call 911? She could have left Sabrina in the woods. It might have been hours before anyone found her."

"She could have just stumbled across the body, panicked, and ran. Didn't want to get involved," Flynn suggested. "But there's still the question of why Sabrina Lin had your name and phone number on this piece of paper." He held up another plastic bag with his contact information visible.

"That's my office number," he murmured, reading the digits. "Not my cell phone. I've been out of the office the last three days. If she called recently, she wouldn't have reached me."

"Maybe she spoke to someone else."

"I'll find out."

Matt pulled out his phone and dialed his former partner, Agent Shari Drummond. She answered on the second ring.

"Matt? Is something wrong? I thought you were taking a vacation before you started your next assignment."

"I was, but I have a quick question. Do you know if anyone named Sabrina Lin called our office, trying to reach me?"

There was a pause. "Actually, yes. She called this morning. I told her you weren't working in our office anymore and asked if I could help. She said she would only talk to you, that she didn't trust anyone else. What's going on?"

"She was found dead in Griffith Park an hour ago. My name was on a note in her pocket."

Shari blew out a breath. "That's terrible. Who is she?"

"I don't know. Did she say anything else?"

"No, she didn't. Sorry."

"Thanks. I'll talk to you later."

"Good luck."

He turned to Flynn as he slipped his phone into his pocket. "Ms. Lin called my office this morning and was told I no longer worked in that unit. She refused to talk to anyone but me. I need to know what happened to her. Are we taking this case? Or will it go to the LA field office?"

"We'll take it. With your name on the victim, and Ms. Lin's refusal to talk to anyone in your old office, it's better if we handle the investigation. I'll let Director Markham know. LAPD will notify Sabrina's family and her employer. We'll go from there."

"First thing we need to do is locate our possible witness."

"Derek is already in the office, running plate combinations. He's one of our best techs."

"Great. I know I'm not officially on the payroll..."

"Just moved your hire date to today," Flynn said with a smile. "Welcome aboard, Matt. You've got your first case."

"Do you want me to work with anyone else? Do I have a partner?"

"As Jason may have told you, we don't have official partners. Whoever is free teams up. We do every job, big or small. That's how we move fast. We don't worry about hierarchy or credit or who's doing what. Whoever lands a case is the lead, and everyone else is backup. Sometimes you're in charge, sometimes you're watching security cameras. You good with that?"

"Absolutely."

"That said, Jason and Agent Andi Hart just wrapped up a case, so they should have some time to help you, depending on where this investigation goes. They'll be in tomorrow morning."

He nodded. "I'll go to the office now and talk to Derek. Hopefully, we can track down our mysterious witness by then."

"We don't hope, we do," Flynn said with a smile. "See you tomorrow, Matt. Oh, and don't bother to wear a suit. We prefer to operate less obtrusively. We find the suit sometimes puts an unneeded barrier between ourselves and a potential witness."

He was fine with changing things up. What he had been doing had not gotten him the results he wanted.

As he made his way back to his car, his mind raced with questions centering on two women: the one who'd run away, and the one who'd died after trying to reach him. That personal connection made the case more important to him. He'd worked homicides before, but this woman had wanted to talk to him, and he needed to know why.

CHAPTER TWO

Haley didn't sleep all night and after tossing and turning for hours, she got up at six on Friday morning, made herself a pot of coffee, and jumped onto her computer. To find the answers to her questions about Sabrina Lin, she did what she always did: she researched.

Now, three hours later, she was sitting at her small dining room table in her fourth-floor Santa Monica apartment. The dining room table, which doubled as her desk since her one-bedroom apartment wasn't big enough for a real office, over-looked the alley behind the building and the back of another apartment complex. There was no beach view, no palm trees swaying in the ocean breeze, just dumpsters and fire escapes and the occasional stray cat. But the rent was cheap, and it was hers. After a chaotic childhood, having her own space mattered more than the view.

As she sipped her third mug of coffee, her gaze swept the table, where she'd compiled notes and printouts on Sabrina Lin and had dug out the dusty box of files she'd put together after her brother's death. She'd known there had to be a connection between Sabrina and her brother, and she'd finally found one.

Sabrina Lin was thirty years old and originally from San Francisco. She had attended UC Berkeley for undergrad, then West-bridge University Law School, the same school that Landon had attended. Sabrina had graduated from Westbridge Law five years ago, and Landon had died six years ago, which meant she'd been in her final year of law school when Landon died. It seemed unlikely they would have known each other, because Sabrina would have been four years older than Landon and probably not a part of the undergrad fraternity party scene. But it was a link she couldn't ignore.

As her gaze moved to Sabrina's phone, she picked it up once more, still staring at the lock screen and the final message Sabrina had gotten. She'd tried everything she could think of to unlock the phone: common number combinations, birthdates she'd found in her research, even the date of Landon's death. Nothing worked. The phone remained stubbornly locked, keeping its secrets and reminding her she never should have taken it. It had been an impulsive decision, and she didn't really regret it; she just wished she could get into it. She'd made friends with a hacker several years ago while working on a story; maybe she could get him to open it for her.

As three sharp knocks suddenly came at her door, she dropped the phone with a clatter, her head swinging toward the door. It was nine in the morning, and no one ever just stopped by.

The knocking came again, more insistent this time. A stern male voice followed...

"Ms. Kenton? FBI. I need to speak with you."

Her blood turned to ice.

FBI? Why would the FBI want to talk to her? Had they connected her to Sabrina's death?

Her stomach flipped over, and a wave of panicked nausea ran through her.

"Ms. Kenton, I know you're in there," the man continued. "Your car is in the parking garage. I need to ask you a few questions."

She got to her feet and grabbed Sabrina's phone. If he saw it, if he knew she'd taken it from the crime scene, she might never see what evidence might be inside. She took it into the adjacent kitchen and shoved it in a drawer as the impatient FBI agent knocked again.

Then she walked to the door. Through the peephole, she saw a tall, brown-haired, broad-shouldered man wearing black jeans and a dark sports coat over a button-down shirt. His hair was wavy and mussed as if he'd been caught in the wind or had run his fingers through the strands more than a few times.

As he glanced directly at the peephole, she found herself looking into piercing brown eyes that seemed like they could see right through her.

"Ms. Kenton..."

She unlocked the door and opened it a few inches, keeping the chain latch engaged.

"Can I see some identification?" she asked.

He pulled a badge from his pocket. "Special Agent Matt Lawson. I need to talk to you about Sabrina Lin."

She tried to keep her expression neutral. "I'm sorry, who?"

"The woman who died in Griffith Park last night. I believe you were there."

Haley's heart pounded against her ribs. "I don't know what you're talking about."

"Ms. Kenton, we have security camera footage of your car leaving the park around the time of Ms. Lin's death. I believe you also placed a 911 call from a burner phone. We need to talk. Let me in."

She hesitated one more second, but she didn't have a choice. She should have realized there might have been cameras in the parking lot. Unlatching the chain, she opened the door and said, "Come in."

———

Matt stepped into the apartment and immediately noticed the chaos of someone who clearly lived and breathed their work, with files and papers dominating the small dining room table. After his gaze swept the room, he gave Haley Kenton another long look. She was much prettier in person than in her DMV photo, although it didn't appear her wavy brown hair had seen a brush yet. She wore leggings and an oversized long-sleeve T-shirt, her face devoid of makeup. But her features were stunning: wide-set light-blue eyes, upturned nose, and a full mouth. He cleared his throat, annoyed at the unexpected attraction to a woman who might very well be a murderer.

"I'll get straight to the point," he said sharply. "Why were you at Griffith Park last night?"

Haley hesitated a fraction of a second too long. "I go walking there sometimes. To clear my head."

"At seven o'clock at night?"

"I like the quiet. It wasn't dark yet," she said defensively.

"Did you talk to Sabrina Lin?"

She stared back at him, folding her arms across her chest, taking a defensive stance. "No."

He waited for her to explain, but she didn't. "No?"

"No," she repeated. "I've never spoken to Sabrina Lin in my life."

His gaze narrowed. "Look, we can talk here, or I can take you in for official questioning. Why don't you stop stalling and tell me why you were in the park."

She stared back at him, conflict running through her gaze as she debated what she wanted to tell him.

"I'm a journalist," she said finally. "Sabrina asked me to meet her in the park. She had a lead on an old story I was chasing."

"But you just said you didn't talk to her."

"I didn't. I saw her on the bridge. I was about twenty feet away when she suddenly screamed and went down. It seemed like she was convulsing. I ran to her and tried to help, but she was already dead. It happened so fast. I heard someone in the brush, and I panicked and ran. I didn't want to be next."

"Why did you wait fifteen minutes to call 911? Why use a burner phone?"

"I just wanted to get away. I was terrified. And I didn't give my name because I didn't want to be targeted. Sometimes 911 calls and witness names get leaked to the press."

There was some truth to what she was saying, but he didn't think he was getting the whole story. "So, you see Sabrina on the bridge. She screams and collapses. Is that it? Did you hear a gunshot?"

"I didn't. That's the thing. I didn't know what happened to her." She hesitated once more. "When I got to her, there was blood on her neck, and I saw what looked like a needle in the skin under her jaw. I think someone shot it into her neck. She died almost instantly."

"Someone? Or maybe you killed her and ran," he suggested.

Her blue eyes widened in shock. "No way. I couldn't kill anyone. How could you think that?"

"Because you're being cagey. You didn't stay at the scene. You didn't identify yourself to the 911 dispatcher. You didn't call in this morning, having had time to calm down and think about it."

"I told you. I didn't want to be a witness. I didn't want to put a target on my back. I don't know who killed her or why."

"If she called you and asked you to meet her there, then you're connected in some way to her death."

"I—I don't know how. But that thought occurred to me, too," she admitted.

"You said she had a lead on a story. What was the story?"

"It was the death of a student at a university six years ago." Her gaze darted toward the files on her table before coming back to him. "But I never spoke to Sabrina. She left me a voicemail to meet her, but she died before she could explain. I've been trying to figure out what connection she might have to that old case, and I discovered this morning that she attended the same university's law school. Her time there overlapped with the death of the student."

Haley's account corroborated what he knew about Sabrina. He also knew that Haley Kenton was a thirty-one-year-old reporter for the *Los Angeles Sentinel*, where she'd worked the past two years. Before that, she'd worked for media outlets in San Luis Obispo and Santa Barbara.

"I have to get to work," she said. "Are we done?"

"We've barely started, Ms. Kenton."

"I don't have anything else to tell you. I don't know who killed her. Was there any evidence at the scene?"

"Our biggest lead is you."

"Then you have nothing."

He was about to press further when there was a knock at the door. Haley jumped.

"Expecting someone?" he asked.

"No. I never have this many visitors. Excuse me," she said, moving to the door. She checked the peephole. "It's my neighbor." She opened the door to reveal a woman in her late fifties standing in the hallway, her curious dark eyes moving from Haley to him.

"Oh, Haley, I'm sorry. I didn't know you had company." She waited, clearly hoping for an introduction that never came.

"Do you need something, Mrs. Gonzalez?" Haley asked.

"I just wanted to let you know a woman came by yesterday looking for you."

Haley tensed. "What woman?"

"She didn't give me her name. But she had straight black hair, very professional-looking. She knocked on your door around eight in the morning. I ran into her in the hallway, and I told her you had already gone to work. She seemed disappointed. Said she'd hoped to catch you before you left."

Matt watched Haley's face carefully. The description matched Sabrina Lin perfectly, and from the way the color drained from Haley's cheeks, she knew it.

"Did she say what she wanted?" Haley asked, her voice carefully controlled.

"Just that she needed to speak with you about something important. She seemed nervous, kept looking over her shoulder. I offered to take a message, but she said she'd call you instead." The woman's curious gaze moved between Haley and Matt. "Is everything all right?"

"Everything's fine, Mrs. Gonzalez. Thank you for telling me."

"Of course. You let me know if you need anything."

As Haley closed the door, he said, "I need to hear Sabrina's voicemail."

"Okay." She picked up the phone sitting on the table next to her laptop and played him the voicemail: *"Ms. Kenton, you don't know me, but my name is Sabrina Lin. I have information about Landon's death. I can't explain over the phone. Would you meet me?"* Sabrina went on to give directions to the bridge at Griffith Park before ending the call.

"Was that the only time she called? May I see your phone?"

"It's the only time she called me, and I don't think I have to give you my phone."

She didn't have to, but he thought her resistance was another sign she was keeping something secret. He thought about the message he'd just heard. There had been anxiety in Sabrina's voice, a definite sense of urgency. But the way she'd said Landon stuck out to him. As if Haley would instantly know who Landon was.

Haley had said the call was about a college kid who'd died six years ago. She hadn't referenced a personal connection to that case. She'd implied that Sabrina had called her because she was a journalist, but he didn't think that was the case. "Who's Landon?"

"He's the college kid who died."

"Right. But who is Landon to you?"

Before she could answer, a phone began to ring, but it wasn't the phone in her hand, nor was it coming from a second phone that was also on the table. The ringing was coming from the kitchen.

Haley's gaze followed his, but she made no move to answer the phone.

"Don't you want to get that?"

"No. It's an old phone. I use that number for spam calls." The phone stopped ringing, and she let out a breath. "I really have to go to work." She'd barely finished speaking when the phone started ringing again.

He headed into the kitchen. She got to the drawer at the same time as him. "You don't have any right to look in my drawers," she said. "You don't have a search warrant."

He gave her a hard look. "Do you want me to get one? If you didn't kill Sabrina and you don't know who did, then why are you so nervous right now?"

She bit down on her bottom lip.

He reached around her and opened the drawer, pulling out the sleek, expensive phone. There was a text across the screen and several missed calls from a number he recognized because he'd called it earlier that morning. It was the number for Sabrina's employer, Adler and Briggs.

His gaze moved from the screen to Haley. "I think I already know the answer to this question, but I'm going to ask it anyway, and I suggest you think carefully about the fact that it's a crime to lie to a federal agent." He paused. "Is this Sabrina Lin's phone?"

CHAPTER THREE

Haley hesitated for a long minute, then said, "Yes. Sabrina dropped it on the ground when she fell, and I grabbed it. I don't know why, except I thought maybe it would tell me why she wanted to talk to me, what information she had to give me."

"And?"

"I haven't been able to open it."

He glanced at the message on the screen. "Who's A?"

"No idea."

"Sabrina was digging into something that could risk her job," he murmured. "Apparently, that had to do with this college kid's death."

"Maybe or maybe not. I'm sure she worked on more than one case."

"Why would her firm be looking into this student's death? They're a corporate law firm. Unless they represent the university?"

"Adler and Briggs doesn't represent the university, but their owner and at least some of their employees, including Sabrina, went to school there."

"So, there's a tie." He gave her another questioning look. "Who is Landon to you, Ms. Kenton?"

"Why is the FBI investigating Sabrina's death?" she countered. "Shouldn't that be the LAPD?"

"The park is federal land. And you didn't answer my question. Who is Landon? You might as well tell me; it won't take me long to figure it out."

"He's my younger brother. He *was* my younger brother," she corrected, pain tightening her expression. "He was six days short of his twenty-first birthday when he ended up dead in a pond in the woods behind his fraternity house."

"Was it a hazing incident?"

"He'd been a member of the fraternity for over a year, so they denied it was anything like that. There was a party the night before. The police believed my brother got drunk, stumbled into the woods late at night, and tumbled into the pond, too inebriated to get himself out of the water."

"But you don't believe that."

"No. My brother was an intellectual. He lived for school. He was always studying. He didn't waste time getting drunk or going to parties. He told me a few times he wished he'd never gotten into the fraternity, because he didn't have time for the nonsense." She paused. "And you know what I told him? I said it's probably a good way to make valuable contacts."

He could see the self-hatred in her eyes and felt a wave of compassion for her.

"That fraternity got him killed," she continued. "I have never believed it was an accident, but I've never been able to prove it was anything else. I don't know why Sabrina Lin called me out of the blue yesterday, why she wanted to meet me, or what she knew, but I need to find out. I need to open that phone. It might tell me how and why my brother died."

His hand tightened on the phone. "Once we get it open, we'll look into anything related to your brother."

"And you'll tell me?" she asked.

"It depends on what we find. I can't jeopardize a murder

investigation by sharing information with the last person to see Sabrina Lin alive."

"I didn't kill her," she said. "Tell me you believe me."

He stared at her plaintive blue eyes, finding it difficult to believe she had a murderous bone in her body. But he couldn't let a pretty face get in the way of logic and reason. "I haven't made a decision yet."

Disappointment ran through her gaze. "Well, I'm the last person who would want her dead. I wanted to know what she found out about my brother."

"Who would want to make sure that didn't happen?"

"I've always been suspicious of some of Landon's fraternity brothers. They seemed to tell the exact same story, as if it was scripted and rehearsed. But I couldn't find a reason why anyone would have wanted him dead. Landon was a mild-mannered guy. He wasn't opinionated or argumentative. He didn't start fights. His girlfriend told me he was friends with everyone."

"He had a girlfriend?"

"Yes, Brooke Mercer. I didn't actually know about her. Landon always brushed me off when I asked about girls. But Brooke was heartbroken when Landon died. She said they were talking about moving in together after graduation."

"Did Brooke think your brother was killed?"

"No. She thought he might have gotten talked into drinking too much, because it was the week of his twenty-first birthday and everyone wanted to party with him."

"Was she at the party that night?"

"No. She was away that weekend." She drew in a breath. "I'm sure you can pull the files on the investigation from the LAPD if you want to know all the details. You might find out more than I did. I drove everyone there crazy with my questions. They got irritated and stopped talking to me. There was one sympathetic detective, but she never came up with anything, either, and the investigation ended very quickly."

"Maybe it was just an accident," he suggested.

"I've tried to make peace with that idea," she replied. "But when Sabrina reached out yesterday, she reignited my suspicions. Her call—her death—they have to be tied to Landon."

"Possibly," he conceded.

"If you can open her phone, then the person who texted her won't be difficult to find. It was probably a friend, maybe someone she worked with."

"Now you're going to tell me how to do my job?"

"In my experience, sometimes law enforcement needs a little help," she said, a bitter note in her voice. "I was deeply disappointed by the investigation into my brother's death. The police deferred to the university security team. It didn't feel like they wanted to find anything. Westbridge is filled with rich kids with powerful parents, and I always wondered if they were pressured not to come up with anything."

"That might be true, but from my experience, victims' families usually don't feel the police have done enough. That's often based on emotion more than facts. And it's completely understandable when you've lost someone young and healthy in a shocking and unexpected way."

Angry sparks ran through her eyes. "I've heard that comment before. If that's all you have to say, then you should go."

"I'll go, but we're not done talking." He pulled a card from his wallet. "Do you have a pen?"

She handed him one from the kitchen drawer, and he scribbled a number on the back of the card. "This is my personal number," he said, handing her the card. "I know you're going to do your own investigation, because you've clearly already started. I won't waste my breath telling you to stay out of this, but I would ask you to share what you find. I would rather work with you than against you."

"Really? You feel more like an adversary than anything else. I just offered to help, and you shut me down."

"No. You asked questions I couldn't answer, and that will probably continue."

"So, it's a one-way street. I give you information. You give me nothing. Sounds like a bad deal."

"I could make it worse. Let's not forget you stole the victim's phone and ran away from the scene of a crime."

"Are you going to turn me in?" she challenged.

"No, I'm going to hold it over your head," he returned. "If you find out something, you tell me. Otherwise, I will charge you for obstructing a federal investigation."

"Got it." She walked to the door and pointedly opened it.

He moved into the hall, then paused to look back at her. "Whoever killed Sabrina won't hesitate to kill again, Haley. Whatever you do, don't forget that."

———

Haley locked and bolted the door after he left, then walked over to the table and sat down, her legs shaky after her disturbing conversation with Agent Lawson. She was lucky he hadn't arrested her, but that could still change if she didn't cooperate. She didn't have a problem with sharing information, but she preferred that information go both ways, and she wasn't going to wait for him to find answers that he might or might not share with her. She needed to talk to someone she could trust, someone who had wanted to help her six years ago, but back then, her hands had been tied. Maybe now she could do more.

She sent a text to the old number she had, giving her name and asking if they could meet this morning to talk about Landon, that she might have new information. She wasn't sure the number was good anymore as she hadn't talked to former Detective Julia Harper in five years. But she got an answer back several minutes later that Julia would love to see her and could meet her at eleven, if that worked for her.

She set up the meeting at her favorite coffee place, then called her editor at the *Sentinel* to let her know she'd be in around noon. Luckily, she'd just completed a series of articles that had required long hours of work, the last of which would be published tomorrow, so she could take a few hours off without feeling guilty.

After changing her clothes, she headed to Culver City, where her favorite café, Grounds Coffee, was located, three blocks away from her office. She'd just gotten coffees for both of them when Julia Harper arrived.

Julia, a tall, fit, dark-haired fifty-year-old, scanned the café with the eagle-eyed efficiency of someone who'd spent twenty years as a homicide detective before retiring five and a half years ago. Dressed in black slacks and a short-sleeved white sweater, Julia possessed an innate energy and drive that didn't appear to have gone away since she'd left the force and opened her own private investigation firm.

Julia caught her eye, gave her a nod, and sat down across from her.

"I got you a coffee," Haley said. "Strong and black, just the way you used to like it, unless that's changed?"

"It hasn't," Julia said. "It's good to see you, Haley."

"You, too. I wasn't sure you were at the same number. It's been a long time."

"It has. You look tired. Still working night and day in pursuit of truth and justice?"

"Pretty much."

"I've been following your career, and that piece on Congressman Merkle was an amazingly detailed exposé, Haley. The way you laid out the story from start to finish...it was impossible to stop reading. You have a gift for making a story come alive."

"Thanks. I worked on that story for several weeks, and I wasn't sure I would be able to generate enough hard, irrefutable evidence to get the paper to publish, but it finally happened, and Congressman Merkle is going to jail."

"Because of you."

"I just put a spotlight on him and hoped law enforcement would do the rest. Thankfully, they did."

"They should have been the ones to uncover the story, not you, but I don't find local law enforcement to be too bold or innovative, especially when it comes to powerful people," Julia said. "One big reason why I left my job after twenty years of service. I was starting to believe justice wasn't the goal anymore." Julia paused. "What can I do for you? You said you wanted to talk about Landon?"

"Yes. A woman named Sabrina Lin contacted me yesterday, claiming she had information on Landon's death. She set up a meet in Griffith Park at seven o'clock last night."

"That's not a good place for a meet," she said, her gaze narrowing. "Why wouldn't you insist on a more crowded setting?"

"I didn't think she was a danger to me. But it turns out she was a danger to herself. I was about to talk to her when she was shot with some kind of poisoned dart. She died within seconds."

Julia's brow shot up as she set her coffee mug down hard on the table. "She was murdered right in front of you?"

"Pretty much. I was a short distance away. I never got a chance to talk to her, unfortunately, and when I heard someone in the woods, I took off."

Julia's expression didn't change, but her posture shifted almost imperceptibly—the cop in her taking over. "You didn't call it in?"

"Not right away. I just wanted to get out of there. And she was already dead. I called 911 about fifteen minutes later." She took a sip of her coffee, even though this was her fourth cup and she was already over-caffeinated. But she felt like she needed it to keep going.

"What do you know about this woman?"

"She was a lawyer at Adler and Briggs."

"That's a top firm with high-end clients. What's her connection to your brother?"

"She was a student at Westbridge Law School when Landon died, but she was older than him. She wasn't connected to him or the fraternity. At least, I don't think she was. I can't figure out why she'd suddenly have information about his death six years later. But I think someone killed her so she couldn't talk to me. The timing seems too coincidental to be anything else."

"It certainly feels like the two events are connected," Julia said. "I don't recall Sabrina Lin's name coming up in my investigation."

"I was wondering if you could double-check your files and see if you ever made a note about her."

"I'll do that. But I don't think her name is in the file, and, as you know, the investigation didn't go on long."

She nodded, still angered by how quickly the police department had accepted the verdict of accidental death. Although Julia had not been so quick. She had been the one bright, shining light back then, someone who actually seemed to care, but the department had forced her to move on to other cases. "I appreciate anything you can do, Julia. Landon's investigation came to an abrupt end, but if we can find out what Sabrina learned, maybe we can get it reopened."

"I'll see what I can find out about what happened at the park last night. I still have some friends in the LAPD."

"The FBI is investigating, not the LAPD. An agent showed up at my door this morning."

"FBI, huh?" Julia murmured. "What's the agent's name?"

"Matt Lawson. Do you know him?"

"No."

She paused, drawing in a quick breath. "I haven't told you everything. When Sabrina fell to the ground, she dropped her phone. I grabbed it and ran."

"You have her phone?" Julia asked in surprise.

"Not anymore. It started ringing when Agent Lawson was in my apartment. He figured out it was hers. He said he could arrest me for obstruction of justice."

"He could. Why didn't he?"

"I'm not sure. I told him about Landon, how I was sure my brother's death wasn't an accident. I don't know if that touched him in some way, or if he just thinks I might provide a future lead because I'm going to dig into why Sabrina wanted to talk to me. He said he wants to work together, but if I don't cooperate, he can still take me in."

"Then you should cooperate."

"I will, but if you can help me at all, I'd appreciate it. I'm happy to pay for your time."

Julia gave a dismissive wave of her hand. "No need. Your brother's death never sat well with me. If I can help you now, I would love to do that."

"Before yesterday, I'd given up on finding out what happened to Landon, but now there's a whole new trail to follow."

"A dangerous trail," Julia reminded her with a serious expression on her face. "If the killer saw you at the park, you could be in danger, Haley. You need to act like you have no idea what's going on. And you might want to look into hiring security."

"I can't afford that."

"I can probably find someone who won't cost you a fortune," Julia said.

"I can take care of myself. I've been doing it for a long time. I'll be smart."

"Smarter than you were last night when you met a stranger in a deserted park?" Julia asked, with a pointed smile.

"I shouldn't have done that," she admitted. "But I was so curious, so desperate to get information, I took the risk."

"You were lucky. You might not be that lucky again. Your desperation makes you a target. You can't fall for someone else telling you they can help you. You can't trust anyone."

"Except you," she said.

"Right. Except me," Julia said, offering her a brief smile. "I'll make some calls. If I find out anything, I'll let you know."

She let out a breath as Julia got up and walked away, happy to have someone on her side.

Sipping her coffee, she checked her watch. She still had time before she needed to get to work. Picking up her phone, she typed in Sabrina Lin. She'd started researching earlier in the morning, but the more she thought about the text message, the more she wanted to find the person who'd sent that text. She just needed to find someone at Sabrina's job or in her friend circle whose first or last name started with *A*. It wasn't much to go on, but she'd started with less before.

CHAPTER FOUR

Matt arrived at his new office shortly after his meeting with Haley Kenton. After parking in the underground garage of a nondescript building in Santa Monica that no one would suspect housed one of the FBI's most successful special units, he headed upstairs, where Flynn MacKenzie introduced him to a mix of agents, analysts, cyber techs, and support staff, mentioning that there were eight other agents working in the field on various cases or not currently in the office.

Everyone was welcoming and friendly, but also all business, which was fine with him. He had a murder case to solve. He'd spent time last night with Derek Blake, their chief tech. They'd gotten Haley Kenton's name and address but very little else. Now that he had Sabrina's phone, he hoped Derek could get it open and they could pick up a new lead.

It did appear that Sabrina's death could be connected to Landon Kenton, Haley's brother, but he also still wanted to know why Sabrina had called him. He hadn't found any connections between them. But they had to have someone in common, someone who would have given her his name, who would have told her to only trust him.

"Matt, you're here," Jason Colter said with a welcoming

smile. "I heard you started last night. Homicide in the park. Way to hit the ground running."

"It's the only way I know how to hit the ground," he said dryly, happy to see one familiar face. He'd worked with Jason on a case about a year ago, before Jason had left the LA field office to work with Flynn's team. He'd always thought Jason was a smart, insightful, proactive agent who deserved all the accolades he'd been given. He'd also appreciated the fact that Jason had never wanted to trade on his family name to get ahead. He'd wanted to make his own path, away from the illustrious FBI careers of his father and grandfather.

"Have you met Agent Andi Hart?" Jason asked as a dark-eyed brunette sipping coffee joined them.

"We just did," Andi said. "I understand you two know each other from the LA office."

"Matt is one of the best," Jason said.

"I would assume so, since Flynn only hires the best," Andi said with a smile. "Speaking of Flynn, he wants us to meet in the conference room in ten minutes to get up to speed on your case, Matt."

"Great. I need to speak to Derek first. I'll see you in there."

After leaving them, he headed into the tech center, which was filled with the latest and greatest technology equipment that more than matched what was available in the LA Field Office. There were multiple monitors and servers humming, and what appeared to be enough computer power to break into any system.

The man sitting in front of one of those monitors was Derek Blake. In his early thirties, Derek was thin, intense, and with the pale complexion of someone who spent a lot of time in this windowless room.

"I got Sabrina Lin's phone," he said shortly, already having learned that Derek wasn't into casual conversation. "It's locked."

"That won't stop me from opening it." Derek took the phone

from his hand, his fingers moving across the touchscreen. A moment later, he said, "Got it."

"That was fast."

"Really? I thought I was a little slow," Derek said, hooking the phone up to the computer so they could look at Sabrina's texts on the monitor.

As he and Derek read through the thread from the unknown *A*, it became clear that this other person was aware Sabrina was looking into something dangerous and warned her to drop it more than once. Sabrina said she couldn't stop without knowing the truth. Neither one mentioned specifically what they were discussing. But one thing was clear: the person who had texted Sabrina felt like a concerned friend, and he needed to talk to her.

He pulled out the chair next to Derek, reading through the other texts while Derek tracked *A*'s phone number. None of the other threads seemed to have anything to do with Sabrina's work or her death. They were about Pilates classes, someone's bachelorette party, and a few texts from family members, making him feel for the loved ones in her life, who had just gotten the worst notification they could ever imagine.

"The phone number traces to Alanna Morris, an attorney at Hartwell and Associates," Derek said. His fingers flew across the keyboard as he put Alanna's name in their system. "Looks like she graduated from Westbridge Law School, same as our victim."

His pulse jumped. Another Westbridge connection. "I need her contact information."

"Texting you her business and personal address now."

"Thanks," he said. "Are you coming to the conference room?"

"Nope," Derek said. "But I'm here for whatever you need."

"Got it."

When he entered the conference room, Flynn, Jason, and Andi were waiting for him. At Flynn's request, he went over his conversation with Haley and the possible connection between

Sabrina Lin and Landon Kenton's death at Westbridge University. Then he got into Alanna Morris and her text message.

"How can we help?" Jason asked when he was done talking.

"I'd like to head over to Ms. Morris's office now and speak to her in person. I need someone to work with Derek to see what else might be on Sabrina's phone. We also need to dig into her employer, the cases she was working on, and if there's a tie between those cases and Westbridge University."

"I don't know about her cases," Jason said. "But Graham Adler, the senior partner and founder of Adler and Briggs, is a Westbridge University alum, and his son Henry graduated from there a few years ago. My father was friends with Graham, and I belong to the same country club as the Adlers. I'd be happy to go with you when you're ready to meet with them."

"Good. Let's do that after I speak to Alanna. I want to chase her down before she gets spooked and runs, unless that's already happened."

"Text me when you're done," Jason said with a nod. "In the meantime, I'll go through the boxes our team brought back from Sabrina's apartment this morning."

"Perfect."

"I'll look into Landon Kenton's death," Andi offered. "I have a friend at LAPD who might be able to offer more insight than what we can find in their files."

He was more than happy to have a team ready to jump in with little direction. "I'll touch base after I speak to Alanna Morris."

———

Alanna's employer, Hartwell and Associates, was located in a three-story office building in Culver City. The commercial neighborhood was middle-class, with a mix of offices and retail space. Matt parked on the street and was almost at the entrance to Alanna's building when he saw a woman approaching from the opposite direction. They reached the door at the same time and the annoyance he felt was reflected in her blue gaze as their eyes met.

"What are you doing here, Agent Lawson?" she asked, a breathless note in her voice.

"I was going to ask you the same question, Haley." How the hell had she figured out who *A* was without Sabrina's phone?

"I'm following a lead," she said, squaring her shoulders as she gave him a defiant look.

"Is that lead Alanna Morris?"

"Yes. I think she's the woman who sent Sabrina that warning text. She went to Westbridge Law School at the same time as Sabrina, and they've seen each other socially over the past few years."

"How do you know that?"

"Internet research. Social media connections, law school class lists, timeline matching." She shrugged. "It's what I do."

He was impressed, but he was also troubled that she hadn't called him with the information. "I thought you were going to reach out to me if you found anything. That was the deal for not taking you in, remember?"

"I haven't found anything yet. I don't even know for sure if Alanna was the one texting with Sabrina."

"She was."

"You got her phone open," Haley said, a new gleam in her eyes. "What else did you learn? Did Sabrina know how my brother died? Did she say who was involved?"

"No. The text messages between Sabrina and Alanna were cryptic, no details, just concern about getting involved in something they never explicitly talked about."

She gave him a speculative look. "Is that true or just what you're telling me?"

"It's both."

"Then we need to talk to her."

"*I* need to talk to her," he corrected. "You need to let me handle this."

Haley immediately shook her head. "You need me."

"Excuse me?"

"I'm the link, Agent Lawson. I know Westbridge. Alanna and Sabrina went there, and the information Sabrina had for me was about my brother. Alanna will be more willing to talk to me than to you."

"You might be the last person she wants to talk to if your brother got Sabrina killed."

Her lips tightened. "I'm speaking to her. You can't stop me."

He could stop her, but she had made a fair point, and he was more interested in getting information than fighting with her. "Fine. You can come with me, but I'll take the lead."

"Got it, boss," she said with a sarcastic edge to her voice. "You lead; I follow. Do you want me to open the door for you so you can go in first?"

She was definitely more of a smart-ass now than she'd been this morning. He grabbed the handle and opened the door for her. "After you. My grandfather told me to never let a woman open a door for herself if I'm standing right there."

"He sounds like a charming man; nothing at all like you."

He couldn't help but smile. "He would agree with that assessment."

"Is he still alive?" she asked as they walked through an empty lobby to the elevator.

"Sadly, no."

"It's weird," she said as she pushed the button for the elevator.

"What's weird?"

"To hear a man talk about his grandfather teaching him something."

"That's strange?"

"To me it is, but I don't know much about families."

He wanted to ask her what she meant by that cryptic

comment, but the elevator doors were opening, and it was time to focus on work.

Stepping into the lobby of Hartwell and Associates, he gave the older woman sitting at the desk a brief smile. "I'm Special Agent Matt Lawson," he said, showing her his badge. "I'm here to see Alanna Morris."

The woman stiffened. "Oh. Okay. I'll see if she's free. Can I tell her what this is about?"

"Just tell her it's important."

She got up from behind her desk and scurried down the hall. A moment later, she returned with a petite brunette in her early thirties, who gave him a wary look. "I'm Alanna Morris. Can I help you?"

"Is there somewhere we can speak in private?" he asked.

Alanna hesitated, her gaze moving from him to the very curious receptionist, to Haley, and then back to him. "I was just going to grab a coffee across the street," she said finally. "We can talk on the way."

CHAPTER FIVE

When they got in the elevator, Alanna looked at Haley and said, "Are you an agent, too?"

"No. My name is Haley Kenton."

Alanna's face turned pale. "Kenton?"

"Yes. My brother was Landon Kenton."

"Oh, God!" Alanna put a hand to her mouth. "I was afraid that's why you came to see me. I told Sabrina to stay out of it. What did she tell you?"

"She didn't tell me anything," Haley said as the elevator stopped at the lobby, and they got off.

"Well, you need to talk to Sabrina, not me," Alanna said, pushing the elevator button to call it back. "I have nothing to say. I'm going back to work."

"We can't talk to Sabrina," he interjected.

"Why not? This is her deal, not mine. I don't want anything to do with it."

As the elevator doors opened, he grabbed her arm. "Wait, Ms. Morris."

"Let go of me," she said, tugging her arm free.

"Sabrina was killed last night." He hadn't meant to deliver the message in such a cold, harsh way, but he needed to stop her from trying to run away from them.

She froze as the elevator doors closed.

"What did you say?" she asked. "That's impossible. I talked to her yesterday when I got off work."

"What time was that?"

"Around five. She said she was going to meet..." Her voice trailed away as her gaze turned to Haley. "She was going to meet you. What happened to her?"

"She was shot," Haley said. "She died instantly."

Alanna shook her head in disbelief. "No. I can't believe this. She's really dead?"

"Yes. And we're hoping you can help us figure out who killed her," he replied. "You sent her a warning text last night, telling her to stop digging into something, that she could lose her job. What were you referring to?"

"Sabrina was trying to do the right thing." Alanna bit down on her lip, visibly struggling to compose herself. "But I was afraid she was getting into something dangerous."

"What was she investigating?" he asked.

She didn't answer as two women came into the lobby. "I can't talk here. Let's get that coffee," she said, heading toward the door, giving the women a quick greeting on the way.

They followed Alanna to a café down the street. There were tables in front of the restaurant, and they sat down together, ordering three coffees from the server.

"Did Sabrina find out something about my brother's death?" Haley asked as soon as they were alone.

Alanna gave them a nervous look. "I really don't want to get involved in this."

"You don't have a choice," Haley said. "And if you don't want Sabrina's death to go unpunished, you need to help us get her justice."

He had to admit that Haley knew which buttons to push, because Alanna straightened at her words. "You're right. She can't have died in vain. Sabrina thought your brother,

Landon, had been murdered. She believed there was a cover-up."

"Why would she think that?" Haley asked.

"She didn't give me specifics. She said she'd come across some new information."

"I don't understand," Haley said, impatience in her voice. "How did Sabrina even know about my brother? He died six years ago. Why would information come up about him now? And why would Sabrina have it?"

"It goes back to law school at Westbridge," Alanna said. "In our final year, Sabrina and I interned at the university legal aid center, helping students with basic legal questions and concerns. One day, a student came in and told us that a friend of his had died a few weeks earlier, and he didn't think it was an accident. He'd gone to the police, but they wouldn't talk to him. He wanted to know what else he could do."

"What was his name?"

Before Alanna could answer, the server returned with their coffees, and he could see Haley's impatience grow until the woman finally walked away.

"His name was Arjun Patel," Alanna answered. "And he was talking about Landon's death. He said that Landon told him some guys in his fraternity were pressuring him, and he was upset about it. A few days later, he was dead after a fraternity party, and Arjun didn't believe that was a coincidence."

"What did you tell him?" Haley asked.

"Sabrina said she'd pass the information on to the head of the legal aid center, and they'd follow up with him, campus security, and the police. After he left, Sabrina spoke to our supervisor. Less than ten minutes later, we were both told that the university and the police had already done a thorough investigation. She suggested Sabrina contact Arjun and encourage him to get counseling, because he was clearly upset about his friend's death."

Haley shook her head in disgust. "How could they not even talk to him? That investigation was a sham."

"Did you know Arjun Patel?" he asked Haley.

"No. I've never heard that name. Landon didn't talk much about his friends. When we spoke, it was mostly about his work or his grades or...me," she said, guilt running through her eyes. "It wasn't until after he died that I realized how little I knew about his life. I should have asked more questions."

"Let's get back to Arjun," he said, turning to Alanna. "Did Sabrina ever speak to Arjun again? Is he the reason she started digging into this after so many years?"

"No. She tried to talk to him after she met with our supervisor, but Arjun had dropped out of school and turned off his phone. He basically disappeared."

"Wait—he dropped out of school?" Haley asked. "So close to graduation?"

Alanna nodded, a grim look in her gaze. "Yes. We both wondered why, but that was the end until a few weeks ago."

"What happened?" he asked. "What was the trigger for all this coming back up?"

"Sabrina asked me to get a drink late one night. That, on its own, was unusual because she worked a million hours at Adler and Briggs and barely had time to breathe. They were slowly sucking the life out of her, but that day she was all lit up. She asked me if I remembered your brother, and, of course, I said I did," she said, looking at Haley.

"What did she tell you?"

"She'd heard something that made her believe Landon's death was not an accident, and she was looking into it," Alanna said. "I asked her for more details, but she said she didn't want to say more until she knew more. But she thought it was all about money."

"Money?" Haley echoed, her expression confused. "My brother had no money. He worked a side job to pay for what his scholarship didn't cover."

"I don't know what she meant; I'm just telling you what she said."

"Did she say anything else?" he asked. "You texted her that she could lose her job. Why would you say that?"

"Because Graham Adler went to Westbridge, and so did his son, Henry. Half the attorneys at that firm are Westbridge grads. If Sabrina had discovered that Westbridge had covered up a murder, her firm would not be happy with her. They are huge donors to the school."

"Did Sabrina consider going to the police?"

"She tried to talk to someone at the FBI, but he wasn't there, and whoever she spoke to said she should talk to the police, that it wasn't in their jurisdiction to look into a death at a private university. They blew her off."

"Who did she talk to?" he asked, disturbed by that answer.

"I don't know, but the person she wanted to talk to was recommended by Anthony Devray. He apparently worked with this guy and said he could be trusted."

"Anthony Devray," he murmured. That was how Sabrina had his number. But Shari had told him that Sabrina hadn't spoken to anyone in his office. And that she'd offered to help, but Sabrina hadn't wanted to talk to anyone but him. Something was off about the sequence of events.

"Do you know Anthony Devray?" Haley asked.

"Yes, but I'm more interested in who Sabrina spoke to at the Bureau. She never gave you a name?" he asked Alanna.

"No, but she was disappointed by their response, which is when she decided to reach out to you, Haley. She knew you were a reporter, and she thought maybe you could get the information she needed."

"Why didn't she come to me right away?" Haley asked.

"She didn't want to raise your hopes in case she was wrong. But when the FBI shut her down, she felt like you had to know."

"I was so close to talking to her," Haley muttered, her expression filled with frustration and anger.

"I can't believe she's dead," Alanna said, her eyes growing moist. "Sabrina was a really good person and a great lawyer. Her firm didn't appreciate her. I told her to leave, but she needed the money to take care of her mom, who has health issues. Oh, God, her mom! She must be devastated."

Both Alanna and Haley were caught up in their pain, and while he sympathized, he needed to keep pushing. "Would Sabrina have confided in anyone at her firm? Did she have a friend there?"

"I don't think so. The firm is cutthroat. All the second-year associates were competing for scraps."

"There's nothing else she told you? Maybe a small detail you didn't think was important," he suggested.

"I'm sorry. I didn't want to know, and she didn't want to put me in danger." She paused, her gaze anxious. "Am I in danger? You two found me. Does anyone else know about me?"

"There's a chance they do," he said honestly. "You should be careful, Alanna. Don't go anywhere alone. Don't take any meetings with people you don't know."

"I can't believe this is happening." Alanna shook her head in bemusement once more.

"We're going to find out who killed Sabrina and who killed my brother," Haley said forcefully. "I promise you that."

"I hope so," Alanna said. "I should get back to work." She got up and gave Haley one last look. "I'm really sorry about your brother."

"Thank you."

When Alanna left, Haley turned to him. "We need to find Arjun and talk to him."

"I'm not against that, but if he'd had more than a hunch, he would have turned it over back then."

"Maybe he did, and someone covered it up. The kid dropped out of school very close to graduation. He was afraid."

"I agree," he said. "It's a good lead, but I need to find out what Sabrina and Anthony Devray were talking about."

"Do you know him?"

"I do. I worked with him on a corporate fraud case. He was acting as a whistleblower. Unfortunately, that case was dropped, and his actions only resulted in him losing his job, not in bringing down the company."

"I thought whistleblowers were protected."

"They're supposed to be. I need to find him, see what he knows about Sabrina."

"Can you call him now?" she asked impatiently.

He hesitated, then pulled out his phone and punched in the number he had for Anthony, but it didn't go through. The number was no longer good. "He must have changed his number. That's not surprising. He was afraid of repercussions the last time I spoke to him."

"Who did he work for? Was it someone who'd gone to Westbridge?"

"I honestly don't know. I wasn't checking school degrees when I was working the case, but I can certainly look into that."

"Okay. You do that, and I'll try to find Arjun Patel."

"Hang on," he said as she jumped to her feet. "This is my investigation. I will handle both Anthony Devray and Arjun Patel."

"It will be faster if I help," she argued. "You said you wanted my assistance."

"In sharing information," he reiterated as he stood up. "But I don't want you getting in the way, and you could easily do that."

"I don't see how."

"You don't?" he asked somewhat incredulously. "You are running on emotion—anger, guilt, sadness, frustration... We have to investigate facts, not feelings. That's the way to get to the truth."

"I hear what you're saying, but I will not be blinded by emotion. I'm a good investigator."

"You may be a good reporter, but you are not an FBI agent. I appreciate your help, but it needs to stay in the background from now on. No tracking down people and going off to see them on your own."

"Fine, whatever you say."

Her capitulation was far too easy. "I mean it, Haley."

"Don't you mean Ms. Kenton? I need to get back to work."

He put some cash on the table to cover their coffees and a tip and then followed her across the street. "Haley," he said as she moved toward her car. "Wait."

She gave him an expectant look. "What?"

"You're not going to stay out of this, are you?"

"Maybe it's better if you don't know what I'm going to do. You seem to have a lot of rules, and the rules haven't worked for me in the past. I'm not going to let them stop me now. If Landon was murdered six years ago, I can't help but think I gave up way too easily. I thought I was fighting, but it wasn't hard enough. I eventually came to believe what everyone was telling me—that Landon's death was an accident. Sabrina died trying to prove it wasn't, so I'm going to do whatever I have to do."

"You could end up exactly like Sabrina. How does that help you get justice for your brother?" he challenged.

"It's a risk I have to take. No one else will fight for him. Sabrina talked to someone at the FBI and was blown off. You could get taken off this case in the next hour, forced to back down like the police did. There's someone powerful who is determined to stop any investigation into my brother's death. But they can't stop me."

"Or me," he said. "No one is shutting down my investigation."

"You just said that happened on another case."

"That was with the LA field office. I'm working with a different unit now. And this isn't just about your brother. It's also about the young woman who was killed last night. Sabrina Lin deserves justice, too."

"I agree. And I hope you don't back down, but I'm not convinced you won't."

Seeing the steel-blue determination in her eyes, he knew he wouldn't be able to stop her, so he needed to find a way to keep her involved but not right in the middle of things. "Okay. You look for Arjun. I'll dig into Sabrina's law firm and see if I can locate Anthony Devray. Then we'll compare notes. If you find anything, call me."

"It can't be a one-way street, Matt."

"And I can't let you get hurt, Haley, or derail this investigation."

"That will be less likely to happen if we share information," she argued.

He let out a sigh. "You are a very stubborn woman."

"I always have been," she said. "I don't know any other way to be."

He could see that, and he could relate, because he could be stubborn, too. "All right. We'll share."

Relief flashed through her eyes. "Are you just saying that, or do you mean it?"

"I rarely say things I don't mean."

"That can't be true. You're an FBI agent. You must say lots of things to get people to talk to you."

"Fair point," he conceded. "But this is different."

"How is it different?"

"I don't know, but it is."

She gave him a considering look, then said, "Okay. I'll let you know when I find Arjun."

She'd said *when* and not if. She wasn't just stubborn; she was confident, too. He couldn't help but like that. What he didn't like was her involvement in his investigation. Unfortunately, there was little he could do to get her out of this case. Her brother seemed to be at the center of everything. And if his death wasn't an accident, then someone was willing to kill as many people as it took to protect their secret.

CHAPTER SIX

After getting in the car, Matt called Jason and related what he'd learned from Alanna Morris about Sabrina's connection to Landon Kenton's death at Westbridge University and a possible cover-up. When he finished the recap, he said, "Are you free to go to Adler and Briggs now?"

"Absolutely," Jason replied. "I'll meet you in the lobby of their building in fifteen minutes."

"See you then." Ending the call, he pulled away from the curb, joining the rush of traffic heading toward Century City, where Sabrina's law firm was located.

When he walked into the gleaming lobby of the ten-story glass tower just before one, he found Jason waiting for him, and they headed to the top floor, where the law firm had its luxury office suite.

The elevator opened directly into the elegant reception area of Adler and Briggs. Floor-to-ceiling windows offered a panoramic view of the city, while the interior was appointed with expensive leather furniture, original artwork, and fresh flowers. The receptionist, an impeccably dressed woman in her thirties, looked up from her computer with a polite but curious expression.

"Good afternoon. How may I help you?" she asked.

Matt stepped forward, showing his badge. "I'm Agent Lawson with the FBI, and this is Agent Colter. We'd like to speak with Graham Adler about one of your employees, Sabrina Lin."

The woman's perfectly composed expression flickered with surprise. "Oh. Sabrina. I just heard the terrible news. I couldn't believe it." She licked her lips, her gaze somewhat nervous. "Let me...let me check if Mr. Adler is available." She picked up her phone, speaking in low tones before hanging up. Then she got to her feet and said, "Follow me."

She led them down a quiet, elegant, thickly carpeted hallway before opening a heavy mahogany door and waving them inside. Adler's corner office with a view of Century City was a testament to old money and Ivy League connections. Diplomas from Harvard Law hung beside photographs of Adler with various politicians and business leaders. But it was the collection of Westbridge University memorabilia that caught Matt's attention —a pennant, several photographs of campus events, and what looked like a framed invitation to an alumni gala.

Graham Adler came around his massive desk to greet them. He was exactly what Matt had expected: silver-haired, sharp brown eyes, with the confident bearing that came from never having to worry about money.

"Jason Colter. It's good to see you again," Graham said. "I wish it were under better circumstances."

"So do I. This is Agent Lawson," Jason said.

Graham gave him a nod. "Please have a seat." He gestured to the leather chairs facing his desk. "I was shocked by the news of Sabrina's death. What a terrible tragedy," he added as he sat down behind his desk. "Such a bright young woman, with her entire future ahead of her." He paused. "How can I help you?"

Adler's expression was appropriately grave, but Matt noticed the way his eyes remained calculating, assessing. "What was Sabrina working on?" he asked.

"I'm not sure. Would you like me to call in her supervisor?"
Adler leaned back in his chair, the picture of cooperation.
"Lindsay can give you more specifics about Sabrina's current
projects. I can't imagine they would have any relevance to Sabrina's death. Do you believe there's some connection?"

"We're looking into every part of her life," he replied.

Adler pressed a button on his phone. "Lindsay? Could you
come to my office, please?"

As they waited for Lindsay, Matt's gaze wandered to the
Westbridge photographs. "Did you graduate from Westbridge,
Mr. Adler?"

"I did my undergrad there. Back then, they didn't have a law
school, so I went to Harvard. The more recent photos are from
my son Henry's time at Westbridge. He did both undergrad and
law school at Westbridge and joined our firm two years ago. I
believe you've met Henry, Jason."

"Yes. At a family golf tournament about ten years ago. Henry
was a good golfer, following in your footsteps."

"He has always tried to do that," Graham said. "He thinks
he's better than me now, but he's not. Are you coming to
Valmont on Sunday for the charity tournament?"

"I might try to get out there."

"You should be playing. Your father won it twice."

"I did not follow in my father's footsteps when it came to
golf."

"Only to the FBI."

Jason nodded. "True."

The door opened, and a woman in her forties made her way
to the desk. She was tall and very thin, with short black hair and
pale skin.

"This is Lindsay Kellerman," Adler explained as Lindsay
stood next to the desk, looking uncomfortable. "She was Sabrina's supervisor. Agents Colter and Lawson would like to know
exactly what projects and accounts Sabrina was handling,
Lindsay."

Lindsay cleared her throat. "First of all, I'm shocked and saddened by Sabrina's death. She was more than a colleague—she was a friend. As for her assignments, she's been working on several client matters, routine due diligence research for IPO filings and patents, mostly. She's very thorough, detail-oriented, and good at her job."

"Which clients?" he asked.

Lindsay glanced at Graham, who answered for her. "I'm afraid we can't divulge that. Client confidentiality, you understand."

"We're not asking for privileged information. If whatever Sabrina was working on got her killed, it's in your firm's best interest to be forthcoming."

"I understand. But I can't imagine her work would have put her in danger. She was a second-year associate. She didn't run cases. Nor was she client-facing. Unless you have a court order, that information will stay confidential to protect our clients."

Graham was polite but firm, and Matt wasn't surprised by his stance. He decided to change tactics. Clearly, Graham and Lindsay had been expecting a question about client work, but they might not be expecting the next one. "Your son, Henry, went to Westbridge. Was he there when a student died? I believe his name was Landon Kenton."

The sudden flare in Graham's eyes told him exactly what he wanted to know. The determination was still there, but the calm had vanished.

"Yes, I am aware of that sad occurrence," he replied. "Henry was in the same fraternity as Landon. I believe his death was an accident. Too much drinking. It's unfortunately not a rare occurrence with college kids these days." Graham's voice carried just the right note of sympathy, but he couldn't help noticing the way Graham's fingers drummed against his desk before he realized the nervous gesture and stilled them.

He turned to Lindsay. "Did you go to Westbridge as well?"

She immediately shook her head. "No, I didn't."

"But Sabrina did."

"Yes," she replied, looking like she wanted to say more but then decided against it.

"Is there anything else you can tell us about Sabrina's last few days?" he asked. "Was she acting differently? Was she getting calls at work? Did she mention any problems in her life?"

Lindsay cleared her throat once more. "As a matter of fact, she did. I noticed she was stressed last week, so I asked her if she wanted to talk about anything. She said a guy she met on a dating app was harassing her and wouldn't take no for an answer. I'm wondering now if he...if he was the one who killed her." She drew in a breath at the end of her statement, a statement that felt far too rehearsed.

"Did she give you this man's name?" he asked.

"No. I wish I'd asked for more information, but honestly, as soon as she said it, she clammed up. She told me to forget she'd said anything."

"What about the dating app?" Jason asked. "Do you know which one she was on?"

"I'm not sure. I think she was on several of them. We didn't talk that much about our personal lives. I was her supervisor. We had some distance between us."

"I thought you just said she was a friend," he reminded her.

"She was a friend, but we didn't talk about men that much," she hastily amended.

"Was there anyone else here she would have confided in?" he asked.

"We're not a particularly social office. We're all focused on work."

"I'll need a list of people Sabrina might have been close to," Jason said. "I'd like to talk to them."

Lindsay glanced at Graham again, who gave a nod. Then she said, "Of course. I'll write down their names. Should I do that now?"

"Why don't you show us Sabrina's desk?" Jason suggested. "Then we'll get the list from you."

"All right," Lindsay said, moving toward the door.

"Thank you for your time, Graham," Jason said as he got to his feet.

"I wish I could be more helpful, Jason," Adler replied. "Let's play golf sometime. I'd like to catch up."

"Sounds good."

Matt simply gave Graham Adler a nod before following Jason and Lindsay out of the office. He'd dealt with enough CEOs to know when to keep his mouth shut. Graham Adler already had his back up, especially since he'd mentioned Landon Kenton.

Lindsay led them to an open area filled with cubicles and smaller offices. "Sabrina worked here," she said, stopping at a neat desk near the windows.

Her workspace was immaculate, only a coffee mug proclaiming a distaste for Mondays sitting next to a dark computer. "Our HR department secured her workspace this morning, as is standard procedure," Lindsay said. "All company-related items were boxed up and packed away. The only personal item was that mug. I don't think she ever drank out of it. She always brought a thermos from home."

"Are you sure Sabrina never mentioned the name of the guy who was bothering her?" he asked, now that they were not under Graham's watchful gaze.

"She didn't, I'm sorry."

"And there wasn't something she was working on that bothered her?" he pressed. "Was a client unhappy with her work?"

"She didn't have contact with clients. Her role was completely internal, as Mr. Adler mentioned," Lindsay replied.

"Is Henry Adler here?" he asked. "We'd like to talk to him as well."

"He's at lunch." Lindsay opened the top drawer of Sabrina's desk and pulled out an empty notepad and a pen. She jotted down three names and handed him the paper. "These people were the closest to Sabrina. I think they're all in a meeting right now, but you could call them later."

Jason took the list. "Thanks. I'll follow up with them."

As they left the cubicle, a young, handsome man in his mid to late twenties came toward them. He had dark hair and eyes and bore a striking resemblance to Graham.

"Jason Colter?" the man asked. "My father said you were here. You probably don't remember me. I'm his son, Henry."

"You've grown about a foot since I last saw you," Jason said, as they shook hands. "Your father says your golf game is impressive."

"I doubt he said that," Henry returned with a smile, before giving him a curious look. "I'm Henry Adler."

"Agent Lawson," he said, shaking Henry's hand.

Henry nodded, his expression turning somber. "We're stunned by the terrible news about Sabrina."

"Did you know her well?" he asked.

"Not well, but we got hired around the same time, so we've worked on projects together."

"Did you know her when you were at Westbridge? You both went to the law school there, right?"

"We did, but she had already graduated from law school before I got in. She worked at another firm before coming here."

"Do you know if she had any problems in her life that could have led to what happened to her?" he asked.

"I heard something about a bad date, but I don't know details," Henry replied. "I hope you find whoever did this to her. She was not only smart but also very caring. She'll be missed. Anyway, I need to run. Hope we can get on a golf course again sometime, Jason."

"I would like that," Jason replied.

"I'll show you out," Lindsay said, escorting them back to the reception area.

As soon as they left the suite, he said, "That dating app story sounded like a deliberate attempt to send us in another direction."

"I agree, but I'll check it out. Graham tensed up when you asked about the kid who died at Westbridge. That was interesting."

"Also interesting that Henry was in the same fraternity. So, you belong to the same country club as these guys?"

"I inherited my father's membership," Jason said dryly. "It's not my scene, but I've kept it because sometimes it gives me entrée into a circle of people that would be difficult to get to otherwise. Speaking of which, there's an event on Sunday. It might be an excellent opportunity to talk to Henry, Graham, and probably a lot of other Westbridge grads in a more casual setting."

"I'll keep that in mind," he said as they took the elevator down to the lobby, then parted company.

On his way back to the office, he stopped to pick up a sandwich and a drink, then returned to work. By the time he arrived, Jason was already digging into the employee list of Adler and Briggs and making calls to the employees Lindsay had called out as being friends with Sabrina. And Agent Andi Hart stopped by to let him know she'd sent him the police file from Landon Kenton's death.

"The file is not thick," Andi added. "It looks like the police wrote off Kenton's death as an accident very quickly. I also couldn't help noticing that every fraternity brother who was interviewed told exactly the same story. Sounds like everyone jumped on a theory and kept repeating it."

"That's what Haley Kenton said. We need to figure out what stones they left unturned and why. If Sabrina's death was tied to Landon's death, then both cases will be important. I assume Derek hasn't been able to trace the shooter at Griffith Park?"

"No. I've been tracking traffic cams as well, and there's nothing. He probably entered the park on foot or possibly bicycle.

Savannah is looking into the dark web to see if we can find any assignments matching that hit."

"Great." As she left, he started looking into the Adler family. It wasn't just Graham and Henry who had gone to Westbridge; it was also Graham's brother, Charles, and his two kids, Trent and Jill, who were the same age as Henry. Considering Sabrina worked for Adler and Briggs, he couldn't help wondering if what she'd heard about Landon had come from Henry.

But Henry and Graham were too smart to talk, especially if they'd been aware of a cover-up six years ago. In looking into the rest of the family, he noted that Charles Adler ran a hedge fund. Trent Adler had been working for his father until two years ago, when he started his own financial investment company. Jill Adler, Trent's twin sister, ran a marketing company in LA, specializing in events and promotions. She seemed to have a client list of celebrities and philanthropists.

Setting the Adlers aside, he checked the police file on Landon's death for a list of fraternity brothers who had been interviewed. Both Trent and Henry were on that list, as well as four other men: Josh Lorrie, the president of the fraternity; Brian Covington who had acted as pledge trainer for Landon's group of pledges; Drew Sanderson, who was Landon's big brother in the fraternity; and Jake Petrie, who had seen Landon stumble out of the house during the party.

He asked him if Landon was okay, and Landon had said he was fine. That was the last time anyone had spoken to him.

As he plugged the students' names into their system, he realized every single one had wealthy and well-connected parents. Josh Lorrie's mother, Eleanor, was a vice president at a media company, and his father, John, was a commercial real estate developer. Brian Covington's father, Edward, was a plastic surgeon for the rich and famous. Drew Sanderson's father, Kent, ran a mutual fund, and Jake Petrie's father was a state senator.

No wonder the LAPD had felt pressure to close their investigation quickly. None of those parents would allow a hint of scandal to touch their kid or their family.

It was also interesting to note that nowhere in the file was there any mention of Arjun Patel, one of Landon's good friends, someone who had allegedly gone to the police with his concerns but had been turned away.

He spent the next hour looking for more details, more information. The police had also interviewed Brooke Mercer, Landon's girlfriend. She'd been out of town and claimed she hadn't spoken to Landon on Saturday night. A review of her phone confirmed that to be true. The police had stopped by the apartment building where Landon lived, but none of the neighbors claimed to know him well, and no one had made a statement.

In terms of the crime, Landon's wallet was in his pocket, but his phone was missing, and no computer was found on his person or in his apartment. That detail should have provided some investigative questions. If Landon's death had truly been an accident, where was his phone? Where was his computer? He was a college kid. There was no way he didn't have a computer and a phone. Someone had taken them. But no one had been questioned about the missing items, or if they had been, their statements had not been noted in the police report.

The deeper he dove, the more he believed Haley was right; the investigation had been deliberately short because no one wanted Landon's death to be anything but an accident.

Clearly Sabrina had found something or heard something. He just wished he knew what that could be. She'd worked with Henry, so maybe he'd let something slip, but he seemed too smart and sly to be that careless. Although it was possible his arrogance had led him into making a careless mistake.

With Sabrina on his mind, he got into her file next. One of their team analysts had already compiled Sabrina's personal information and family history. Her father was an architect, her mother, a high school teacher, currently on leave as she battled cancer. Agent Hart had spoken briefly to Sabrina's father, Daniel Lin, who claimed he knew nothing about Sabrina's case work and their conversations had been focused solely on her mother's health issues.

So, Sabrina hadn't spoken to her parents, but she had called the FBI. He picked up his phone again and punched in Shari's number, wanting to clarify exactly how that call had gone. But Shari didn't pick up, so he left her a voicemail to call him as soon as she got a chance.

Next, he got back on the computer to try to track down Anthony Devray. But it felt like Anthony had dropped off the face of the earth in the last month. He'd closed his bank accounts, his credit cards, moved out of his apartment, and disconnected his phone. But at some point, he'd spoken to Sabrina. Maybe in tracing Sabrina's movements over the past few days, he could find Anthony. But that could take some time, and, clearly, Anthony was doing everything he could not to be found.

Frowning, he considered what to do next. As if on cue, a text from Haley popped up on his phone that made his pulse jump.

Found Arjun. He's in the Valley. I'm going to try to see him now. Just sharing my info.

He immediately texted back. *I'll pick you up.*

Already on my way. Here's the address. She texted an address in North Hollywood, which was a good forty-five minutes to an hour away in Friday afternoon traffic.

He checked his watch. It was almost 4:30. *I can be there in an hour. Don't go inside until I get there.*

She didn't answer right away, and he texted again.

I mean it, Haley. Wait for me.

She sent back a thumbs-up emoji, which wasn't particularly reassuring, but it was all he was going to get.

CHAPTER SEVEN

It was just before five thirty on Friday evening when Haley pulled into the parking lot of what looked like an abandoned warehouse in North Hollywood. The building was nondescript gray concrete with no visible signage, just a small neon sign that read "CIPHER" in electric-blue letters above a heavy metal door.

She'd found Arjun through a combination of old university records and some creative social media stalking that had suggested Arjun was now going under the name AJ Patel and ran a multiplayer video game club out of this building. She was eager to talk to him, but she'd promised Agent Lawson that she'd wait for him. Although she still wondered if she shouldn't have made this trip on her own.

Alanna had said that Sabrina had contacted someone at the FBI, who had blown her off. And Matt seemed to know the man Sabrina had gotten her referral from, which made her wonder how much she should trust Matt Lawson. Did he really want to find the truth, or did he want to stop her from finding it?

That dark thought made her nervous, especially now that she was sitting in a spooky, shadow-filled industrial area. She forced herself to breathe and focus on the facts. Matt had wanted to talk to Alanna. He'd told her he was going to speak to Sabrina's employer. He'd certainly acted like he wanted answers, and he hadn't charged her for stealing Sabrina's phone, so that was another plus in the pro column. She didn't completely trust him, but she could use an ally, especially one with the resources of the FBI.

She jumped when her phone rang. It was Julia, returning her call.

"Hi," she said. "Thanks for getting back to me. I wanted to fill you in on a few things."

"What's going on?"

"I found the person who sent the text to Sabrina Lin. Her name is Alanna Morris. She went to law school at Westbridge with Sabrina."

"That was fast. I thought all you had was an initial."

"I did, but I was able to figure it out from there. Alanna and Sabrina interned at the legal aid center on campus the year Landon died. During that time, they met with a student named Arjun Patel, who was confident my brother's death was not an accident. Arjun was desperate to get someone to investigate and wanted to know if Sabrina could help him get the authorities to keep looking for answers. Sabrina passed on his request, and the university and police said the matter was closed. A few days later, Arjun dropped out of school and turned off his phone." She paused. "Did you ever interview Arjun? Did he ever talk to you?"

"He definitely didn't speak to me, and I don't remember anyone by that name being interviewed. But, as you know, the investigation only lasted a few weeks before the brass told us to shut it down. There was no evidence leading to anything other than an accident."

"If you and the others had been able to spend more time looking for evidence, you might have found some," she said, still bitter about that.

"I don't disagree. Did this woman tell you what Sabrina found out?"

"Unfortunately, no. All Alanna knew was that it had to do with Landon. I'm hoping Arjun will be able to tell me more."

"Do you want me to track him down?"

"I've already done that."

"Of course you have," Julia said with an amused tone in her voice. "You should be working with me as a private investigator."

"I like being a journalist. I'm about to go see Arjun now. I'll let you know what I find out."

"Please do. I know I haven't helped you at all yet, but I want to. I've been wrapping up another case today, so I haven't had time to get into what we talked about this morning. I'm sorry about that. I'll have more time tomorrow."

"No problem. I just dumped all this on you."

"I kept copies of the file from your brother's investigation, just in case. I was going to look over them tonight. I'll see if Arjun's name is in there. Where are you now? Do you want me to talk to this man with you?"

"I'm in North Hollywood at a club called Cipher, which Arjun apparently owns, although he goes by AJ Patel now. I'm waiting for Special Agent Matt Lawson to join me. As I mentioned earlier, he's holding my theft of Sabrina's phone over my head. If I don't share information, he'll charge me with obstruction. So, I'm sharing." She paused as a car pulled into the lot and parked several spots away from her. "He's here now. I'll talk to you later."

"Be careful, Haley. I don't want you to end up like your brother or Sabrina."

"Me, either." She ended the call, then got out of the car to meet up with Matt.

He gave her a skeptical look as he took in their surroundings. "Where are we?"

"It's an interactive gaming club called Cipher. I couldn't find much information about it online. It seems to be for serious gamers."

"Was your brother into video games?"

"Very much so," she said. "But I was not. I was never interested in the fake world of battles; I had enough real-life wars to fight."

"Someday, you're going to need to tell me more about you and Landon and how you grew up."

"Maybe later. Let's go."

They walked to what appeared to be the front of the building and a large door, which had no handle—just a digital keypad and a camera above it. As they approached, the screen flickered to life with text:

WELCOME TO CIPHER. TO ENTER THE SANCTUM, YOU MUST FIRST PROVE YOUR WORTH. ARE YOU READY TO BEGIN?

Two buttons appeared: YES and NO.

"Well," Haley said, pressing YES, "this should be interesting."

The screen changed to display a message: *ENTER THE PREPARATION CHAMBER. YOU HAVE 45 MINUTES TO ESCAPE, OR YOU WILL BE ASKED TO LEAVE. GOOD LUCK.*

The heavy door clicked open, revealing a dimly lit corridor lined with exposed brick. They stepped inside, and the door sealed behind them with an ominous thud. She felt a shiver run down her spine. "Gotta say, I've never been big on enclosed spaces." Her heart was already starting to race, and her palms were beginning to sweat.

"It's an escape room. We'll be fine," Matt said.

"If we can escape," she said tightly.

He gave her a sharp look. "Are you okay?"

"I might have a little claustrophobia."

"You're going to be fine. And I have always been able to escape any situation I've been in."

She'd found his confidence arrogant and irritating before, but now it felt comforting. "What do we do?"

"Let's walk to the end of the hall."

The corridor led into a small room that looked like something between a medieval dungeon and a high-tech laboratory. Stone walls were fitted with electronic panels, and chains hung from the ceiling alongside fiber optic cables. In the center of the room sat an ornate wooden chest.

A voice came from hidden speakers: "Welcome. You seek an audience with the Architect, but first you must prove you can think beyond the obvious. Your first challenge: Unlock the chest using only what you observe."

Matt approached the chest, running his hands along its carved surface. "No keyhole," he said. "But look at these symbols." He traced his finger along a series of carved images: an eye, a hand, a mouth, an ear. "I think these represent four of the five senses."

She tried to focus on what he was saying instead of the panic slowly rising within her.

"What do you think, Haley?"

His voice broke through her anxious brain fog. "Uh, I don't know."

"Look around. I need your help," he said forcefully.

His tone snapped her out of her paralysis, and her gaze moved to wall. "Over there—a hand scanner, some kind of audio input, a camera, and..." She paused as she looked at the last device. "Is that a breathalyzer?"

"Looks like it."

"I think we need to match the symbols on the chest with the sensors, probably in order."

"Okay. You read them off; I'll push the buttons."

When they'd activated all the sensors, the chest clicked open to reveal a key and another message: *Trust is the foundation of all knowledge. Proceed together.*

"That seems a little on the nose," she murmured.

"You're supposed to trust me."

"Or you're supposed to trust me."

He smiled. "Let's see what the key opens."

She handed it to him. "You can lead."

"Now you want me to lead, when there's probably a trapdoor ahead," he said dryly.

"I'm just doing what you asked me to do before."

He stepped up to the lock and inserted the key, then turned the knob and slowly pushed the door open.

She felt a little trepidation, but nothing jumped out at them, and the floor did not fall away. Instead, they walked into a closet-sized library with towering bookshelves and a large mahogany desk positioned in the center. The desk's surface appeared to be made of dark glass or polished black stone, completely smooth and reflective, with no visible controls or markings. It looked elegant but also mysteriously high-tech.

"What now?" she asked. "I was hoping that first part was it."

"There must be a secret door somewhere." He examined the shelves, then reached for a book titled *Medieval History*.

When the book left the shelf, the desk's surface came alive. A grid of twenty-five squares appeared on what she now realized was an interactive display, and one square in the upper left corner glowed green. When she took out a different book, a blue light appeared in the center of the grid.

"It's a logic puzzle," Matt said. "Each book corresponds to a specific square. We need to figure out what pattern we're supposed to create."

"There are a lot of books. Do you think we have to pull them all out?"

"I doubt it." He grabbed another book, and a light flickered, then went off. "Or maybe we do," he said, setting the book back in its place.

"This could take forever," she groaned, impatient to get out of this room and find Arjun Patel.

"Then we better keep going," he said pragmatically, lifting another book off the shelf that lit up a green square and also a digital readout that flickered to life: *ILLUMINATE THE PATH: 7 SQUARES REQUIRED.* "Looks like we just need four more."

The idea of being done spurred her on, and they worked together, pulling out books. While some books lit up the grid, they didn't create a path, so they had to keep going.

As Matt reached across her for a book with a gold spine, his hand brushed her arm, and she found herself noticing the subtle scent of his cologne, the breadth of his shoulders. Her pulse sped up again, but it wasn't anxiety raising the temperature; it was the FBI agent, whose very attractive qualities she hadn't really noticed until now.

She moved away from him, and he gave her an odd look. "Are you okay?"

"Just feeling hot. There's not a lot of air in here."

"You'll feel better once the door opens."

"If it opens," she said a little desperately.

"Try the red leather book," he suggested. "It's right behind you on the sixth shelf. The colors of the spines could be important."

She grabbed the volume in question, and he was right—a gold square lit up on the grid. The lighted squares were actually one step delayed, so a gold book lit up a white square, and a red book lit up a gold one. She looked at the books they had already picked out and put on the desk and realized the last clue. "We need blue," she said.

Matt was already ahead of her, grabbing a blue book to light up a yellow square and complete the path.

The entire grid flashed green, and they heard a mechanical click as a section of the bookshelf swung inward, revealing the door to the next room. She was so excited to leave the chamber, she collided with Matt and stumbled.

He put his arm around her waist to steady her. "Okay?" he asked.

She was definitely not okay, but she couldn't begin to tell him she'd suddenly become very aware of him as a man and not an FBI agent who could charge her with obstructing justice. "I have to get out of here," she said.

"After you." He waved her through the door.

As she stepped into the room, she let out a breath. Facing them was a hostess stand leading into what looked like a bar.

The woman, who had pink hair and tattooed arms, gave them a smile. "Congratulations. Welcome to Cipher." She waved her hand toward the spacious room behind her.

Inside, the club was much more elegant than the drab exterior had implied, with exposed brick walls, comfortable seating areas, and the soft glow of multiple computer screens. People sat in small groups, some playing elaborate board games, others hunched over laptops or engaged in what appeared to be virtual reality experiences. A bar along one wall served drinks in beakers and test tubes, giving the whole place the atmosphere of a mad scientist's social club.

"Table for two?" the hostess asked. "Or are you joining friends?"

"Actually, we're looking for AJ Patel," Haley said. "Is he here?"

The woman's expression shifted, becoming more guarded. "Who's asking?"

She knew Matt was about to flash his badge, so she put a quick hand on his arm, not wanting to scare anyone off. "Tell him it's Haley Kenton, Landon Kenton's sister. It's very important I speak with him."

"All right. Wait here."

As the woman moved into the large room behind her, she turned to Matt. "I was afraid if you said you were FBI, he'd cut out before we could talk to him. But if he really was my brother's friend, maybe he'd speak to me."

"It was a good call," he agreed.

"Thank you."

A few minutes later, the woman returned. "AJ will see you. Follow me."

She led them through the club room, down a hallway, and opened a door marked Private.

The room appeared to be an operations center. Multiple monitors lined the walls, displaying everything from security camera feeds to what appeared to be complex code. There was a man sitting in front of the monitors, but he had to be in his mid-forties, much older than AJ would be, unless she had the wrong man.

He turned to face them, then raised his hand and waved them toward a door leading into an office. As they stepped into that room, the man who got up from the desk appeared to be in his mid-twenties, around Landon's age, with dark hair and eyes and a full beard.

"You're Landon's sister," he said with a nod. "I saw you at Westbridge six years ago and on the local TV news, begging for information about Landon."

"But I didn't see you. And you were his friend, right? You're Arjun Patel?"

"I go by AJ now. Who's this?" He tipped his head toward Matt, a question in his gaze.

"I'm Agent Lawson with the FBI," Matt replied.

AJ stiffened. "What's this about?"

"We need to talk to you about Landon's death," Matt said.

"Now? Now the FBI wants to talk to me?" AJ shook his head in disgust. "That's crazy. Six years ago, I couldn't get anyone to listen to me."

"Well, we want to listen to you now," Matt said. "What do you know about it?"

"I know it wasn't an accident." His gaze moved to her. "I'm sorry for what you went through. I'm sorry no one would help you."

"Why didn't you help me? Why didn't you talk to me? I was on campus for two weeks after he died. I was in his apartment. I talked to his friends, his girlfriend, his teachers, but no one mentioned you. Why is that? How come I didn't know about you until now?"

His gaze narrowed. "How do you know about me now?"

"Alanna Morris, who worked in the legal aid center with Sabrina Lin, told us you came to see them a few weeks after Landon's death, and you were convinced it wasn't an accident."

"I went to the police, too, but they told me unless I had evidence, I had nothing to offer, and all I had was a bad feeling."

"You had more than that," Matt put in. "You told Sabrina and Alanna that Landon had been having problems with his fraternity brothers and wanted to drop out of school. What was that about?"

"He wasn't specific, but he said the guys in the fraternity were pressuring him to give them test questions, answers, or maybe even share his work so they could get better grades. He said they'd told him it was one for all and all for one, that the group was more important than the individual, that the network, the way they helped each other, resulted in rewards for everyone."

"They wanted him to cheat," she murmured.

"Yes," AJ said. "And who better to help than him? Landon was brilliant—genius-level brilliant. We met in a computer science class our junior year, and he blew me away. I always thought I was the smartest kid in school, but I was nothing compared to him. Landon also worked as a TA and had access to test questions. Some of his frat brothers were in that class."

"He wouldn't have cheated," she said. "Landon had a very heightened sense of right and wrong, and he wouldn't have chosen the wrong path."

"That was the problem," AJ said. "Or at least part of it. I got the feeling they wanted something more than just help on changing their grades."

"Like what?"

"Landon had a special project he was working on. He didn't tell me much about it, but he did say it was a forecasting algorithm that could change the way people invested in the markets, portray various risk scenarios so smaller investors could avoid pitfalls."

Her throat tightened. She knew exactly why Landon would have wanted to protect investors. "He never told me about that," she said, but deep down, she knew why he hadn't said anything. It would have been a painful reminder of a tragedy they had both lived through.

"I think," AJ continued, "that some of his fraternity brothers found out about his project and saw potential dollar signs."

"Which fraternity brothers?" Matt asked. "Do you know who he was close to?"

"Drew Sanderson was his big brother. Trent Adler seemed like a friend. But, like I said, he didn't really hang out with them that much, especially toward the end of senior year. He was over the whole fraternity experience."

"I talked to both of those guys. They were actually the most communicative of the group. Drew expressed a lot of sadness and regret. Trent, too."

"Were those guys at the party?" Matt asked.

"Drew was. Trent wasn't. Drew said he'd talked to Landon earlier in the evening but had lost track of him. He also said Landon was drinking a lot that night, and he thought it was unusual. One of the other guys, Josh Lorrie, said that Landon was definitely wired. He seemed stressed out and wanted to drink his troubles away."

"I met Lorrie a few times," AJ said. "I wouldn't trust anything he had to say. Seemed smart but shady. I was in a class with Drew once. He wasn't too sharp academically, but Landon said he was funny and had been cool about not pressuring him during the whole hazing thing when he first joined. Frankly, I don't know why Landon ever rushed. He wasn't into that scene. And I can't believe he got so drunk he didn't know where he was. He rarely ever drank more than one beer. He was always thinking about his work, his classes, his job. He was a serious dude. It never made sense to me."

"He wanted to make connections. I encouraged that," she said heavily. "I shouldn't have."

"You weren't wrong. He did make connections," AJ said. "With a bunch of rich kids with influential parents."

"Were there any other friends you remember Landon mentioning?" she asked.

"What about Henry Adler?" Matt interjected. "Trent's cousin."

"Henry was a cocky, know-it-all. The kind of guy who always wants to talk while everyone else listens. I didn't know either him or his cousin well. I think one of them had a sister, too."

"Jill Adler," she said. "Trent's twin sister."

AJ nodded. "That's right."

"What about Landon's girlfriend, Brooke Mercer? Did you know her?" she asked.

"I met her once. I didn't think they were boyfriend-girlfriend until I saw the news articles calling her his grieving girlfriend. That seemed strange to me. I didn't think they'd gone out more than a few times. She was a sorority girl, and she really liked the frat parties. They seemed very different to me, but she was hot."

"It doesn't sound like you cared for her that much," Matt commented.

"She didn't care much for me. She thought I was just some lab rat computer nerd. Not that Landon wasn't the same thing, but he was better looking."

She hadn't known what to make of Brooke, either. She'd certainly acted like she was heartbroken, often breaking down in tears. They'd spent some time together that first week until Brooke's mom had shown up and suggested Brooke take a few days away from it all. Which reminded her that AJ had left school a few weeks later. "Why did you drop out of school, AJ? Alanna told us Sabrina tried to find you, and you were gone. You had left school and disconnected your phone just a few months before graduation. Why?"

"I was scared. I was one of the few people outside the frat who was close to Landon. When I realized the university would not do anything that would jeopardize the reputation of the institution and the endowments of their alumni, I thought I might be in danger. I didn't know anything, but maybe someone would think I did. A couple of times, walking home from the lab late at night, I had the feeling someone was following me. That's why I left. I finished my degree at another university, and I never looked back...until now." He paused. "Why are you digging into all this? What changed?"

"Sabrina Lin reached out to me yesterday morning," she answered. "She said she had information about Landon's death and asked me to meet her, which I did. Before I could talk to her, someone killed her."

His jaw dropped as he gasped. "What? Sabrina is dead? I can't believe she was even looking into Landon's death. It's been six years. What about the other woman I talked to at the legal aid center? You said you spoke to her. What does she know?"

"Nothing. She said Sabrina was short on details."

"But she told you about me," AJ said with alarm. "Now I need to be worried. Damn! Why did you come here? Why did you bring me into this?"

The fear in his eyes was very real, but she hoped it wouldn't stop him from helping her. "I think you cared about my brother, and I need your help, AJ."

"If I had proof of something, I would have laid that out six years ago."

"You could have told me about Landon's project before. You could have talked to me."

He gave her a guilty look. "I did think about it, but I didn't know what to say. You were so devastated, and in the beginning, I wasn't sure if I was just making up an excuse for him to be dead because I didn't want to believe he was a guy who would drink himself into oblivion." He ran a hand through his hair. "I thought you might come looking for me back then, but I guess Landon didn't mention me."

"He might have mentioned you, but I was spinning with grief. Names were a blur to me. I didn't know who to trust. The kids I spoke to painted a picture of my brother that felt completely false."

"Because a dead drunk kid was a better explanation than anything else," AJ said harshly. "I wish I'd been braver, talked louder, but I didn't know what to do. The police turned me away. No one wanted to hear what I had to say."

She couldn't really blame AJ. It wasn't like he had a smoking gun, either, just a theory that, like other theories could be wrong. But it was something to look into.

"Do you have any idea where Landon might have kept his research files?" Matt asked. "I understand that his computer and phone were missing."

"That was another reason I didn't believe it was an accident," she said, looking to AJ for his answer to Matt's question.

"I didn't know they were missing, but he was always writing stuff in black notebooks. He had at least six of them. He kept all the information on his algorithm there," AJ replied. "You cleaned out his apartment. You probably have them."

She shook her head. "I don't remember any black notebooks."

"Do you still have his things?" Matt asked.

"Yes. I have his boxes in a storage unit in my building. But there weren't any black notebooks." She frowned. "This is why you should have talked to me back then, AJ. No one else mentioned notebooks to me."

"Like I said, I went to the police, and they weren't interested in what I had to say. And Sabrina told me the same thing when I went to the legal aid center. I started to think I was the crazy one."

She couldn't really blame AJ, but she still wished they'd had this conversation six years ago.

"Look, I'm sorry," AJ continued. "I really am. I liked Landon. I respected him. But I don't want to get dragged into this. Does anyone know about me?"

"As far as I know, just Alanna. But Alanna said she didn't know where you were. I don't think you need to be worried."

"Except you're both here now, and I'm going to be in an FBI file." He turned to Matt. "Can you keep me out of this? I don't want to end up like Landon and Sabrina, especially when I don't know anything."

"I understand," Matt said. "I'll do my best to keep your name out of it."

"How good is your best?" AJ challenged.

"Very good," Matt returned. "I don't want anyone else to get hurt, especially not someone who's trying to help. We appreciate your candor, Mr. Patel."

"I wish you'd never come here. Someone might have followed you."

"No one followed us," Matt said firmly.

"You need to go," AJ said. "Do whatever you need to do, just keep me out of it."

"Thank you for sharing," she said. "Thank you for being my brother's friend. It's nice to know someone cared about him."

"I wish I could go back in time and do things differently."

"So do I," she said heavily. "We'll go. We don't have to escape again, do we? Because that was a little harrowing."

He smiled. "No. There's an exit next to the bar. I'm surprised you didn't enjoy the entrance. Landon loved escape rooms. We'd travel miles to try out a new one. He liked the challenge. Not that any of them were much of a challenge for his big brain, but they were always fun."

Something else she hadn't known about her brother.

"Stay safe," AJ added as he opened the door. "Landon wouldn't want you to die looking into his death."

"I need to get justice."

"Justice won't bring him back. Maybe you should let this go."

"I can't let it go until I know what happened to my brother, until I make whoever took his life pay for what they did."

"Then I'll just say good luck."

When they left the club, the cool night air was instantly refreshing, and she sucked in several welcome breaths before turning to Matt. "AJ gave us a few things to think about."

"He did," Matt agreed. "I'd like to take a look at Landon's boxes."

"We can do that, but I really don't remember packing up a half-dozen black notebooks. However, my mind was in a fog then, so it's possible I just thought they were class notes and no longer important. I haven't looked in those boxes in probably five years."

"Let's do it now. Are you hungry?" he asked. "We could pick up a pizza on the way to your place."

"Okay," she said, a little surprised he wanted to do it now. But that was probably because he didn't want her looking into Landon's boxes without him. "What do you think about what we just heard?"

"That we have more to figure out."

"Because I found AJ. I told you I could be a valuable asset."

"You did," he acknowledged. "AJ was helpful. But you still need to stay in your lane, Haley."

"I'm not very good at that," she said candidly. "And I hate to make a promise I know I can't keep, because I'll do whatever it takes to find Landon's killer."

"That's what I'm worried about. Because *whatever it takes* could put you in danger."

"I'm willing to take that risk. Why don't you get the pizza? I'll eat anything, and I'll meet you at my apartment in an hour or whenever you get there."

"All right. But if you get into those boxes before me, don't hide what you find. I'm on your side, Haley."

She gave him a long look. "I hope so, Matt. I really need law enforcement to step it up this time. I'll see you in a while."

As Haley got into her car, Matt headed toward his vehicle, already having second thoughts about suggesting dinner together. He wanted to see what was in her brother's boxes, but spending more time with Haley felt like a bad idea. They were getting too close to each other, too involved. She was a witness, and he was an FBI agent. They weren't friends. They shouldn't even be calling each other by their first names. But that wasn't what was bothering him the most; it was just—her. She was pretty and smart...fierce at times, vulnerable at others. And he found that both attractive and a little too dangerous.

He never mixed business with pleasure, not unless he was undercover, playing a role. But that wasn't happening here. He was himself. She was herself. And there was an unexpected attraction between them. He'd seen the recognition in her gaze when they'd bumped into each other in the escape room. But he wasn't going to act on it. And neither was she. They were investigating two murders: one old, one new. There was no time for anything else.

He needed to get his head together before they met up again, and the best way to stop thinking about her was to focus on the case. He believed that Landon's death and Sabrina's were tied together. But he didn't have the piece that connected them. What he did have was more information about Landon. Maybe he had to start in the past in order to figure out the present.

AJ had raised some interesting possibilities: Landon's passion project that might have been of interest to someone, and the cheating operation that had been part of the fraternity culture could have contributed to his death. A lot of fraternities seemed to be able to get their hands on prior tests and worked together to keep their GPAs high enough to avoid probation. But Landon's fraternity had had an even better option: a TA who was one of them, who could actually change grades.

Landon had balked at that request. That provided at least one motive for murder but seemed like an extreme resolution for a problem with a grade.

He pulled out of the lot and headed back to Santa Monica. About a mile away from the club, he saw Haley's car stopped at the nearest light, a black SUV behind her.

The light changed, and both cars proceeded through the intersection, as did he.

For the next ten minutes, despite several turns, the SUV stayed right on Haley's tail, and as Haley entered the Hollywood Hills, his gut tightened.

His phone rang, and he took the call on speaker.

"Matt?" Haley's voice was tight with tension. "I think someone's following me."

"So do I," he said grimly.

CHAPTER EIGHT

"What should I do?" Haley asked. Her heart hammered against her chest as her gaze darted to the rearview mirror.

"Just keep driving for now," Matt told her. "It could be a coincidence. Leave your phone on."

She prayed it was just a coincidence, but as she navigated the twisty curves of the Hollywood Hills, the headlights of the car behind her loomed large in her rearview mirror, a constant, menacing presence. As she got deeper into the hills and away from the city lights, the road narrowed, with one lane in each direction, the canyon walls pressing close on either side.

"I don't like this, Matt. It's getting darker, and there's no one on this road but us."

"Just keep driving. Once we get through the canyon and into West Hollywood, we'll go somewhere very public and lit up."

"Okay," she said, forcing herself to focus on the road ahead. The guy behind her probably wouldn't try anything with someone else behind him, even if he had no idea it was an FBI agent. But as his lights suddenly blazed in her mirror, she realized he was very close.

"He's right on my bumper," she said, her voice rising in pitch.

"Speed up a little," Matt said, "as if you've just noticed he's crowding you."

She pressed down on the gas, but the SUV immediately closed the gap. A second later, the car behind her hit her bumper, giving her a hard jolt. "Oh, God! He just hit me, Matt."

"I've got you, Haley. I'm coming up beside him. I'm going to slow him down. But you've got to drive faster. Give me some room."

She pushed the gas pedal to the floor, and her car jumped with the force, flying down the road. Her gaze moved to the rearview mirror. Matt's vehicle was coming up next to the SUV, crowding him, forcing him to slow down so Matt could slide in behind her.

But the other guy wasn't backing down, and she soon realized in horror that there was a car coming in the opposite direction, heading straight for Matt.

It was now or never. Matt must have realized the same thing and bumped the SUV hard, forcing him to the side of the road, but the other guy hung on, pushing Matt back into oncoming traffic.

Matt was forced to retreat, and her tail was behind her once more.

A hundred yards later, she saw a turnout on her right. It was risky to pull over, but if she took it fast, maybe the guy behind her wouldn't be expecting it. And she felt like she had to do something. She waited until the last second, then swerved into the turnout, hitting the brakes so hard her car skidded toward the rail. She braced for impact from either the rail or the car behind her, but her brakes held, and her tail was moving too fast to stop in the turnout, disappearing down the road in front of her.

Matt pulled up beside her and jumped out of his car, his gun drawn, as if he expected the car to return, but the road remained empty. Then he put his gun away and opened her door. Hands trembling, she undid her seat belt and climbed out, falling into his strong arms.

He held her tightly against his broad chest. "Are you all right?"

"I think so. I can't seem to stop shaking." She looked down the road, but there was still no car in sight in either direction. "Is he really gone? I thought he was going to knock me through the railing."

"You made a fast move. Very quick thinking, Haley."

"I wasn't sure it would work. Thank God it did." She paused. "He probably didn't want to have a witness, and he couldn't take out both of us at once." She blew out a breath of relief. "I've never been so scared in my life."

He gave her a reassuring look as he gazed into her eyes. "You're safe now, Haley."

"I can't quite believe it. I'm still shaking."

He pulled her back against his chest, and she buried her face in his shoulder, breathing in his scent, letting his steady heartbeat calm her racing pulse. She might be safe now, but what about later? What about tomorrow?

After a few minutes, she pulled away from him, looking into his eyes. "Do you think he followed me from Cipher?"

"Probably."

"AJ could be in danger. We have to warn him. We did exactly what he was worried about; we led someone straight to him."

She let go of Matt to grab her phone off the console and punched in the number for Cipher, asking the woman who answered to get her AJ, that it was urgent, a matter of life and death.

"I'm sorry," the woman said. "But AJ is gone. He left twenty minutes ago. He said if anyone called to tell them he was going on a trip, and he didn't know when he'd be back."

"Okay. Thanks." She looked at Matt. "He's gone. He left right after we did. He had a bad feeling."

"Well, that's good."

"Is it good? Is anything good? Because things appear to be getting worse."

"That just means we're getting closer. Are you going to be able to drive home?" he asked.

"I don't think I have a choice. I can't stay here."

"I can get someone to come and get your car, or we can come back tomorrow and get it."

"I can drive. Just don't let anyone get between us."

"I won't. I'll follow you all the way home, and we'll order a pizza when we get to your place."

"If he followed me to Cipher, he must know who I am, where I live. Am I going to be safe at home?"

He frowned. "I don't know. But let's check the boxes you took from Landon's apartment. Then we'll figure out what to do next to keep you safe."

———

Her shaking had stopped by the time she got home. Matt had kept his promise and stayed right behind her. He parked in front of her building, then got out of his car and got into hers as she pulled into the underground parking garage. It seemed a little silly to need him to do that, too, but he'd offered, and she was grateful for his presence.

It was odd how quickly they had gone from wary adversaries this morning to reluctant allies this afternoon, and now, after what had just happened, he felt like a friend, someone she could actually count on. There had been very few of those people in her life. Which was why she quickly reminded herself she shouldn't get carried away.

He might have just saved her life, but that's because he was an FBI agent. He was trained to protect people, and he'd done for her what he would have done for anyone else. He was still the same controlling guy who wanted to be in charge and wanted her to stay in her lane. She probably shouldn't forget that.

They took the stairs to her apartment. "The elevator only works half the time," she told him. "After I got stuck in it once for fifteen minutes, I decided I'd stick with the stairs."

"That must have been a long fifteen minutes for someone with claustrophobia."

"I chewed every one of my fingernails down to the quick. Thankfully, the manager was able to get it restarted fairly quickly." She paused. "Do you have any phobias?"

"A few things scare me, but I wouldn't say I have a phobia about anything in particular."

"What would be one of the things that scares you?" she asked as they made their way down the hall to her front door.

"I don't like sharks. I see a fin in the water, and I'm getting out, even if it's a dolphin."

She smiled, sensing he was not being serious. "Have you ever actually been close to a shark?"

"Not the kind that live in the water," he returned.

"They might be less dangerous than the other kind."

"You are probably right."

She inserted her key in the lock and opened the door, stepping across the threshold with some trepidation, but everything appeared exactly the way she'd left it. Matt followed her inside, and she turned the deadbolt behind him.

"I was a little afraid to open the door," she said. "I wasn't sure what I'd find."

"It's good for you to be cautious. Mind if I look around?" he asked as he moved toward her bedroom.

"That won't take long," she said as he popped into her small bedroom and bath and returned to the living room. "It's not exactly a mansion."

"It's comfortable," he said as he returned to the living room.

She smiled. "I think so. My furnishings are pretty much sourced from flea markets and thrift stores, but everything is cozy and makes me happy."

"That's the most important thing."

She moved toward the kitchen. "Do you want some water or a glass of wine? Because I'm going to open a bottle."

"I'll take a glass of wine," he said, pulling out his phone. "How about I order us some pizza?"

"That would be great. Get whatever you want. I like everything." She grabbed a bottle of red wine from her cabinet and opened it, filling two glasses with generous portions as Matt ordered dinner.

Taking the glasses into the living room, she sat down on the couch and let out a sigh as she took a sip.

Matt slid into the chair across from her, picking up his glass.

"It's not super expensive wine, but I like it," she said.

"It's good." He gave her a thoughtful look. "Do you think I'm a rich guy, Haley?"

"I don't know. I haven't thought about it."

"You just pointed out your furniture is used and your wine is cheap, as if you needed to defend it."

"I guess I like to get the judgment out of the way," she muttered.

"I wasn't judging anything."

"Oh, come on. You've been judging me since you showed up here this morning." She let out a breath. "I can't believe that was just this morning. So much has happened since I went to the park last night."

"That's for sure. And I did judge you for taking Sabrina's phone. I wasn't completely sure you were telling me the truth, but the events of the day have convinced me you were just hoping for information."

"We did get information from the phone. We found Alanna, and she led us to AJ."

"Who pointed us to the boxes. Where are they again?"

"They're in a storage unit in the garage. We should have gotten them when we were down there. We can go now."

"In a minute. Take a breath." He paused as he glanced down at his phone to read a text.

"Is that about the case?" she asked.

"It's about the car that followed you. I sent the license plate to my team. The vehicle is registered to Steven Holliday, a seventy-three-year-old man who resides in Torrance. One of my team members called him, and he said he doesn't use the car anymore. He gave it to one of his grandkids on their sixteenth birthday last month."

"The guy following me was not seventy-three or sixteen."

"I would agree. One of my team members will follow up with the teenager and see if he lent his car to anyone."

"We should warn Alanna that things might be heating up. AJ was smart enough to take off as soon as he spoke to us. I'm afraid for her now."

"I'll give her a call." He punched in her number, but after a moment, he left a message, saying, "Alanna, this is Agent Lawson. Give me a call back. I'd like to talk to you about ways to increase your security." He left his number, then ended the call.

"Can't you get her protection?" she asked Matt.

"Unfortunately, our resources for protecting people who are not in immediate danger are limited."

"But she could be in immediate danger."

"I'm more worried about you at the moment."

"Well, I'm worried about both of us. She didn't answer her phone. Something could have already happened to her."

"I'll send someone over to do a welfare check."

As he made another call, she settled back on the couch, feeling better that they were doing something to ensure Alanna was all right. The fact that someone had followed her from AJ's made her wonder if that person hadn't been following her all day.

Matt ended the call and said, "Someone from my team will check on Alanna."

"Thanks for doing that."

He took a sip of wine, then said, "Tell me more about you and your brother. Let's start before he went to college. What was your family life like?"

"Why does that matter?" she challenged.

"Because it will help me understand who Landon was."

"You don't need to know who he was to find his murderer."

"His past could be relevant. When AJ talked about Landon's pet project, you got an odd look on your face. You said you didn't know about it, but there was something that resonated with you. What was it?"

"I don't like to talk about my past."

"We're talking about Landon's past."

"His past is my past, and it's painful."

He leaned forward. "I wouldn't be pressing if it wasn't important. You need to talk to me, Haley. The more I know, the more I can be effective in getting you the answers you want."

He was right, but she hated going back in time.

"I'm not going to judge you," he added. "And you can trust me."

"I trust the barista to make my coffee right, but trusting someone with big things…I don't do that."

"Because someone broke your trust," he said, making it a statement and not a question.

"Among other things. My brother and I didn't have a happy childhood."

"Tell me about it."

She hesitated, then gave in. He could find out about her past whether she told him or not, so she might as well save the time. "My father worked as a stockbroker and made some very bad bets for himself and some of his clients. They all lost a lot of money. My dad was embarrassed, ashamed, and devastated. He couldn't see a way out. It was too much for him to cope with, so he killed himself when I was twelve years old and Landon was seven."

"Damn," Matt muttered, his gaze filling with compassion. "I'm sorry, Haley. I had no idea."

She averted her gaze, not wanting to see the pity in his eyes, as she continued her story. "My mother fell apart after my dad's death. To be honest, she was fragile even when he was alive. But after he was gone, she spiraled, turning to alcohol and drugs to medicate herself. She couldn't keep a job. She had trouble getting us to school. She disappeared for days at a time. We got kicked out of apartments. We lived in a car for a while. And when I was sixteen, she disappeared for a month. A neighbor turned us in to social services. They put Landon and me in separate foster homes, and it was the worst few weeks of my life. I couldn't stand losing my brother, too. I knew how scared he must be."

"What did you do?"

"I went looking for a blood relative, and I found my mother's aunt. She hadn't been close to us in years, but she lived in Los Angeles in a nice enough house. She was divorced and had a good job. I told her I would take care of Landon. I would clean the house. I would do whatever she needed to have done. All she had to do was become our guardian. She finally agreed. But it almost didn't happen because my mother showed up again. She had some fantasy of us all being together. I begged her to let us live with her aunt so that Landon and I could stay together while she got better. In a moment of sanity, she agreed. I think, in some ways, it was a relief."

"What was it like living with your great-aunt?" he asked, making no comment on what she'd just told him.

"She was nice, somewhat indifferent. She'd always been up front about never wanting kids, and she liked to travel, so she was gone a lot, but she gave us a roof over our heads and money for food. It all worked out."

"And you raised your brother. That was a huge burden to take on, Haley. I can't begin to imagine how you felt, having to raise yourself and your brother. Your parents really let you down."

"They did. But raising Landon was easy. He was a good kid and so smart. He got straight A's all through high school. He was just brilliant. I went to the community college and worked so I could pay for extras for us. Sometimes, Landon would help me with my homework because he was so far ahead for his age, it was crazy. He got into a gifted program and won a full scholarship to Westbridge. It was the dream school for him—for both of us, really. We knew that they really helped their graduates get into good jobs, so it felt like we could finally see the future." She paused as a wave of sadness swept through her. "He was so close to graduation when he died." She shook her head. "I still can't believe what happened to him. He was such a sweet guy. Who would want to kill him?"

"Maybe someone who saw a possible fortune in his project, a project he might not have wanted to share with the one for all, all for one group."

"But why kill him? What would that get them? He had the brains, the knowledge for what he was doing."

"If they wanted what he refused to give, then he had to go," Matt said. "I'd like to talk to Landon's girlfriend. What was her name?"

"Brooke Mercer. I have no idea where she is."

"I'll find her," he said confidently.

"I might be able to find her, too," she returned.

He smiled. "From what I've seen so far, I don't doubt that. Why did you get into journalism?"

"I always loved to write, and I liked the idea of standing up for people who didn't have a voice, revealing truths that someone might have tried to bury."

"I looked you up. You've done some excellent work, Haley."

"Thanks. I looked you up, too. I found your name on corporate fraud cases. Why are you on a murder investigation now?"

"Because Sabrina had a piece of paper with my name and number on it in her bag, courtesy of Anthony Devray."

"Did you find him yet?"

"No, but I will."

"Why did your fraud case get shut down?"

"We got a new director three months ago. She wanted to

reorganize, cut cases that were taking too much time and didn't have enough evidence to go the distance—her words, not mine."

"Do you think there was more than just efficiency behind her decision?"

"Yes. I think she might be a director who caves to political pressure, and that won't work in the white-collar crime division."

"So you left. And your new team?"

"Very impressive. And they operate without a lot of oversight, which will be refreshing. At least, that's my hope. Time will tell." He paused as his phone buzzed. "Our pizza is ten minutes away. Why don't we go down to the garage and get those boxes before our food arrives?"

She was more than happy to do something other than talk about her past, although bringing Landon's boxes back into her apartment would probably be worse.

CHAPTER NINE

The storage unit was cramped and dusty, filled with the remnants of her brother's life. She'd never put anything else in there. In fact, she'd never even opened the door in the past five years. But now, she had to go back in time. She grabbed the large box while Matt pulled the two smaller ones out, and they took them upstairs, setting them on the floor by her coffee table.

"These are dusty," Matt commented.

"I haven't opened them since I put them in there a few weeks after I moved here, which was about ten months after Landon died. I'm kind of afraid to look in them now, but I know I have to."

"You have a few more minutes," Matt said as he glanced at his phone. "The pizza is here. I'll run down and get it. We'll eat and then tackle the boxes."

She was relieved by the delay. "Sounds good."

After he left, she cleared her files off the dining table, then got plates and napkins from the kitchen. She had just grabbed the bottle of wine and their glasses from the coffee table when Matt knocked on the door a moment later. She checked the peephole just to be sure, then let him in. The delicious aroma of garlic and onions followed him through the door, and she realized she hadn't eaten all day. "That smells good."

"It is good. One of my favorite places in Santa Monica."

She looked at the box. "Luigi's. I've never been there."

"Once you taste this pie, you'll want to order it again and again."

"You are very confident in your choices," she said dryly. "Even when it comes to pizza."

"Especially when it comes to pizza," he said as they sat down at the table.

She took a slice from each box, happy to eat, and Matt seemed to feel the same way. When she'd finished her third slice, she sipped her wine and said, "I feel better."

"Me, too."

She sat back in her chair. "We've been talking a lot about me, and I know next to nothing about you. What's your story, Agent Lawson?"

"I thought you researched me."

"I didn't have time to look that deeply, and you have no social media presence, so that didn't help."

"I don't like social media. I see no value in posting photos of my food or looking at other people's photos of their food."

"It's not always about food," she said with a smile. "It's about sharing your life."

"I'm an FBI agent. Being covert is part of my job."

"Sure. But we're working together, so I should know more about you. Where are you from? What was your childhood like? Do you have family?"

"I have a family. I was born in a small farming community in Central California called Millbrook. Population about 10,000. My dad was an agricultural inspector for the state, and my grandfather was the sheriff. My mother was a teacher, and my grandmother worked at the quilt store."

"Sounds like a beautiful family growing up in an idyllic place."

"It was great until I was nine years old. That's when my

father filed a complaint against the food-processing plant that employed sixty percent of the residents of Millbrook. After that, our family was basically shunned by the locals. No one would talk to us. Kids were beating me up in school. My grandmother's quilt store was getting vandalized, and my grandfather had to go out and arrest people who hated his family. My mother was furious with my dad for ruining everything."

"But he was just doing his job, which was to protect food safety, right?"

"Exactly. He was being responsible. There were a lot of safety violations at the plant, and the company had been polluting the local rivers and streams. Even though people understood why my father did what he did, their lives got worse, and they needed someone to blame. That was him."

"They should have blamed their employer."

"The plant was shut down for almost a year. Thirty percent of the population was gone within six months, including my family. My parents separated. My mom moved to San Francisco. My father took me to San Diego. My grandparents stayed in Millbrook another few years, but my grandmother's shop eventually shut down because she didn't have enough business. Then they moved to San Diego to be near me and my dad. By then, my parents were divorced, and I shuttled back and forth on a plane between them far too many times to count."

"That's rough."

"It was what it was," he said with a shrug. "After a few years, they both remarried. My mother had another baby, a son. My father had twin girls with his new wife. So, the family got bigger but also further apart."

"How did you feel about it all?" she asked curiously. "You're giving me a lot of facts but not feelings."

"It didn't matter how I felt. They couldn't stay together, and I couldn't change that."

"It should have mattered how you felt."

"Well, it didn't. And that's that."

"Are you really that pragmatic?"

"I really am," he said.

"Okay, fine. What about your stepparents? Did you like them? Are you close to your half-siblings?"

"Not really. I'm eleven years older than my half-brother, who is twenty-three, and thirteen years older than my half-sisters, who are just turning twenty-one. Frankly, after I got out of high school, I barely saw any of them. Once I was eighteen, and it wasn't court mandated that I spend time with my parents, it was easy not to."

Despite his matter-of-fact tone, she suspected his feelings about his family were more painful than he wanted to say, maybe even wanted to admit to himself. But the picture he'd painted of a life lived between two families that were growing without him made her feel for the lonely little boy whose happy life had been completely upended by circumstances beyond his control.

"Anyway, that's my story," he finished. "I told you it wasn't that interesting."

"I think it's very interesting. You said your grandfather passed away. What about your grandmother."

"She died a few years before he did."

"I'm sorry. What did your grandfather think of you being an FBI agent?"

For the first time since he'd started talking about his family, a smile lifted the corner of his lips. "He used to rag on me for not being a cop, thinking the feds were better, but he was proud, and he set high standards. I always wanted to live up to them."

"Like opening a door for a woman."

He tipped his head. "Like that."

"He sounds like a great grandfather. Did you ever think about being a cop instead of an FBI agent?"

"No. I didn't have a clue what I wanted to do when I went to college. I majored in business and accounting and went into finance after graduation. I thought money meant security and stability, but three years in that field was three years too many. It was dull, and I didn't feel like I was accomplishing anything. But with my expertise in corporate accounting and knowing how to follow money, I was a good candidate for the FBI."

"And you've worked with whistleblowers like your father. Having lived that experience as a family member, that must make it easier for you to understand the mindset, the fear of speaking truth to power."

"I do have a better understanding and appreciation for my father's bravery in telling the truth," he admitted. "I didn't always appreciate it, but time gave me perspective."

"It must have felt a little lonely to have one foot in your dad's world and another foot in your mom's world. Did you feel like a wishbone, each one trying to pull you in their direction?"

"Only in the beginning, when they were fighting to keep me. After they moved on with their lives, it didn't feel like either one of them was trying to pull me in their direction. Not that they didn't love me. They just had a lot of other people to love. Anyway, I made peace with it all a long time ago."

She wondered if that was true, or if he'd just buried his feelings so deep, he didn't think they were there anymore. "Making peace is not easy," she murmured.

"Did you do it with your parents?"

"Not completely. I still have anger for both of them. But what I have never been able to come close to making peace with is Landon's death."

"I'm beginning to understand why you feel so frustrated. I'm sorry the police and the school let you down."

"Julia Harper said the brass forced her and the other detective to shut it down. Otherwise, she would have kept going. She was the only one who listened to me, who heard me, who wanted to explore other options, but her hands were tied."

"I saw her name in the file. I'd like to talk to her."

"You should. I contacted her earlier today after I spoke to you. I hadn't talked to her in several years, but I knew she was a private investigator now, and I thought she might be able to help me figure out what Sabrina knew."

He straightened, a frown on his face. "This is an FBI investigation, Haley. I can't have a PI getting in the middle of it."

"She could be an asset, just like me. She was there six years ago, working in the police department. She's the only one who tried to help."

"I'll talk to her. But is it possible she was part of the cover-up and just didn't play it that way in front of you?"

Now, she was the one who was frowning. "I don't believe that. She genuinely cared about me and my brother. You just said you had a case shut down by the higher-ups, so why couldn't that have happened to Julia?"

"It could have, but I would prefer to keep the circle of information tight. From here on out, don't tell her anything without speaking to me first. Someone tried to run you off the road tonight. And I don't want to trust anyone unless I've vetted them first."

"She wouldn't have tried to run me off the road." She paused, suddenly realizing that Julia was one of the few people who had known she was at Cipher. But she still didn't believe Julia had had anything to do with that attack. She was just letting Matt's doubts get into her head. "Let's focus on my brother."

"If we're going to do that, it's time to get into his boxes. Are you ready?"

"As I'll ever be," she muttered as they got up from the table. She grabbed a pair of scissors from a drawer and then moved into the living room, kneeling next to the big box. She slit the tape and opened the box. "This has academic stuff," she said, waving her hand toward the textbooks, notebooks, and papers inside. "But there aren't any black notebooks. And definitely no computer, no phone."

"I'll start there. Maybe there's something written down about his passion project."

"Okay." As Matt looked through that box, she opened the

other, finding Landon's favorite Westbridge sweatshirt on top. She picked it up and held it to her, thinking it still smelled faintly of her brother, or maybe that was just her mind wanting the connection.

"Your brother took a lot of notes in his classes," Matt said. "And old school, too, handwritten on binder paper. I bet his grades were never less than an A."

"Never," she agreed. "He would freak out if he got a B. Controlling how he did in school was his way of dealing with the unpredictability in our lives."

"Makes sense."

"Landon didn't voluntarily drink himself to death, Matt. I knew him better than anyone. I raised him. That wasn't who he was. He didn't use alcohol to drown his sorrows, not after watching my mother chase the highs only to fall even lower when they ended."

He looked up from the box and met her gaze. "I believe you, Haley."

"Really?" she asked in surprise. "You do?"

He nodded. "I do."

His words touched her deeply because no one except Julia had ever believed her, and even Julia had expressed doubts at times. She'd always felt so alone in her fierce defense of her brother. "Thank you," she said, blinking away the moisture in her eyes. "That means a lot to me."

"But we still have to prove it."

She looked back in her box and pulled out a couple of framed photos that had been in Landon's room. Her heart twisted again at the first one, which was a picture of her and Landon in Hawaii.

"What did you find?" Matt asked.

She showed him the photo. "I took Landon to Hawaii for his high school graduation. I scrimped and saved for months. It was the first time either of us had left the state. We could only afford four nights in a cheap motel, but the beach was beautiful, and we felt like we were starting a new chapter." She shook her head and let out a sigh, then picked up the next photo. "This is Landon and Brooke, his girlfriend."

"I'd like to see that." She handed him the photo of Brooke, a very pretty brunette wearing a tight mini dress, her hand on Landon's chest, as they smiled for the camera. In the background, there were Greek letters on a banister, but they weren't at the fraternity house. "I think that was taken at one of Brooke's sorority events," she said. "They look happy."

"Your brother doesn't look exactly like you, but there's definitely a resemblance," Matt commented.

"That's true. Landon had dark-blond hair like our mother, while I inherited the brown hair from my dad. But we both had the same blue eyes." She paused for a moment. "I looked at the photo a bunch of times in the first few days and told myself that I should be happy that Landon was smiling and had a girlfriend and was enjoying his life. But after talking to AJ, I wonder if this moment captured his true feelings."

"Are there any more photos?"

"Just this one," she said, picking up a loose, unframed photo. "It's a picture of all the guys in the fraternity house. I guess everyone must have gotten one. I circled the faces of the guys I talked to." She handed him the photo.

"I met Henry earlier today at Adler and Briggs."

She started at his comment. "That's right. You were going to go to Sabrina's law firm. I never asked you what happened."

"Not much. I met Henry and his father, Graham, and Sabrina's supervisor, a woman by the name of Lindsay. The company had already secured Sabrina's files and refused to discuss the clients she was working with. It wasn't a productive meeting. I did bring up Landon's death, but Graham immediately insisted it was an accident."

"I'm sure no one is going to change their story now, not unless we find evidence to prove they are lying. What did they say about Sabrina?"

"They expressed the appropriate amount of concern. They presented a theory of Sabrina being stalked or harassed by someone on a dating app, but no one had a name, just random comments Sabrina had made about someone bothering her. Her manager claimed Sabrina was a friend, then almost immediately recanted, saying they only had a professional relationship."

She met his gaze. "Interesting that they already had their own theory ready to go. They want you to start looking for Sabrina on dating apps, talk to people she might have matched with, look through her texts for men she dated."

"You're very quick, Haley. You have an investigative mind."

"Journalism requires research. It's easy to get distracted by a shiny penny when someone puts it right in front of you."

"I wasn't distracted. I immediately recognized their theory as a ploy to steer my investigation in a specific direction. I wasn't going to fall for that."

She liked that Matt was sharp, too. They needed to be at the top of their game if they were going to get justice for Landon and Sabrina. "I'm glad you saw through them."

"It wasn't difficult." He looked back at the photo. "Thanks for putting names next to faces."

"You're welcome, but as you can see, I only spoke to about eight out of forty guys in that house."

"Trent Adler has lighter hair than his cousin Henry."

"He's nicer, too, and he comes across as more genuine than Henry. But that could have been an act. Honestly, I felt like they were all acting when I met them. I couldn't tell who was genuinely sad and who was just saying the right things. I do know that Trent was not at the house that night. His alibi was confirmed. As was Brooke's. The others at the party didn't have alibis. But no one seemed interested in confirming their whereabouts through photos or eyewitness accounts."

"I noticed the timeline was vague. And there were also a lot of drunk kids at the house that night, not just the fraternity brothers. There were plenty of girls there, too."

"I'm sure it was a chaotic scene, but I still believe someone knew something or saw something. They were just afraid to come forward."

"Did you talk to Landon the day he died?"

She shook her head, more anger and guilt running through her. "No. It had been a few days since we'd spoken. We were planning to get together the following week for my birthday. I was working in Santa Barbara at the time, at a small newspaper, and I was going to drive down to have dinner with him."

"Santa Barbara, huh? Did you move to LA after his death?"

"About ten months after he died. I needed to be busier. Santa Barbara was too quiet. The *Sentinel* was a better place to escape. After I got that job, I moved in here, and that's the last time I looked in these boxes." She dug through the rest of the box, but aside from some of his favorite hats and childhood mementos she hadn't been able to throw away, there was nothing of significance. "There isn't anything here," she said.

He gave her a sympathetic smile. "I'm sorry I'm making you look through all this, Haley."

"As soon as Sabrina contacted me, I knew it was all going to start up again. I just thought I'd have more information to go on." She opened the last box, and her breath caught in her chest. "Oh, my God. I forgot about this."

"What is it?"

She pulled out the small white box carefully. It was tied with a blue ribbon and had a birthday card taped to the top, her name written in Landon's careful handwriting.

"Landon had gotten me a birthday present. I found it in his room when I was cleaning up. I couldn't bear to open it at the time. Or even later. I'm not sure I can do it now."

"You don't have to."

"No, I should. It's been long enough." Her hands trembled slightly as she opened the card, her eyes blurring with tears as she read his note.

"Do you mind telling me what he said?" Matt asked.

She nodded, then read aloud. "You know you've always been my North Star, Haley. Whenever I felt lost, I looked to you, and I knew where home was. You're the only person I've ever trusted completely, and that will never change. When I saw this, I had to get it for you. I hope you'll think of me when you wear it. Love, Landon."

She opened the box and found a heavy silver star pendant on a long silver chain with intricate designs around its shimmering edges. She pulled it out to show Matt.

"It's beautiful," he said.

"I can't believe he found this." She put the necklace on, fingering the pendant as she gazed down at it. "He told me I was his North Star when he went to Westbridge. And I told him that I felt the same way about him. It had always been the two of us. When we were together, wherever that was, that was home." She blew out a ragged breath. "I'm sorry for getting so emotional. This is more difficult than I thought it would be."

"Don't apologize for loving your brother, for grieving him. I'm glad you have something to wear to remember him by."

She gave him a teary smile. "Me, too. I should have opened the gift before. I just couldn't do it. Then I forgot about it. I tried to forget about everything because it hurt so much." As Matt's phone buzzed, her thoughts returned to the present. "Has something happened?"

He looked up from the text he was reading. "Alanna boarded a plane for Melbourne at four o'clock this afternoon."

"As in Australia?" she asked in surprise.

"Yes. She apparently wanted to get as far away from LA as she could. Anyway, we have one less person to worry about."

"That's good." She looked back into the box, pulling out some of Landon's favorite books that she'd also kept for no real reason, except she had fond memories of him reading before bed. "There's nothing else here that can provide us a clue."

"Nothing here, either," he said as he leaned back in his chair while she got up to sit on the couch.

"I didn't really think there would be, but it was good we looked," she said with a tired yawn.

"I would like to go over the notes you made at the time. I noticed a big stack of files on that chair over there."

"You're welcome to look through them." She couldn't help yawning again. "Sorry. I guess the day is catching up to me."

"It's been a long day. You should get some sleep, Haley."

"Do you think I'm safe here after what happened earlier? Should I go to a hotel?"

He gave her a thoughtful look, then said, "What do you think about me sleeping on your couch?"

"I think you'd be pretty uncomfortable."

"I'm not worried about that. I can sleep anywhere."

"It's not necessary. I can take care of myself," she said. "I've been doing it for a long time."

"I know you have, but I'd feel better if you weren't alone."

As he finished speaking, her phone rang. She didn't recognize the number, but with everything going on, she decided to answer. "Hello?"

"Stop," the robotic voice said. "Stop before it's too late."

She paled as the call ended.

"Who was it?" Matt asked.

"I don't know. It sounded like a bot. They said, 'Stop before it's too late.'"

His lips tightened as his serious expression met hers. "I'm definitely sleeping on the couch."

"Maybe you should," she agreed. "I'm surprised you didn't suggest I do what they asked, that I stop looking into my brother's death. Why didn't you?"

His brown eyes darkened. "Because it's already too late."

His honest but harsh words stole the breath from her chest.

"Sorry. I should have sugarcoated that," he said, reading her expression.

"No. I want you to be honest, and you're right. They're already worrying about what I know. That's why they tried to run me off the road tonight. If they get an opportunity to silence me, they will."

"I won't let that happen."

"I like your confidence," she murmured.

"I'm going to remind you of that next time you think I'm taking over."

"I said confidence, not controlling attitude."

"I'm afraid they go together. Go to bed, Haley. I promise you'll be safe tonight."

She got to her feet. "Okay, thanks for staying. But if you have to leave, if you get a call or something, or you're just too uncomfortable and you need to go home, can you tell me before you go? I'd rather wake up and be told you're leaving than just find you gone in the morning." It was the closest she'd come to sharing that particular fear with anyone. Hopefully, he would relate it only to the extreme circumstances they were in and nothing else.

"I won't leave without telling you. You can count on that."

"Thank you. I'll get you a pillow and a blanket," she said as she headed into the bedroom. She'd stopped counting on people a long time ago, but maybe tonight she would let herself count on him.

CHAPTER TEN

Matt woke up Saturday morning to the sound of coffee brewing and the soft shuffle of bare feet on hardwood floors. For a moment, he forgot where he was, then the events of the previous day came rushing back. Haley's couch was about as comfortable as advertised—which was to say, not at all—but it wasn't the lumpy cushions that had kept him awake. It was Haley.

After reading through her notes on her brother's death, he'd finally gone to sleep around two, having developed an even greater appreciation for her investigative skills and also her fierce love for her brother. He hated that law enforcement had let her down. He hated that it had taken six years for someone to try to get information to Haley, only to be killed before she could do that.

More than anything, he hated the way Haley had grown up— her father dead by suicide, her mother's descent into alcohol and drugs—leaving Haley to raise herself and her brother. She had a strength that had been forged in fire, but there was still a vulnerability to her that made him want to protect her. He'd seen that last night when she'd asked him to tell her if he had to leave. She hadn't wanted him to disappear, probably because too many people in her life had vanished without a word. It had taken courage for her to express that thought. He'd seen the shame in her eyes and had wanted to tell her it was okay. But it had seemed better to just assure her he would be there and hope she would believe him.

She'd definitely had it rough growing up, far worse than he had. And it made him realize how lucky he'd been to have two parents who, while rarely focused on him, had made sure he had a place to live, plenty of food, and money to take care of his needs. But Haley had been the one to give all that to her brother.

Knowing what he knew now, he felt even more determined to help her get the truth about her brother's death, because he didn't believe it was an accident any more than she did. It was time for law enforcement to step it up, and he intended to do just that. He just had to make sure she was safe while they were unraveling the truth, which meant he should try to get her into a safehouse. She'd balk at the idea, but she'd almost lost her life last night. If he hadn't been right behind her, he didn't know what would have happened.

Thankfully, he'd been there to save her, to hold her in his arms, to comfort her. And that memory reminded him of the dreams he'd had about her last night—dreams that were definitely not appropriate for an FBI agent to have about a witness in an active investigation. Haley Kenton was brave and beautiful, but she was also vulnerable and directly connected to his case. He couldn't forget that.

Taking a breath, he opened his eyes, knowing he needed reality to chase away the lingering dream images. Turning his head, he saw Haley walking toward him with two mugs of coffee in her hands, a bright smile on her face and light in her striking blue eyes, and his resolve to keep her at a distance immediately fled. She'd put on worn jeans and a tank top that clung to her curves, and her hair was pulled back in a ponytail, which emphasized her natural beauty. He was instantly attracted.

"Do you want coffee, Matt? It's black, but I can add creamer if you want, or a touch of vanilla."

"Black is fine." He desperately needed a shot of caffeine to clear his head. He sat up, swinging his legs to the floor, and accepted the mug with a grateful smile. "Thanks."

"I also made breakfast. Nothing fancy—just scrambled eggs and toast." She settled into the chair across from him. "I thought you might be hungry. There's also leftover pizza if you prefer that."

"The eggs are fine. You didn't have to cook for me."

"You didn't have to stay and protect me. Breakfast was the least I could do." She sipped her coffee. "Did you look through my files?"

He was grateful for the question, for the opportunity to think about something other than how much he wanted to kiss her. Clearing his throat, he said, "I did look through them. They were certainly more detailed than the file we got from the police."

"Did anything jump out at you?"

"No, but your notes about Brooke definitely make me want to talk to her."

"I actually looked online for her this morning. Brooke works for a marketing firm owned by Jill Adler."

"Of course she does," he said dryly. "The Westbridge grads like to hire their own. What does their client list look like?"

"Companies with Westbridge grads in the CEO chair. Not all, but a lot."

"This is starting to feel incestuous."

"It is," she agreed. "According to the company's social media page, they're sponsoring a charity event today at the Sheridan Art Museum. Feel like looking at some art?"

"I can't think of anything I'd rather not do," he said dryly.

"Really? Not an art fan?"

"It all looks like kids' scribbles to me. But I haven't spent a lot of time in museums."

"You've missed out. I love museums. They're so clean, controlled, beautiful. Even the air is exactly the right temperature and level of humidity. And when you look at art that was created sometimes hundreds of years ago, it gives perspective."

He could hear the passion in her voice and was surprised. "I wouldn't have guessed you liked art so much."

"I used to take Landon to free days at museums. We'd spend hours roaming the big exhibition rooms. It was a safe place for us to go." She shrugged. "Anyway, that doesn't matter. We need to talk to Brooke, and that's where she'll be. Plus, there will be others there as well, including Jill Adler and maybe some of her relatives. I can spring for the tickets."

"I can cover that," he said. "But first, I need to change clothes and check in with my team. Do you feel comfortable staying here while I do that? Then I can come back and pick you up."

"Sure," she said, hesitation in her voice. "That makes the most sense."

"Don't leave the apartment, Haley. Don't answer the door. If anything feels off, call 911 and then call me."

"I'll be fine. But why don't you eat before you go? I've got the eggs in the oven. They're warm."

"Great. I'm starving."

As she got up and moved into the kitchen, he put on his shoes and then joined her at the table. After breakfast, he would put a little more space and time between them. He just hoped his decision to leave her alone wouldn't prove to be a bad one.

———

Matt had left at ten, and it was now noon. In the past two hours, Haley had cleaned the kitchen, made her bed, read through her files, and walked back and forth to the window a few dozen times to make sure there was no one in the alley, no one watching her window.

She still had an hour and a half to go before he'd be back, and she needed to find something useful to do so she could stop worrying about the danger she was in. She also needed to stop thinking random, inappropriate thoughts about Matt, who had looked less like an FBI agent sleeping on her couch and more like a very attractive man with ruggedly handsome features and a fit, powerful body that she'd found comfort and safety in after almost being run off the road.

But it wasn't so much gratitude that was dominating her thoughts; it was the feeling of attraction, chemistry...both completely inconvenient emotions, considering the man was a federal agent who could still lock her up for obstructing justice. Not that she thought he would. They'd moved beyond that. But she still couldn't allow herself to think he was anything more than an agent trying to do his job.

It wouldn't be so difficult if she hadn't gotten to know him better last night. She'd heard about his family and related to his emotions as a lonely boy caught between his divorced parents and their new families. While her childhood had been much different, she'd also felt very lonely in her role as Landon's second mother.

She'd wished a million times that her father hadn't taken the easy way out, because it had certainly seemed that way to her, even though as an adult she could logically understand he'd had mental issues and deeply painful emotions. But even knowing that, she still blamed him for leaving her alone to fix everything.

At least Matt's father had done something heroic, even if his actions had also cost the family their idyllic living situation.

Her phone rang, startling her out of her thoughts, and she was grateful to focus on someone other than Matt. "Hello, Julia?"

"Did you talk to Arjun? I thought you were going to call me last night after you spoke to him?" Julia said, with an edge to her voice.

"I'm sorry. There was a lot going on. I did speak to Arjun— AJ, as he calls himself now."

"Did he tell you anything new?"

"He said that my brother was working on a passion project, some kind of algorithm, and AJ thought the frat brothers might have been trying to get their hands on it."

"What would this algorithm do?"

"I don't know. AJ said Landon was secretive about it."

"Well, I'm not sure his frat brothers would have been smart enough to do anything with his research without him being there to explain it."

"I don't know. AJ said Landon told him the guys were pressuring him to do something he didn't want to do. He was angry and worried to the point that he was thinking about dropping out of school. Then he died a few days later. That's why AJ didn't believe it was an accident. He knew Landon didn't drink and that he didn't like those guys anymore and wasn't interested in their parties."

"So, AJ believes someone in the fraternity wanted your brother's research, his algorithm?"

"Yes. And that makes sense when you consider the fact that Landon's phone and computer were missing. He also mentioned that Landon had written a lot of his project research in a series of black notebooks. I didn't see those at his apartment. I think they were stolen, too." She paused. "Unless the police took the notebooks into evidence?"

"No. There weren't any notebooks. Maybe I should follow up with AJ. You told me he runs a gaming club in North Hollywood?"

"Yes, Cipher. But he's gone, Julia. AJ left his club right after we did. I think he got scared by my questions and the fact that Sabrina Lin is dead."

"That's too bad. He might have known more that he didn't say."

"I agree, but I don't think we're going to find him."

"Did he say anything else to you?"

"That was it. But something happened after we left the club.

I was followed into the Hollywood Hills, and someone tried to run me off the road. Luckily, Matt—Agent Lawson—was not far behind me. He saw what was happening and tried to get between us. It was pretty scary. I thought one or both of us was going to crash into the canyon, but eventually, I was able to pull over, and the guy took off."

"That must have been terrifying, Haley."

"I still shake when I think about it. I've never had anyone go after me like that before. I think he was trying to kill me."

"You need security. Can you get the FBI to put you up in a safehouse?"

"I don't know. Matt spent the night on my couch. I'm okay now."

"Is he there with you?"

For some reason, Julia's question gave her pause. It seemed like Julia should be more interested in talking about the case than about where she was and who she was with. But that was silly; Julia was just concerned about her. She couldn't let Matt's doubts color her thoughts. She knew Julia better than he did.

"Matt will be back shortly," she said. "We're going to a charity event hosted by Jill Adler today."

"I doubt she'll confess anything at a public event."

"No, but maybe she'll reveal something we don't already know."

"Or you'll make someone see you as more of a threat than they already do. You should take a page out of Arjun's book and get out of town."

"And do what? I have a job. I can't hide. And I'm not sure they wouldn't track me down anyway. They don't know what I know, and that makes me dangerous to whoever killed my brother and Sabrina. Anyway, I'll be careful, but I'm going to keep trying to figure this out. Agent Lawson believes Landon was murdered, so he's willing to help me."

"I heard his unit pulled the file."

"Were you forced to leave anything out of that file, Julia?"

"No. I was forced to stop asking questions and to find evidence to support what the university claimed happened."

"Who do you think was putting pressure on the police?"

"Someone from Westbridge, probably the dean, who was most likely being pressured by alumni parents and donors."

"Why would they have power over the police department?"

"The deputy police chief, Alan Matson, had political aspirations. Now, he's a state senator."

"I forgot about that," she murmured.

"I can't say for sure he was the one being influenced. He was several levels above my supervisor. I was just told to shut things down, and unless I had hard evidence otherwise, we couldn't pursue it." Julia paused. "I'm glad the FBI is involved now, and Lawson has a good reputation as a solid agent."

She was reassured by that information, because she was definitely going to need Matt's help. "I'm happy to hear that."

"Keep in touch. I'll be curious to hear what Brooke has to say now."

"So will I."

CHAPTER ELEVEN

The Sheridan Art Museum occupied what had once been the Beverly Hills estate of silent film producer Harold Sheridan, and the building still retained the grandeur of 1920s Hollywood royalty. As Matt drove through the iron gates of the estate, the three-story Mediterranean villa rose from perfectly manicured grounds, its cream-colored stucco walls and red tile roof speaking to an era when movie moguls built palaces to rival European nobility. Palm trees created a canopy over the circular drive, where valets in crisp white shirts efficiently whisked away luxury cars.

"I feel like I should have worn something fancier," Haley said as they got out of the car.

"You look great," he said, silently noting how the light-blue dress highlighted her eyes and her curves.

"You don't look so bad, either," she muttered, her gaze sweeping down his gray suit and maroon-colored tie. "But you might be hot. It's supposed to be low eighties today."

"I had a feeling this was a suit and tie event," he replied. And he was right. Every man within his view was formally dressed.

He put a hand on her back as they walked up the steps to the main entrance to enter the building through a pair of massive oak doors flanked by marble columns. Inside, the lobby hummed with quiet chatter as guests checked in at the reception desk and then accepted glasses of sparkling champagne from waiters moving through the rotunda.

The interior was breathtaking. Soaring twenty-foot ceilings were supported by hand-carved wooden beams, while crystal chandeliers cast warm light over polished floors inlaid with intricate geometric patterns. After checking in with the receptionist, a woman in a silky gray dress directed them toward the main gallery, where the special exhibition was housed.

"The contemporary pieces are in the east wing," the woman said with a practiced smile, "and the garden reception is just through those doors." She gestured toward a wall of floor-to-ceiling French doors that opened to a spectacular view.

Through the glass, Matt could see the museum's crown jewel —formal gardens that would have made Versailles jealous. Geometric hedges formed perfect patterns around a central fountain, while ancient oak trees provided shade for elegantly dressed patrons browsing the silent auction tables scattered throughout the space.

They accepted champagne from a nearby waiter, then headed farther into the museum.

"There she is," Haley said suddenly, nodding toward a woman near a large abstract painting that looked like someone had thrown red and black paint at a canvas. "That's Brooke Mercer."

Brooke was even more striking than she'd been in the picture he'd seen last night. Her dark hair was swept into an elegant updo, and in a champagne-colored dress, she had the kind of polished beauty that came from expensive skincare and professional styling.

"She's very attractive," Haley commented. "Probably the prettiest woman Landon ever dated. He was a shy, nerdy kind of guy, but he did blossom when he got to Westbridge. He gained confidence."

"Enough confidence to get himself a beautiful girlfriend," he murmured.

"I still think it's strange he never told me about her."

A tall, skinny blonde woman interrupted Brooke's conversation with the older couple. And as the two of them moved away, the blonde gestured toward the entrance, as if she were displeased about something. Brooke nodded in response and walked back to the check-in desk. As the blonde turned her face in their direction, he realized he recognized her. "That's Jill Adler, isn't it?"

"Yes. Trent's twin sister and Henry's cousin."

"She looks stressed. And she seemed annoyed with Brooke about something."

"Events like this are probably always stressful. Should we try to talk to Jill?"

"Let's start with Brooke and let Jill calm down a bit."

They walked quickly back toward the hostess. As Brooke finished her conversation, she turned around and then halted when she saw Haley.

"Oh my God," Brooke breathed, her hand flying to her throat. "Haley? Haley Kenton? I can't believe it's you. It's been so long since I've seen you."

"Hello, Brooke," Haley said. "You look wonderful."

"I...thank you. You do too." Brooke's gaze darted between Haley and Matt, clearly trying to process this unexpected encounter. "What brings you here? Are you interested in contemporary art?"

"Actually, we came to see you," Haley said. "This is Agent Matt Lawson with the FBI. We'd like to ask you a few questions about Landon."

If Matt had thought Brooke looked pale before, she went absolutely white now.

"FBI?" she repeated, her voice barely above a whisper. "I don't understand. What could you possibly want to know about Landon now? He died so long ago."

"We're following up on some new information," Haley said.

"New information?" Brooke's voice cracked slightly. "About Landon's death? But it was ruled an accident."

"Could we speak somewhere more private?" Haley asked, glancing around at the crowded entry, where their conversation was beginning to attract curious looks.

"Of course," Brooke said quickly. "Let's go into the garden."

Brooke led them to a quiet, secluded corner of the museum's sculpture garden, which was adjacent to where the outdoor event was being held.

"What kind of new information?" Brooke asked again, her body stiff with tension.

"We can't discuss the details of an ongoing investigation," Matt said. "But we'd like to ask you about your relationship with Landon. How well did you know him?"

"We dated for a few months. Haley already knows our story." Brooke gave Haley a look, as if begging for intervention.

"Agent Lawson wants to hear it from you, Brooke," she said.

"It was a whirlwind romance," Brook said, turning her attention back to him. "An instantly perfect relationship. We just... clicked. Landon was different from the other guys. He was quieter. More serious. I liked that."

"You told me you were planning to move in together after graduation," Haley said. "I have to admit I was surprised to learn you were so serious, because Landon never mentioned you to me."

"Really? I thought he had. He said he couldn't wait to tell you about us." She paused. "Actually, I think he said you'd gone through a recent breakup, and he didn't want to rub our newfound happiness in your face. I guess he never had a chance to tell you." She took another breath. "I couldn't wait for graduation. I was excited to plan a future with Landon away from school."

"What kind of future?" he asked.

"Oh, you know. Living together. Taking a trip to celebrate graduation."

"A trip where?" Haley interrupted.

"Uh, well, Landon really wanted to go to Costa Rica. He'd seen a documentary about the rain forests and became obsessed with seeing them in person."

Matt noticed Haley stiffen beside him, her blue eyes sharpening. "Really? Costa Rica?" Haley questioned.

"Yes," Brooke said. "We thought it would be fun."

"Interesting," Haley commented.

Clearly, she found it more interesting than he did, but he'd follow up with her on that later. "Did Landon ever talk to you about his work?" he asked. "His research projects? Maybe something he was working on outside of his classes?"

Brooke's brow furrowed. "He did talk to me, but to be honest, I rarely understood anything he was saying. I was an English major, and his tech talk was way over my head."

"One of his friends said he was working on a personal project, and he would write down details about his research and his experimentation in a black notebook. He wrote so much, he had filled up probably six of them that year. Did you see him doing that?"

"Yes. He said he was working on stuff for his classes. I was surprised how much he liked to scribble in his notebooks. I preferred the computer."

"Did you see the notebooks after he died?" Matt asked.

"I don't remember." Brooke's gaze turned to Haley. "You cleaned out his apartment."

"I didn't see them," Haley said. "You were in his apartment when I arrived. I wondered if you had taken them or if someone else had been there before me?"

"I didn't take them," Brooke said. "And I didn't see anyone else come into the apartment. Are you accusing me of stealing something?"

"I'm just trying to figure out where his notebooks went."

"I have no idea. And what do notebooks have to do with him drinking too much?"

"That's another question I have," he said, drawing her gaze back to him. "Haley tells me her brother wasn't a drinker. Obviously, a sister might not know as much as a girlfriend. What was your reaction when you heard he'd fallen into a pond and drowned because he was staggeringly drunk?"

Brooke drew in a deep breath. "I couldn't believe Landon had gotten that drunk, because he wasn't a big drinker. Haley isn't wrong about that. But he was stressed out that week. He said he had some decisions to make, and he needed time to figure things out. I felt a little annoyed with his reluctance to confide in me. That's why I went away that weekend. But after what happened, I felt guilty. If I had stayed that weekend, he might not have died."

Brooke's emotion seemed genuine, the guilt in her eyes, the pain in her voice. But he still wasn't sure he trusted her, and he didn't know why. There was just something off.

Before he could ask her another question, a male voice rang out.

"There you are," the man said as he joined them. "I've been looking all over for you, Brooke." He gave Brooke a kiss and then turned to them with a warm and easy smile. "Hello. Sorry to interrupt. But I need Brooke to tell me what painting I'm supposed to bid on." He slipped his arm around Brooke's shoulders, clearly indicating they were together.

"This is my fiancé, Kyle Vance," Brooke said. "Kyle, this is Haley Kenton. She was...Landon's sister."

Kyle's expression immediately shifted to surprise, then sympathy. "Oh. I'm so sorry. Brooke told me about Landon. He sounded like an amazing guy."

"Thank you," Haley said tightly.

"And this is Agent Lawson," Brooke continued. "The FBI has some new information about Landon's death."

Kyle's eyebrows rose slightly, but his smile remained in place. "Really? I thought it was an accident."

"It wasn't," Haley put in.

"How could it be anything else?" Brooke asked.

"We can't get into details," he interrupted, not wanting Haley to give away too much. "Did you know Landon as well, Mr. Vance?"

"No. I didn't go to Westbridge. But I've heard a lot about him from Brooke. He was important to her. Sometimes, that makes me a little jealous. Not easy to compete with a saint."

"Landon wasn't a saint, just a good guy," Brooke said quickly.

"He impressed a lot of people who knew him, that's for sure," Kyle said. "I work with Drew Sanderson. He was also a big fan of your brother."

"What do you do?" Matt asked.

"Financial analysis," Kyle said. "Are you nearly done? I need to steal Brooke away for a few minutes."

"I'm sorry I couldn't be more help," Brooke said. "It was good to see you again, Haley. I hope...you find whatever it is you're looking for."

"I don't know what to think about her," Haley said as soon as they were alone. "She was very convincing about loving Landon and feeling guilty, but I think she was lying when she told me they were going to take a trip to Costa Rica."

"Why?"

"Because Landon was a germophobe. He was freaked out about tropical diseases, especially mosquito-borne diseases, because he always got bitten. When he learned in high school that mosquito bites can kill you, he was constantly spraying himself down whenever he went outside. Trekking through the jungle of Costa Rica? There's no possible way that was his dream vacation."

"Maybe he was willing to risk a mosquito bite for his very attractive girlfriend."

"I don't buy it. I think she was lying. In my experience, when

I stumble upon a truth, it's usually because of a small lie someone didn't think would matter."

"Like the simple question of what were you planning to do after graduation."

"Exactly. But when Brooke started talking about how she could have prevented his death, it felt like she was being real, so I'm confused. What do you think?"

"Brooke knows more than she's saying. I'm also interested in her new boyfriend, Kyle Vance, who works with Drew Sanderson, Landon's fraternity big brother. The Westbridge gang has stayed close. Let's see who else is here. With Jill and Brooke running this thing, I could see some of those other guys showing up."

As they reentered the building, Jill immediately came toward them. "Haley Kenton?" she asked. "I'm Jill Adler. I don't know if you remember me."

"I remember you," Haley said.

"Brooke just told me you were here. I couldn't believe it. How are you?"

"I'm doing all right. This is a lovely event. I understand Brooke works for you."

"She does. We started working together last year." Jill turned to him with an inquisitive smile. "And I understand you're an FBI agent."

"Matt Lawson," he said, shaking her hand.

"And you came here to talk to Brooke about Landon? Something about his death not being an accident?"

It was clear that Brooke had made a beeline for Jill as soon as she and her boyfriend had left them. That was interesting. *Why the pressing need to fill her in so quickly? Had Brooke wanted to warn Jill about something?*

"How well did you know Landon?" he asked.

"Not particularly well. He was in my brother Trent's fraternity, and we partied together a few times. Trent and my cousin,

Henry, were devastated by Landon's death. It was so sad and shocking."

"Are Trent and Henry here today?"

"Trent is supposed to be. I haven't seen him yet. Can I ask why you're here now, wanting to talk about Landon's death? Has something happened?"

"We have some new evidence. But I can't get into it."

"All right. I understand this is important, but this is also a charity event, one crucial to raising money for the Children's Hospital. I would request that you be as respectful as possible. You're not planning to arrest anyone, are you?"

"Is there someone I should arrest?" he countered.

"Of course not. I just don't want the event to be disrupted in any way. I hope that doesn't sound callous, because, of course, I want you to find out what happened to Landon. I just don't think anyone here can help you."

"We're just asking a few questions. I doubt anyone will be concerned or bothered, unless they have something to feel guilty about," he said.

Anger sparked in her eyes, but she had a tight grip on her composure, and her expression returned to neutral very quickly. "Then I won't worry. Thank you for the reassurance. Excuse me."

"She's strung tight," he commented.

"And Brooke filled her in very quickly. If we were hoping to take anyone by surprise, that opportunity has vanished. Should we try the patio and see who's out there?"

"Sure," he said as they moved toward the main patio where the silent auction was being held next to a crowded bar area. "Do you want something to drink?" He suddenly paused, his gaze catching on a familiar face. "What is she doing here?"

"Who?" Haley asked.

"The woman with the dark-red hair in the tan dress," he replied. "That's someone I used to work with—Shari Drummond." He moved forward to cut Shari off, and her expression stiffened when she saw him.

"Matt," she said in surprise. "I didn't expect to see you here."

"Likewise. Are you working, or is this pleasure?"

"Pleasure. I love art."

"I didn't know that about you," he commented.

She shrugged. "I guess it didn't come up. Are you going to introduce me to your friend?"

"This is Haley Kenton. Agent Shari Drummond. We worked together until a few days ago."

"Nice to meet you," Haley said.

"You, too."

"I'm going to get us some drinks," Haley interrupted. "I'll be back."

He wasn't sure why Haley had left, but he was happy to have a moment alone with Shari.

"Are you dating her?" Shari asked curiously. "She's pretty."

"No. She's a...friend," he said, stumbling a little over the word.

Shari caught that immediately, giving him a questioning smile. "Really? Why don't I believe you?"

"You should believe me, because it's true. Do you remember when I asked you about a woman named Sabrina Lin?"

"Yes. The woman who called the office looking for you and ended up dead in the park. I remember. Why?"

"Well, she apparently did speak to someone in the office, someone who told her that the information she had regarding an old murder at Westbridge University wasn't of interest to the Bureau. You said she refused to talk to anyone but me and hung up. I'm confused as to who she had a conversation with."

"How do you know she talked to anyone else?"

"I have credible information that she did," he said carefully. "Any thoughts?"

She considered his question, not looking particularly concerned. "There were a couple of other agents in the office when I took the call. Bill and James were there. I think Bill asked me who I was talking to, and I said it was a woman wanting to speak to you. I didn't give him her name or number."

"But her number would have been logged into our system," he said.

"Sure, but I don't know why he would have bothered to look it up. He didn't act that interested, and she didn't say why she wanted to talk to you." Shari paused. "Although Bill was always jealous of you getting the big cases. Maybe he thought this was an opportunity. What's going on?"

"I'm not sure, but something isn't adding up."

"All I know is that she asked for you, and I said you weren't there. She didn't want to speak to anyone else and hung up. Can you tell me more about what's going on? You mentioned a murder at Westbridge?"

"Yeah, it happened about six years ago."

"And that case is connected to the woman who called, the woman in the park."

"It looks that way."

"If I can help, I will. We may not be officially working together anymore, but you always had my back, and I had yours. I would like to hope that hasn't changed, Matt."

"It hasn't."

Relief entered her eyes. "Good. I'm going to miss working with you. I know you were frustrated with the lack of support on our last case. I hope you get more of that with Flynn's group."

"I hope so, too." He paused, giving her a speculative look. "Why are you really here?"

She gave him sly smile. "You know me too well. I'm working on something I can't talk about now that we're no longer partners. I guess neither one of us can be completely open anymore. That will take some getting used to. Before I go, tell me about Haley. Who is she?"

"She's a reporter at the *Sentinel*."

"You're dating a reporter?" she asked with surprise.

"I said we were friends. I didn't say we were dating."

"Maybe that's just as well. It's difficult to believe an FBI agent and a reporter can have a relationship when one will surely want to ask questions the other can't answer."

"Like I said, she's a friend."

"Too bad. It's about time you had a woman in your life." Shari gave him a smile and a playful pat on the shoulder. "I'll see you around."

As Shari moved away, Haley returned with two glasses of sparkling water.

"I didn't know if you wanted something alcoholic, but I thought you might be thirsty," she said.

"This is perfect. Thanks," he said as he took the glass from her hand.

"I also thought you might want a moment alone with your ex-partner. That she might tell you something if I wasn't standing right next to you."

"Unfortunately, she did not. She still claims she told Sabrina I wasn't there and that was the end of the call, but she did mention there were other agents in the room, so I don't know. It doesn't add up, but I've never had a reason to doubt Shari. We worked together for a year."

"Does it seem odd to you that she's here, though?"

"She told me she's working on something."

"Do you believe her?"

"Well, she's part of the white-collar crime division, and there are a lot of CEOs wandering around, so it's possible." He paused as his gaze caught on the man stepping onto the patio with Jill. "Isn't that Trent Adler?"

"It is. And it looks like Jill is pointing him in our direction, which means she's not trying to hide him from us, which probably means he doesn't have anything to hide."

"Or the best defense is a good offense," he murmured.

CHAPTER TWELVE

Haley considered Matt's rather cynical statement as she watched Trent move in their direction. Trent was of average height, dressed in an expensive dark-blue suit, his light-brown hair styled, his boyish, charming face giving him a rich boy-next-door kind of look. The last time she'd seen him, he'd been wearing jeans and a T-shirt, his eyes red from lack of sleep and maybe even some tears for her brother. He'd been twenty-one then and had seemed completely overwhelmed when she'd met with him the day after her brother's body had been found. He'd been nicer to her than some of the others. He'd actually given her a hug and told her how much he'd liked Landon.

"Haley," he said, giving her a compassionate smile. "Trent Adler. My sister told me you were here. I was surprised, but it's good to see you." His gaze ran down her simple blue dress. "You look better than the last time I saw you."

"I was going to say the same thing. This is Agent Matt Lawson."

He nodded, turning to Matt. "I heard you have some new information about Landon's death. Henry also told me yesterday that an associate of his died, and you were there asking questions about her. Are the two incidents related?"

She was surprised by his direct questions, but maybe Trent was smart to go on offense because he didn't appear at all threatened by their presence.

"I can't answer that," Matt said. "It's an ongoing investigation."

"Well, your appearance here suggests a connection, whether you can answer or not. What do you want to know? How can I help you?"

"Did you see Landon at the party? Did you witness his excessive drinking? Was there any kind of fight?"

"I wasn't at the party. I was at a friend's house that night, but my friends told me Landon was drinking heavily, that he started early on his twenty-first birthday celebration." Trent paused. "Landon was a good guy. He got along with everyone. I can't imagine anyone wanting to hurt him. He was very well-liked."

"I heard he was having problems with fraternity brothers wanting him to help them cheat by changing their grades or giving them test answers in advance," she interrupted. She didn't miss the sudden shift in his expression, although he quickly tried to cover it up.

"I don't know about that. I can't imagine Landon would help anyone cheat. He was very ethical."

"If he was being pressured by someone in the house, who do you think would have led that charge?" Matt asked.

"Are you suggesting that one of my fraternity brothers killed Landon?" Trent asked, bewilderment in his voice. "Because he wouldn't help them cheat?"

"I'm just asking questions," Matt said.

"The questions are insulting. And, no," Trent said with a decisive shake of his head. "I don't believe anyone was pressuring Landon, and I certainly don't believe anyone killed him. Whoever is feeding you that information doesn't know what they're talking about."

"Who doesn't know what they're talking about?" Henry Adler interrupted. "Agent Lawson, we meet again."

"Mr. Adler," Matt said, with a tip of his head.

"And Haley Kenton," Henry added with a nod in her direction. "It's been a long time."

"Yes, it has." Henry had been the least forthcoming of anyone she had spoken to about Landon. Even at twenty-one, he'd seemed slicker than the others.

"What are you talking about?" Henry asked.

"Landon's death," Trent said.

"I thought you were investigating Sabrina Lin's murder. How does that tie to Landon?" Henry asked with an inquisitive gleam in his eyes.

"I can't say," Matt replied.

Henry gave her a hard look. "What about you? Do you believe they're connected, Haley?"

"I don't know if there's a connection, but I believe my brother was murdered." It was the first time she'd said that to any of them. She'd said it many times to Julia and the police but never to one of the fraternity members, and it felt good.

Both Henry and Trent appeared taken aback by her words, an awkward silence developing between them.

"I hope that's not true," Henry said finally. "That would make his death even more terrible."

"You don't really believe that, do you, Haley?" Trent asked, his gaze more shadowed than it had been before.

"I do. And now, with the help of the FBI, I'm going to prove it."

Henry nodded. "Good," he said. "If it wasn't an accident, then Landon needs justice. And we are happy to help. But we'd also like to hear evidence not just speculation."

"We'll get evidence," she said confidently. "And we'll follow it wherever it goes."

"As you should," Trent put in, his gaze troubled. "It feels like you don't think we're on the same side, Haley, but we are."

"I hope so."

Henry cleared his throat. "Is there anything else? Because Jill wants Trent and me to put in some bids to get the auction action going." He turned to his cousin. "She especially wants to see your name at the top of every list, Trent. She said it's your brotherly duty."

"As long as I don't actually have to buy any of the art, I'll put my name down," Trent grumbled.

"Your place could use some art," Henry said. "It's about time you stopped decorating like a twenty-year-old. You should use my mom's interior decorator. She'd turn your apartment into something worthy of art."

"The last thing I want to do is live in an apartment that reminds me of your mother or mine," Trent said. Pausing, he turned to her with a sympathetic smile. "I'm sorry all this is coming back up again, Haley. I understand why you're desperate to get answers. I just don't think you're going to find your answers here. We were your brother's friends."

"Trent is right," Henry said. "Landon was our brother. And his death was a blow to everyone who knew him and cared about him."

They both had just enough sincerity to make it difficult to call them outright liars, but she still didn't believe a word they were saying.

"At any rate, we should help with the auction," Henry continued. "Are you going to bid on anything, Haley? Or are you just here to question people who went to Westbridge?"

"I'm not sure," she replied. "I haven't looked at the auction items yet, but I might be interested in something."

"They pay you pretty well at the *Sentinel?*" Henry asked.

It bothered her that he knew where she worked, although it was hardly a secret. "Of course not," she said, sensing his comment was also meant to put her in her place, remind her she wasn't one of them. And she couldn't help but wonder if he'd done the same thing to Landon.

"There are some inexpensive items," Trent put in. "Jill likes to make sure that the auction is accessible to all levels of donations."

"I'll keep that in mind," she said.

"Good luck with everything," Trent said, pausing for a moment as Henry left. "And I really do hope you find answers. I always thought it was an accident, but if it wasn't, then someone needs to be held accountable."

"Thank you," she said as Trent headed to the patio.

"Well, those two are night and day," Matt muttered.

"Not just in looks but in personality," she agreed. "Henry is dark and shady. Trent is open and light."

"Or at least that's who they want you to think they are."

She turned and met his gaze. "Henry wanted to remind me I wasn't of his class."

"I noticed that. Did it bother you?"

"No. I've been poor my entire life. I don't need some rich kid to remind me of that. I'm very aware of the size of my bank account." She let out a sigh. "I feel like we go around in circles in every conversation."

"Because Henry is right. We need evidence, not speculation," he said. "And it kills me to say Henry was right because I don't like him."

"Me, either. But I guess being a sleazy, arrogant prick doesn't necessarily make him a murderer."

Matt smiled. "No, it doesn't. But it also doesn't exonerate him. Do you want to get out of here?"

Despite the hopeful note in his voice, she shook her head. "Not yet. Let's go look at some art. I could use a break from the pointless conversations we've been having."

"They haven't been that bad. I'm getting a better idea of who everyone is now. Out of those we've met so far, I'd say that Brooke and Trent would be the most likely to help, while Henry and Jill have much sharper edges."

"What about Kyle?"

"Not sure about him. He wasn't at Westbridge when Landon was killed, so he's of less interest to me."

"That's true. But he's engaged to Brooke, and he works with Drew, so he's connected to the group in multiple ways."

"Have you seen Drew Sanderson?"

"No. Not yet. Maybe he's also looking at the art." She smiled as Matt let out a resigned sigh. "It really won't be that painful."

"We'll see."

As they entered the exhibition area, her tension immediately eased as they wandered through the rooms, admiring the art pieces. She knew Matt was probably bored, but the art soothed her soul, the way it always had. And it made her feel closer to Landon, to the times they'd shared at museums all around the city.

"Are you dying of boredom?" she asked about thirty minutes later.

He shrugged. "I'm fine. Some of it is...okay."

"Okay is not good enough. You have to look closer." She stopped before a painting of a woman at a window, her expression unreadable. "This one is layered with emotion."

"She just looks sad to me."

"But why is she sad? Look at her hands—see how tightly she's gripping the windowsill? And the way the light falls across her face, half in shadow. The artist could have painted her crying, made it obvious, but instead, he's showing us her restraint. The way she's holding herself together, even though something's breaking inside her." Haley's voice grew passionate. "You can feel the weight of whatever she's carrying. Sometimes the most powerful emotions are the ones people try to hide."

Matt gazed at her, then back at the painting. "You think she's waiting for someone?"

"Or she just realized he's never coming back." She blinked away a tear.

"I thought art was supposed to make you happy," he commented. "You're talking about yourself, not her."

"Maybe both of us," she said, giving him an emotional smile. "And it does make me happy. Because she's not just sad; she's strong. She's not giving up. She's going to move on. She's not the type of person to quit."

"You get all that from this painting?"

"Well, I suppose it's possible that we see what we want to see. And that's okay, too. Because art is supposed to inspire, not just depict."

"I have to say, you've given me a different perspective."

"Then the art did its job."

"Or you did," he said with a smile. "For the record, I happen to think you're also a strong woman who is never going to give up, never going to quit, because that's not who you are."

"It's not. Especially not when it comes to family." As they moved past the painting, she stiffened as a silver-haired man walked into the room with Matt's former partner at his side. "That's Senator Alan Matson. He was the deputy chief of police when Landon died. Why would your partner be with him?"

"She said she was working this party. Maybe he's part of an investigation."

"I think it's a weird coincidence, Matt. Shari is the one who takes Sabrina's call and says she never talked to her. Now she's here with Senator Matson, the one who shut down my brother's investigation..."

He frowned at her words. "How do you know Matson is the one who shut down your brother's investigation?"

"Julia said she thought he was behind it when I spoke to her earlier."

"You spoke to Julia today?"

"She wanted to find out what AJ told me."

"And you shared information after I told you not to?" he asked, disappointment in his gaze.

"I didn't tell her much of anything," she said defensively. "I couldn't just cut her off. And I trust her, even if you don't."

"Did you tell her where we were going today?"

"Yes," she admitted.

He let out an exasperated sigh. "Haley, you have to stop talking to her. If you aren't willing to do that, then I'll have to reconsider what I tell you."

The last thing she needed was for Matt to cut her off from the investigation. "Okay. I won't tell her anything else." She paused as her phone began to vibrate. She pulled it out of her bag. "That's weird. It's my neighbor. She wouldn't call me unless there was a problem." She moved toward the hallway behind them to get away from the crowd, and Matt followed. "Hello? Mrs. Gonzalez? Is everything all right?"

"No, it's not," her neighbor said in a tense voice. "I saw someone running away from your apartment, wearing a hood over his head and dark glasses, and he had some tools in his hand. He knocked me down and called me some swear word and then disappeared. When I looked at your door, it was hanging on the hinges."

"Oh, no," she said in alarm. "You're saying he broke in?"

"Yes. I called the police. They're on their way. I didn't know if you were in there, and I didn't want to go inside, but I called your name and you didn't answer. Eli said he thought he heard you leave earlier."

"Thank you so much for letting me know. I hope you weren't hurt."

"No. But I don't like what happened."

"I don't, either. I'll be home soon." She ended the call and turned to Matt. "Someone broke into my apartment. I have to go home."

"We'll leave now."

"This is bad, isn't it?" she asked, meeting his gaze.

"Let's go," he said, not answering her question, but then, he didn't have to.

CHAPTER THIRTEEN

Haley's stomach twisted with fear as Matt drove to her apartment. The twenty-minute drive felt like an eternity. She couldn't stop picturing her apartment torn apart, her private sanctuary violated by someone who wanted to hurt her—someone who had already killed her brother and maybe Sabrina, too. Her hands were clenched so tightly in her lap that her knuckles had gone white, and she could feel Matt glancing at her every few seconds as he navigated the familiar streets of her neighborhood.

When they turned onto her street, she could see a single empty patrol car parked in front of her building. No officers in sight.

"They must be upstairs," Matt said as they got out of the car and hurried toward the entrance.

They jogged up the stairs two at a time, and when they reached the second floor, Haley could hear voices. As they rounded the corner, her heart sank as she looked down the hall. Her apartment door hung at an odd angle, held in place by only the bottom hinge. The doorframe was splintered. Wood fragments were scattered across the hallway carpet.

Mrs. Gonzalez was standing nearby talking to one officer,

while another headed into her apartment. Tim, a musician, who lived in the apartment on the other side of her, was also there, hovering near his door in shorts and a T-shirt, clearly trying to figure out what was happening.

"Oh my God," she whispered. "It's worse than I thought."

"Haley," Mrs. Gonzalez said. "Thank God you weren't home. I was so worried when I saw the door. I was afraid you were inside."

She drew in a deep breath, giving her neighbor a reassuring smile. "I'm fine. Thank you for calling the police."

Matt flashed his badge to the officer talking to Mrs. Gonzalez. "I'm Special Agent Matt Lawson, FBI."

"Officer Connelly," the older man said, surprise in his eyes. "You live here?"

"I do," she interrupted. "I'm Haley Kenton."

"This break-in is most likely connected to an ongoing federal investigation," Matt said. "I'll be taking it from here."

"Okay, got it. My partner, Officer Cruz, is checking the inside." He'd no sooner finished speaking when Officer Cruz stepped into the hallway.

"All clear," he said.

"FBI is taking over," Officer Connelly told his partner, then turned back to Matt. "We'll let you take it from here. You can finish talking to the witness."

"Thanks," Matt said, turning to Mrs. Gonzalez as the officer left. "Can you tell me what happened?"

Mrs. Gonzalez nodded vigorously. "I was coming back from the market. I had just gotten to the top of the stairs when I saw a man coming out of Haley's apartment. He looked like he was running away from something. He had tools in his hands—a crowbar or something metal. When he saw me, he pushed past me and knocked me down right there in the hallway." She gestured to the area near the stairwell. "Called me a name I won't repeat."

"Can you describe him?" Matt asked.

"White man, maybe five ten, average build. He had brown hair—I could see some of it sticking out from under his hood. He had a beard, kind of scruffy. Dark glasses and one of those black face masks. And gloves—black gloves, like people wear when it's cold. He was very scary looking."

"Did he say anything else?" Matt asked.

"No. He was moving fast."

"Was he carrying anything but a crowbar?"

"Actually, he had a big backpack, too. It was hanging off his shoulder." She paused, looking at Haley with concern. "Are you in trouble, Haley? Don't I always tell you to stop stirring the pot with your news articles?"

Haley gave her a tense smile. "You do. I don't think this is related to that, though."

"Then what's it about?"

"I'm not sure. Thank you again for calling me right away."

"Is there something else I can do? What about your door? You can't stay there with a broken door."

"We'll take care of that," Matt told her. "You can go home."

"All right. You call me or knock on my door if you need anything, Haley."

"I will." As Mrs. Gonzalez moved down the hall, she stepped into her apartment and was shocked at the chaotic scene. Her living room had been turned upside down. Couch cushions were slashed open. Books had been swept off shelves, papers strewn everywhere. In the kitchen, every cabinet door hung open, dishes pulled out and left in haphazard piles.

"He really went at it," Matt observed as he followed her inside.

"My files," she whispered, rushing toward the dining room chair where her files on Landon had been sitting, but they were no longer there. Her computer was also missing. Everything was gone. "All my notes, all the copies of police reports, everything about Landon's case is gone, not to mention the research I had on my computer about other stories I've been working on."

Matt gave her a grim look. "Do you have a backup?"

"For most of my computer files, but not my personal hand-written notes." As she gazed at the rest of Landon's things that were strewn on the floor, she realized that the personal items had held no interest for the burglar. "I'm going to check my bedroom."

She moved into her small bedroom with a sense of dread, and her worst fears were confirmed when she saw that her dresser drawers had been pulled out and overturned, clothes scattered everywhere. Her mattress had been flipped, her closet ransacked. But the burglar had missed the hidden compartment in the top of her dresser, which contained her jewelry, passport, birth certificate, and two hundred dollars in cash. She'd also put the necklace she'd gotten from Landon into the compartment before she'd gone to bed and was thrilled that the last gift her brother had given her was still in her possession.

"Anything missing?" Matt asked from the doorway.

"I'm not sure. He missed this compartment in my dresser with my jewelry, papers, and cash. I guess that's good, but I can't believe I lost all my files and my computer. That's going to be expensive to replace." She blew out a breath, knowing there was no point in crying over what was already done. She had most of her work backed up, so that wasn't an issue, and she'd find a way to buy a new computer. But she still felt a wave of loss for the notes she'd composed after Landon's death. "I remember almost everything from my investigation into Landon's death, but it still hurts to lose my thoughts from that time."

"I understand. You have every right to be angry and upset."

"It won't get me anywhere. I don't know what to do now."

"Do you have a building manager?"

"Yes. His number is on the side of my cabinet in the kitchen."

"I'll call him and see if he can get someone out here to fix your door and change the lock. In the meantime, pack a bag. You're not staying here tonight."

"They won't come back. They took what they wanted," she said. "They got everything."

"Not everything," he said, meeting her gaze. "They didn't get you, and I'm going to make sure that doesn't happen."

"I don't want you to stash me in some hotel. I won't feel any safer."

"Until I can figure out a safehouse, I'm taking you to my apartment. I live in a security building. It will work for at least tonight."

She wasn't sure how she felt about going to Matt's place, but it was better than being left in a safehouse with agents she didn't know. Hopefully, it would only be for a night or two.

———

Thirty minutes later, after throwing clothes into an overnight bag, along with toiletries, her passport, birth certificate, cash, and her jewelry, Matt drove her to his apartment. When they'd left, the manager was already working with someone to fix her door and locks, so she was happy not to have to leave her apartment open.

Matt's apartment building in Santa Monica was a modern high-rise with a uniformed doorman and the kind of understated luxury that whispered rather than shouted wealth. After parking in the secure underground garage, they rode the elevator to the twelfth floor. Matt's unit was at the end of the hall, and stepping into his apartment felt like walking into a showroom at a furniture store. The open-plan living area featured sleek, stylish furniture in shades of gray and black, with splashes of navy blue in the throw pillows and an area rug. Floor-to-ceiling windows offered a distant view of the Pacific Ocean, the water glittering in the late afternoon sun.

"Guest room is down the hall," he said, setting her bag down. "Bathroom is right across from it. Make yourself at home. I'm going to check in with my team."

"Thank you," she said, meaning it. "I know this is above and beyond, Matt."

"It's no problem. I want you safe. And where I can keep an eye on you."

She felt a flutter in her chest at his protective tone, but she pushed it aside. This was about the case, nothing more.

While Matt disappeared into what she assumed was his home office, she explored the apartment. The kitchen was small but efficient, with high-end appliances. The refrigerator and freezer were surprisingly well-stocked, as were the cabinets and a spice rack. It was the only room so far that felt like it was used.

The living room had a large flat-screen TV, a leather sofa, and built-in bookshelves that held mostly nonfiction—biographies, true crime, and books about financial fraud. No novels, no poetry, nothing that revealed the man behind the badge.

The sliding glass door led to a small balcony with a bistro table and two chairs. Haley stepped outside, breathing in the ocean air and letting the stress of the day fade. With the water in the distance and the sound of traffic muted by the height of the building, she started to relax.

The door slid open, and Matt joined her by the rail. She gave him a questioning look. "Anything new?"

"No. Just filling my team in on what happened. They'll check security cameras in the area to see if we can find your burglar."

"Your team works weekends?"

"There's always a support staff on duty."

"The man in my apartment didn't sound like a Westbridge grad, more like someone who was hired."

"I agree. I doubt any of the Westbridge boys do their own dirty work, but there could be a money trail."

"The files they stole aren't worth anything to them. They'll soon see I don't know that much. Maybe that will make me less of a target."

"Maybe," he said in an unconvincing tone.

"I really wish I knew how Sabrina got new evidence. If she found something, why can't we?" she asked in frustration.

"We're not done, Haley."

"It feels like we are."

"It's just a setback."

"Someone destroyed my apartment. It was a vicious attack. It felt like they weren't just trying to steal my stuff; they were sending me a message."

"I know. I understand why you're upset," he said, meeting her gaze. "But try to look at this another way."

"There's another way?" she asked doubtfully.

"Every action they take gives them more exposure. We have another lead to follow."

"Well, happy I could help."

He smiled at her sarcasm. "You should scream."

"What? Why?"

"Because you need to let the stress out."

"I'm not going to do that."

"It might help."

"Screaming into the wind has never helped, but I am going to sit down." She let out a sigh as she took a seat. "Sorry to be a downer. I just need a minute. I'll bounce back."

"I know you will," he said, taking the seat across from her.

"This is a nice view," she said, as the ocean view calmed her anger. "It's peaceful out here. It feels like we're above it all."

"This balcony is what sold me on the place. When I come home, I usually need peace."

"Is your job dangerous? Are you always doing things like this? Bringing people here to protect them?"

"I've never brought anyone here. There's some danger, but it's just part of the job."

"I think you're downplaying it."

He gave her a faint smile. "You've had enough danger talk for the time being."

"You're right. So, did you hire a decorator, because there aren't a lot of personal touches in your place?"

"I hired a very lovely woman named Pam, who picked out everything."

"She did a nice job, although I would have gone for a warmer look. How long have you lived here?"

"Two years."

"Seriously?" she asked in surprise. "That long? Don't you want to make it a little more your own?"

"I don't spend that much time here. I work a lot. Sometimes I'm gone for days or weeks at a time on a case."

"Doesn't sound like you have much time for a social life."

"I don't. My job is not great for long-term relationships."

"Mine is the same way, or maybe it's that way because burying myself in work is better than going home alone," she said candidly. "I feel good when I'm being productive. Too much time alone usually makes me think too much. My imagination can get too active."

"Was Landon the same way?"

"No. He was more pragmatic than I was. I tried to shield him from the worst stuff; I didn't always succeed."

"I'm sure you gave it your all."

"Sometimes that wasn't good enough."

"Growing up the way you did, I can understand why you and Landon were so tight." He took a breath. "There is something Brooke said that made me curious."

"What was that?"

"She said Landon hadn't told you about their relationship because you'd recently broken up with someone, and he didn't want to rub their happiness in your face. Was that true?"

She frowned at the question. "I had broken up with someone probably three or four months before Landon died. It wasn't recent, and it wasn't like I was devastated. It was just one of those relationships that ran its course. We were together about six months before we both realized we didn't have much more in common than the fact that we were both reporters. Jared worked as a sports reporter for a local news station, and he lived and breathed sports on his personal time, too. He bet on games, played all the fantasy teams, hung out at sports bars, and painted his face and chest for playoff games." She shook her head. "It was too much for me. It's not that I don't like sports, but not at that level, and he couldn't talk about anything else. So, we ended it. I really didn't have a broken heart. I don't know why Landon would have thought that."

"Maybe Brooke was just making excuses for why you hadn't heard about her. Perhaps there wasn't that much to hear."

"She had a key to his apartment, so there was something going on between them."

"When you got to the apartment that day, what was she doing? Was she cleaning? Packing up her things? Did she help you go through Landon's belongings?"

She thought back to that horrible day. "I got to the apartment around five. Brooke was packing some stuff in a duffel bag. I wasn't really paying attention to what she was taking. She said she couldn't bear to stay there after what had happened. We talked a little, but we both kept breaking down. She finally left, and I spent the night on Landon's couch, thinking it was all a horrible nightmare."

He frowned. "Okay. That's enough. We don't have to keep talking about this now."

"If it helps you to understand, then I'll talk about whatever you want. As for Brooke, I don't know that I trust or believe anything she said, including her description of their relationship. She and Landon seem so different. I don't even see how they got together."

"She's a beautiful woman. I can't imagine any young man not being flattered by her attention. Maybe she was part of the frat's plan to loosen Landon up, distract him, get him to let down his guard. Love or lust can be blinding, especially when you're twenty. If the frat wanted something from Landon, maybe Brooke was their way in."

"That makes sense, but how can we prove it? Do we talk to Brooke again?"

"At some point. I want to keep moving around the circle. We don't want any one person to think they're the sole target of the investigation. Better to make everyone a little nervous."

"Out of the fraternity group, we haven't talked to Drew Sanderson yet. Or Josh Lorrie or Brian Covington."

"We also haven't talked to the professor that Landon worked for."

"That was Justin Harrington." She paused. "There's also the dean, who shut down the investigation. His name is Robert Haas. He was of absolutely no help to me. In fact, I thought he was rather rude. And then there's the former deputy police chief turned senator, Alan Matson. Can you talk to your former partner about him? She seems to know him."

"I will if that makes sense."

"What about Sabrina's contact referral—Anthony Devray?" she asked. "You said his phone was disconnected. Is there any other way to find him?"

"Maybe."

"There's a lot to do. And what we've done up to now hasn't gotten us very far."

"We've gotten far enough to make people nervous. And nervous people make mistakes."

"I hope that mistake happens soon. We need a break."

Matt's phone buzzed. "This is my team. Hopefully, we just got one."

CHAPTER FOURTEEN

"Jason, what do you have? Did you find who broke into Haley's apartment?" He put the phone on speaker so Haley could hear the update. She was right in the middle of everything and could possibly help with any questions that might arise.

"Not yet. Derek is still working on that. But we just got results back on the compound injected into Sabrina's body," Jason replied. "It was a modified neurotoxin with two synthetic stabilizers not available in commercial production. We matched one of the agents to a restricted chemical manufactured by a research-grade compounding lab in Pasadena."

"And the buyer?" he asked, excitement running through him.

"We were able to match plates on a vehicle seen at the lab the day before Sabrina was shot with a vehicle seen exiting the park. The car had fake plates, but we were able to get facial recognition on an ex-Army lieutenant, Gareth Pike, who was dishonorably discharged last year and now resides in Pasadena."

"Do you have Pike in custody?"

"No. He's dead. Overdose—probably staged. No phone, no wallet, no computers at the scene."

He let out a heavy breath as disappointment ran through him. "Someone's covering their tracks."

"It looks that way. Gareth Pike was a hothead and a drug addict. But he was a skilled marksman, and it's clear he was hired to do a job. We're digging into Pike's life, see if we can find a contract."

"Good. Now, didn't you say there's an event at your golf club tomorrow? Haley and I shook some of the Westbridge grads up today at the charity event, but we didn't meet with everyone. I'm especially interested in Drew Sanderson."

"Sanderson and his father, Kent, are playing in the tournament," Jason said. "Along with the Adlers."

"Can you get me in?"

"Of course."

He paused as Haley pointed to herself. Then he said, "I'd like to bring Haley as well. I need to keep an eye on her, and she makes our suspects uncomfortable. They have a more difficult time refusing to answer questions when she's there."

"I'll see you both tomorrow at two."

"See you then." He met Haley's gaze as he put down his phone. "We're making progress."

"The shooter is dead, so it doesn't feel like progress. I knew it was unlikely one of those rich guys would have actually shot Sabrina, but we've hit another wall, another dead body."

"It's almost impossible not to leave some kind of trail or a digital fingerprint on a job like this. It's usually buried under layers of encryption and secrecy, but my team is good, and they'll continue working as hard as they can to locate the employer."

"The Westbridge group has money and connections, Matt."

"True, but they're not invincible."

"I hope not."

"Are you hungry?"

"I...I don't know," she said with a helpless shrug. "I hadn't thought about it."

"Well, you don't have to think about it. I'll cook. You relax."

She gave him a questioning look. "You cook?"

"I'm not in line for a Michelin star, but I can throw something together. Why don't you settle in and take a few minutes to breathe? It's been a rough day. I know that finding your apartment in that condition was disturbing."

"It feels so personal now. It's weird. Someone tried to run me off the road last night, which was far more dangerous, but the way they went through my things...it really bothered me."

"Well, make yourself at home. You can watch TV, take a nap, a shower. Whatever. I'll get started on dinner."

"You're being very nice to me, considering it was only two days ago that you wanted to arrest me."

"Taking that phone was stupid and illegal. But I understand why you did it. We've moved past that."

"Yes, we have. Into a world that feels very topsy-turvy." She paused. "Thanks for taking me in. I think I will jump in the shower. It usually helps clear my head."

"Go for it. And your presence here will actually justify the money I spent on having a guest room because no one else has stayed there."

"Then, you're welcome," she said with a tired smile before heading into his apartment.

He couldn't stop himself from watching her every step of the way. He'd never felt so personally connected to someone involved in an investigation. He had always been able to separate his personal life from his professional one, but there was something about Haley that felt different, and he was a little concerned about the shift in his priorities.

He wasn't thinking as much about Sabrina's death and finding her killer as he was thinking about Landon, about helping Haley get the answers she'd spent six years searching for. He told himself it didn't matter that the line was blurring, because the cases were connected, but deep down, he knew the line he was walking was getting thinner, and he could get to a point where he wouldn't be able to see a line at all.

But that point wasn't now, he reminded himself. All he had to do right now was make dinner.

———

Haley couldn't believe what Matt managed to whip up in an hour and a half. When she sat down at his dining room table a little after seven, she was surprised to see a restaurant-quality plate of food in front of her. "What is this? It looks amazing."

"Chicken thighs sautéed in garlic and ginger with rice and chili bok choy," he said, as he sat next to her and picked up a bottle of white wine. "Would you like a glass?"

"Yes," she said, immediately scooping up a bite of his chicken dish. The spicy flavors had a nice heat to them, and she quickly went back for more. "This is amazing."

"I'm glad you like it," he said as he filled her glass.

"Do you cook like this every night?"

"No. But when I have some time, I like to eat in. It's a nice change from grabbing food on the go."

"I would eat in more often if I could cook like this."

"This isn't difficult," he said with a smile that seemed to be warmer every time he flashed it at her. His hard exterior had definitely softened over the past few days.

"I'll take your word for it. Did your mom teach you to cook?"

"My father was the chef in our house, at least before the divorce. His second wife cooked more than he did, and my mother never seemed interested in more than the basics. Luckily, her second husband liked to cook, so she never had to get better. What about your parents, before everything fell apart?"

"My mom would cook, but nothing that complicated. My dad would throw things on the grill. He knew his way around the barbecue, but not the stove or the oven."

"You haven't said much about him, beyond his death. Were you close?"

"I thought I was, but I was a kid. I had no idea what was going on in his head. I still don't, to be honest."

"I'm sorry," Matt said.

"I don't want you to be sorry for me. It doesn't make me feel better," she said candidly.

"How does it make you feel?"

"Ashamed."

"Why?" he asked with surprise. "You were a kid. You weren't responsible for the choices your parents made."

"I know, but after my dad's death, everywhere we went, people were whispering. I'd go to school and kids would stop talking whenever I got close. My mom felt it, too. Her friends didn't know what to say to her. I think that drove her need to escape." She paused as she thought about the past. "My dad was free, but we were trapped under this dark cloud that never seemed to pass."

"When did it get better?"

"Surprisingly enough, when we got to my great-aunt's house. That's when I felt like I could see the sun again, or, at least, the possibility of sunshine. It was kind of scary being away from my mother. Even though she was unpredictable, we knew what we were getting with her. We didn't know what we'd be getting with my great-aunt." She picked up her fork and took another bite, feeling a little of the tension ease now that they had moved on to happier memories in her life.

"You don't have to keep talking about this," Matt said. "Unless you want to. I'm happy to listen."

She smiled at that comment. "I didn't think you were going to be the greatest listener when we first met and you were barking questions at me."

"Hey, you ran away from the scene of a murder, and you stole the victim's phone. I didn't know what I was dealing with."

"Fair enough. Anyway, as I was saying, once it was just Landon and me living in my great-aunt's quiet, comfortable house, the world opened up. Landon did well in high school, winning all kinds of merit awards and acing the SATs. He got a full scholarship to Westbridge, and it felt like the future was going to be so much brighter."

"It sounded like he was happy there for most of the time."

"I think he was the first three years and maybe even the first half of his senior year, but in retrospect, that Christmas he seemed more subdued than usual. I thought he was just stressed about school and getting perfect grades. But now I know there was more going on."

"Everything looks different in the rearview mirror."

"I suppose. I just wish Landon had gotten to have a future. It's so unfair. And I hate that I'm even saying that because I learned a long time ago that life isn't fair. But I don't get to escape. I don't get to take the easy way out."

"You're talking about your dad's suicide now?"

"Yes. Sorry."

"Don't apologize. Just say what you're thinking."

"I've never really talked to anyone about it. I don't know why I'm talking to you."

"Because I'm a good listener," he said lightly, reminding her of what she'd just said.

"I had a lot of anger about my dad taking his own life. Of course, it was mixed with horrific sadness, too. But I was conflicted. It felt like he abandoned us. And I didn't understand how anyone could do that to their family. I could never do that. I could never leave the people I loved so unequipped for the future. Not if it was my choice."

"You're a stronger person, Haley. Maybe because of what happened."

"Maybe," she admitted. "I definitely grew up fast after that. I tried to tell myself he wasn't in pain anymore, and I should be happy about that."

"Except that you were still in pain," he said, meeting her gaze.

"I was. Along with Landon and my mother. I couldn't understand why my father wouldn't have been able to predict that my mother would fall apart, that Landon and I would suffer without him. Or maybe he did consider that and just didn't care."

"If he was in emotional pain, he wasn't thinking clearly."

"I have tried to accept that, and mostly I have. But sometimes my anger overwhelms me."

"I can't begin to tell you how to feel about what your father did. But I can say this; you're not just angry with him."

He was right. "My mother is also on the list," she conceded.

"But she's not at the top. You're in the number one spot. And that's the anger you need to let go of, Haley."

"I don't blame myself for what happened to them."

"But you do blame yourself for what happened to Landon."

"What happened to him is my fault. I wanted him to go to that school. I encouraged him to join the fraternity. I thought the connections would be valuable. I didn't know they would kill him."

"How could you know that?" he challenged. "And you weren't living on the campus. You weren't around him all the time. The information you got came through text messages and phone calls and a few visits a year, right?"

"Yes, but we were so close. I should have known."

"Do you think he'd want you to feel angry and guilty, to blame yourself?"

"No. He'd be pissed off."

"I get why you take it all on, Haley. How could you not? You became the caretaker in the family, not just of Landon, but of your mom."

"I failed with her, too."

"You didn't fail; she did. Why are you so hard on yourself?"

"Because look where I am. I didn't save any of them."

His gaze softened with compassion. "It wasn't your job to save them, especially not your parents. And Landon's death was at the hands of someone evil. You weren't there. You didn't know what was going on." He paused. "I know you can hear me, but I can see that you don't believe me. When I look at you, I don't see a failure; I see an incredibly determined, loving, fiercely loyal daughter and sister."

Despite her stubborn refusal to ever let anyone make her feel better, she had to admit his words were a soothing balm to her soul. Sometimes, she felt bruised and battered by her own rough edges. "Thank you for saying that. It does mean something to me." She paused, giving him a smile. "A man who listens and can cook—how are you still single?"

He grinned. "A beautiful woman who fights for truth and justice for her family—I could ask you the same question."

"Sometimes I can be too intense, too single-minded."

"Same," he said with a nod. "And then I'm not cooking or listening to someone else. Work has always been my anchor."

"After a childhood of flying back and forth between parents and cities. That makes sense."

"Yeah, I'm sure a psychologist could see a connection between that and how I live my life now."

"Oh, please, a psychologist would think you are incredibly normal. They would have a field day with me and all my craziness."

"Not craziness," he corrected. "You're a survivor, Haley. But you go beyond basic survival. You're trying to make the world a better place for everyone. That's what your reporting does. I have to confess, I'd almost forgotten there were people like you in the world."

She cocked her head to the right, giving him a questioning look. "Really? Why?"

He shrugged. "I've gotten jaded. I've seen too many people cut too many corners lately. But you remind me that sometimes the fight for truth and justice is shockingly pure and clear-cut."

"Sometimes. But this case isn't at all clear-cut. It seems like any one of the people we've spoken to in the last few days could have been involved in my brother's death, and I can't help thinking I missed something big six years ago. I thought I had overturned every stone I could see or that the police had. But there was a clue we missed, a clue Sabrina obviously found."

As she spoke, her hand crept to the necklace Landon had

bought for her birthday. It was ironic that he'd thought of her as his North Star, because in many ways, his presence had guided her, too. She'd had to be strong for him. She'd had to set an example. He'd kept her grounded. They'd both been home for each other.

Her finger suddenly caught on one edge of the star, and she was surprised by a sharp unevenness. She ran her finger back and forth, feeling like something was off.

"What's wrong?" Matt asked.

"I'm not sure. There's something sharp." She reached behind her neck and unhooked the latch, then held the star pendant up in front of her, seeing the sharp edge on the back side of the thick star. "It looks like a latch," she murmured, running her fingers over the area in question. She pushed on the pointed edge, and it opened the back side of the star. "Oh, my God!"

"What is it?" Matt asked.

She pulled out a tiny silver square. "This was inside. I don't know what it is."

"I do. It's a drive."

"For a computer? But it's so small. And why would it be inside the necklace?"

Matt's eyes blazed with excitement. "Because Landon wanted to put it somewhere safe, and where would be safer than in the necklace he was giving his sister?"

She stared at the tiny drive in shock, a mix of fear and excitement running through her. They might be about to find out why her brother had died and maybe who had killed him.

CHAPTER FIFTEEN

"May I have it?" Matt asked.

She handed him the drive. "Can you open it?"

"I can. Let's go into my office."

She tossed down her napkin and followed, her stomach churning with a mix of anticipation and dread.

Matt sat down at his desk and powered on his laptop. She stood behind him as he handled the tiny silver square with surprising gentleness, easing the microdrive into a card reader attached to an adapter.

The screen blinked once. Then a message came across the monitor: *Drive Locked. Encrypted Volume.*

"This is a good sign," Matt said. "If it's encrypted, it means there's something valuable on it."

"But how are we going to open it?"

His fingers flew across the keyboard. Several windows opened, with black and white code scrolling across the screen, and then another message: *Enter Password.*

He paused, glancing back at her. "Any ideas?"

"He wouldn't have picked something easy. It could be a string of code. I have no idea. He was the computer whiz, not me." She felt a wave of helpless frustration. "I don't know what to tell you.

He was always on me to change my passwords, to use a password-locking app, to be more careful."

"But you weren't always careful, were you?"

"No. I try to be better, but I'm sure most of my passwords could be guessed by someone who knew what they were doing."

Matt gave her an assessing look.

"What are you thinking?" she asked.

"That Landon would have figured you'd be the one to find this, to have to open it. He'd want you to be able to figure it out."

She stared at the monitor. "I don't know, Matt."

"What's your favorite password, one he might have teased you about?"

"There were a couple. I used one of our old addresses with some exclamation marks for a while."

He pushed his chair back to give her access to the computer. "Give it a shot."

She typed in the address, hands sweating. The denial message hit her like a slap in the face.

"Try another one."

She did as he suggested, but it was wrong, too.

"Did you have a nickname? A dog? A favorite food? An inside joke?" Matt asked. "Could it be something with North Star? He thought of you as home. What else did you do that made him feel safe?"

She thought for a moment. "Hot fudge sundaes on Sunday night," she said. "I'd melt a piece of chocolate to make the fudge, and sometimes when we couldn't afford ice cream..." Her voice cracked as an old memory ran through her mind. "One Sunday, on Landon's tenth birthday, my mom had told us there would be a cake and ice cream, but she left on Saturday night and she didn't come home the next day. Landon was so sad. I told him I was going to make it all right. We went to the store, but I didn't have enough money for it all, so I...I bought the chocolate bar, and I stole the ice cream, just one of those small cups, just enough for Landon. I put it in the pocket of my jacket, and I was so scared the manager was going to say something. He gave me a really sharp look when I gave him money for the chocolate bar, but he let us go. And when we got home, I made Landon a sundae, and I sang Happy Birthday to him."

Matt's lips tightened. "Your mother should have been prosecuted."

"I was the one who stole the ice cream."

"Because of the horrible circumstances you were left in. You were fifteen, right?"

She nodded. "Yes. It wasn't the only time I stole something, but I tried not to. I knew it wasn't right, and I didn't want Landon to see me. That day, I made him stand by the door, so he wouldn't notice." She paused. "But I think he might have figured it out."

"Maybe the password is *hotfudgesundae*."

"No. I think it's Finley's. That was the name of the market. We always said, 'Let's go to Finley's'. And if he had to use numbers, maybe that date." She typed in *Finleys* without the apostrophe and the date of Landon's tenth birthday. The cursor blinked, then the screen opened. "It worked."

"Let's see what we've got," Matt said, moving his chair closer to the computer as he started to type.

She held her breath as the folder structure came to light: Project_K – tests, logs, drafts, security.

He clicked into the first sub-folder, labeled *Tests*, but all of the individual files needed new passwords.

The log folder contained screens of data and numbers that made no sense to her.

"This is all encrypted," he muttered.

"Can you get through the encryption?"

"Not on this computer."

He opened the next folder labeled *Drafts*, and, finally, she saw a regular-looking paragraph. It appeared to be notes for some kind of paper. *Timing is key. It's not the market that creates volatility;*

it's perception. The model isn't about reaction. It's about pressure, causation, and sequential actions. Worldwide markets collide. Money moves. Power shifts. Who's in control?

"He's talking about something predictive, some kind of forecasting model," Matt said. "It feels like it might be about manipulating financial markets."

"Arjun said something about that, but it doesn't make sense."

"Doesn't it?" he challenged. "Your father committed suicide after losing all his money and some of his clients' money in a stock market fall."

"That's true. But Landon never expressed any interest in financial markets. He thought investing was a losing proposition, that it was like gambling. The house always wins."

"Maybe he found a way to ensure the house doesn't always win."

"You think he was trying to game the markets?"

"Or trying to understand how they work."

"He might have wanted to prevent someone else from suffering that kind of loss," she said. "I can't see him trying to concoct some scheme to make money for himself."

"Why not, Haley? You grew up poor. You stole ice cream to make sundaes. Why wouldn't Landon want to make money? And look where he was—Westbridge University, a private college inhabited by rich kids, probably flaunting their wealth. Maybe he wanted to have that life for himself, to take care of you for a change."

She wished she could refute his theory, but a part of it did resonate, especially the part about Landon wanting to take care of her. "He used to say one day he'd pay me back for everything I'd given him. Of course, I told him that wasn't happening, that I could take care of myself, and I just wanted him to have a good life."

"He wanted the same for you."

"I still don't know if that's what he was doing. He certainly didn't have extra money at the time of his death."

"Maybe that's because he hadn't used the algorithm yet, or whatever he was working on was stolen from him."

"Possibly," she admitted, her brain swirling with new questions. "What's in that last folder? The one labeled *security*."

"Let's find out."

As Matt opened the folder, four video files appeared. He clicked on the first one, and her breath caught in her chest as the grainy images appeared to show a bedroom. "That's Landon's apartment. What is this?"

"Looks like he set up a security camera."

For several seconds, there was no movement. Then a woman walked over to Landon's desk. She pulled open a drawer and then stopped, looking over her shoulder. As she did so, the camera caught her very pretty face.

"That's Brooke," she breathed, feeling Landon's sense of betrayal as clearly as if it were her own. "What is she doing?"

"She's looking for something." Matt pressed play on the next video.

It had to be a different day or later that night, because the light was different. It was darker, no light coming from the windows, which made the details more difficult to make out. Brooke went back to the desk and dug through the drawers, pulling out papers, file folders, and several black notebooks.

"There they are," she exclaimed as she watched Brooke toss the notebooks into a backpack and zip it up. A man came up behind her, but all she could see was a shadowy figure, an arm, reaching for the pack. "Damn, we can't see him."

"There's a ring on his finger, maybe a class ring."

"Can you lighten the image?" she asked.

"Not on this computer."

They watched for another moment. After Brooke gave the backpack away and the man disappeared, Brooke turned and looked at Landon's bed. She wrapped her arms around herself as if she were upset. She shook her head several times and then, with her head down, she turned and left the room.

"She stole Landon's notebooks and gave them to someone else," she said.

"And your brother knew it. He saw these files before he put the drive in your necklace."

"He knew she'd betrayed him. But how long did he know?"

"I'm not sure. There's no date stamp on these." Matt clicked the next video, which was from a camera in a different bedroom, one she didn't recognize, but it was a smaller room with sports paraphernalia and clothes strewn about.

"Where's this?" she muttered.

"Maybe a room at the fraternity house?" Matt suggested.

They watched for several long seconds and then a man came into view. He looked like he'd just gotten out of the shower, shirt off, hair damp, towel around his hips. As he turned his face, she realized who it was. "That's Drew Sanderson, Landon's big brother." She watched as Drew picked up a phone from the bed, read a text, and then tossed it back down. "I wish there was sound," she said in frustration. "Why would Landon put a camera in Drew's room?"

"There had to be a reason. There might be a way to zoom in on that phone and see what that text said," he murmured as Drew walked over to answer the door. "But again, not on this computer."

She watched the video as Drew held the door partway open, but they couldn't see who was on the other side. Whoever it was, Drew wasn't happy to see them. He waved one hand in the air in apparent anger or frustration. Then he shut the door and slammed it with his fist before walking out of view.

"What's the last video?" she asked, impatient to find more answers.

Matt opened the file to reveal another scene from Drew's room. This time there was another person with Drew, a woman who looked like Jill Adler. "That's Jill." She watched as Jill and Drew talked, and then the door opened again, and Henry walked in. The three of them appeared to be arguing. Jill was very animated. Drew seemed annoyed, and Henry seemed to be watching it all with a smile.

"I really hate his smug grin," she said.

"I'd like to wipe it off his face," Matt agreed.

The door opened again, and another guy walked in. He had a stocky build and had been a star high school quarterback before going to Westbridge. "That's Josh Lorrie, the president of the fraternity." She paused as Josh put his arm around Jill. She shrugged it off and stormed out of the room. The three guys seemed to share some moment of mutual agreement, although no one said anything. Then all three of them walked out, and the video ended. She turned to Matt. "That didn't tell us much. They could have been arguing about anything. Why would Landon have kept this particular clip?"

Matt thought for a moment. "I don't know, but he set up a camera in Drew's room for some reason. We just have to figure out what it was."

"It might have been Drew and Trent's room," she said. "I think they were roommates at the time, if I'm remembering right. But Trent isn't in any of these videos, so..." Her voice trailed away as she let out a sigh. "More questions but no answers."

Matt glanced down at his watch. "It's late. We should table this until tomorrow."

"Really? I thought you had tech support working around the clock."

"Derek is the best one we have, and I know he went home a while ago. We can get him to look at this tomorrow."

"I don't want to wait that long," she said impatiently.

He smiled with sympathy. "I understand that feeling. But it's probably going to take a little time to get the files open. Even if he was working tonight, this isn't going to be a five-minute thing. Your brother put some heavy-duty encryption on this drive."

"Waiting is my least favorite thing."

"And you've been waiting too long. I get it. But this drive

was a big break. It's going to tell us what Landon was working on and why someone was willing to kill for it."

"And they didn't just kill my brother. They killed Sabrina, too. They also tried to run me off the road, and maybe if I'd been home earlier today, I wouldn't have survived the break-in. We have to move as fast as we can, Matt. They're going to keep trying to kill me and anyone else who gets in their way."

"We are moving fast. And you're not alone anymore. I'm behind you, and so is my team. I'm not going to let anything happen to you."

"I want to believe you, but we don't know how many are on their side, and what they're trying to protect, because it has to be more than just my brother's death. Sabrina wouldn't have tried to contact the FBI if it was just about a cold-case murder. It had to be something the Bureau would care about."

"It probably has to do with whatever is on Landon's drive, whatever he was working on. Maybe whatever he created was stolen and is now being put in play."

"Which is why we're running out of time." She could hear the edge in her voice, and so could he.

"I really shouldn't tell you to calm down, should I?" he asked dryly, a gleam in his eyes. "I don't know a lot about women, but I know that usually doesn't go well."

"You should definitely not tell me that."

"Okay, then I think we should find a way to distract ourselves. We could watch a movie."

She immediately shook her head. "I can't settle into some other story, not with this one raging through my head."

"You could go to bed. When you wake up, we'll be able to take the drive down to Derek and keep going."

"There's no way I can sleep. I feel too wired, too restless."

"I know some yoga poses that could help."

She raised an eyebrow, surprised by his words. "Seriously? You know yoga?"

"Why is that strange? Yoga is good for the mind and the body, especially when someone is stressed out."

"I just didn't picture you as a meditative kind of guy."

"It's not my favorite workout," he admitted. "I usually hit up a bootcamp or a boxing class or go for a run, but I have found that yoga gets to parts of my brain that other exercises do not. Have you ever taken a class?"

"Sure. But I'm super tight. I can't even touch my toes."

"You just have to practice."

"I'm not big on practicing. I like to get right into something," she said.

A smile spread across his face. "You like to compete, to win."

"Well...yeah," she admitted. "You do, too."

"I do. But I haven't had as many wins as I would have liked lately, so I've had to find ways to cope with that frustration. And there's a good yoga studio on Fourth Street, by the beach, called Karma. You should check it out sometime."

"Maybe after all this is over." She took another circle around his office, then said, "I do have one idea of something we could do to distract ourselves."

His eyes glittered as his gaze met hers. "Not that," he said sharply.

"Not what?" she challenged, intrigued by his immediate reaction.

"There's a bad idea going through your head right now."

"Reckless, maybe. Bad? I don't think so."

"Do you play cards?" he asked, a somewhat desperate note in his voice.

"What?" she asked, surprised by his abrupt question.

"Gin? Poker? What's your game?"

"I can play gin and some poker, but I'm not good at bluffing."

"Let's go back to the dining room, and we'll find a responsible way to pass the time."

She frowned. "You don't even want to know what I was going to suggest a minute ago?"

"Haley—"

"Ice cream sundaes," she said, interrupting him. "They always helped me pass the time before. And we didn't have dessert. I'm pretty sure I saw some ice cream in your freezer."

A mix of emotions ran through his eyes. "I have ice cream. But I don't know about chocolate."

"I have a bar in my bag. I'm never too far away from chocolate. So, we're set. We'll make sundaes."

As he got up, he gave her a quizzical look. "Was that really what you were going to suggest, Haley?"

She gave him a secretive smile. "I guess you'll never know."

CHAPTER SIXTEEN

As they made their way to the living room, Haley found herself looking at Matt with new eyes. When he'd first shown up at her apartment, she'd seen him as just another authority figure who wanted to keep her in the dark, to use her for information but not share any in return. Now she was beginning to see that beneath his FBI agent exterior was someone who genuinely cared about getting to the truth, not just closing a case. And maybe someone who also cared about her, about Landon. She might be reading too much into his protectiveness. He was the kind of man who was going to do his job to the best of his ability, no matter what. She really shouldn't forget that.

"I'll get the ice cream," Matt said. "You get the chocolate."

She grabbed the chocolate bar out of her bag and took it into the kitchen, where Matt had pulled out a carton of vanilla ice cream and two bowls. Breaking the bar of chocolate into small squares, she tossed them in a saucepan, then turned on the heat to simmer. "This works better with milk if you have it."

He retrieved a carton of fat-free milk. "This is all I have."

"It's perfect." She poured in some milk and then stirred it into the melting chocolate. "Why don't you dish out the ice cream? This is almost ready."

After Matt scooped ice cream into two bowls, she poured the warm chocolate over the top. "This would be better with nuts and cherries, but this will work." She didn't take a bite until Matt had spooned up a mix of chocolate sauce and ice cream. "Well?"

He nodded with approval. "It's good."

She took a bite and let out a sigh of pleasure that came not just with the warm chocolate taste, but with the memories that came with it.

Matt gave her a smile. "You look like you've been transported."

"I don't have a lot of happy memories, but the ones I have are usually connected to an ice cream sundae."

"Let's take these into the living room," he suggested.

"Okay." She followed him into the other room and curled up on the couch with Matt sliding in next to her, although keeping a good amount of space between them. "So, what's your favorite childhood memory?" she asked.

"It doesn't involve a sundae."

She smiled. "I didn't expect it would. Tell me."

He thought for a moment, then he said, "I was pitching in a baseball playoff game. I was twelve, and it was the final game of the tournament. My team was up by one going into the bottom of the ninth. I just had to get through three batters, but they were the three best hitters on the other team."

"Well, don't keep me in suspense," she said as he paused for a long moment. "What happened?"

"I was more nervous than I'd ever been. The first batter hit a ground ball to second, and we got the out. The second batter hit a short fly over the shortstop's head and was safe at first."

"You remember a lot of details," she said with amusement.

He grinned and gave an unapologetic shrug. "It was an exciting game. The next batter got a hit, and suddenly there was one out with two on base. I saw my win sliding away. I looked to the stands, but no one from my family had been able to come that day. I wasn't going to get any moral support. I had to do it on my own."

"And..."

He smiled. "I told myself to calm down, focus."

"So, you react well to being told to calm down," she teased.

"When I'm the one saying it. Anyway, I struck out the next two batters, and we won the game."

"You were the hero. No wonder it was a good memory. But a little sad that no one from your family was there."

"I had given up on that long before that game."

"Did you stay mostly with your mom or your dad?"

"My dad during the school year, and my mom in the summers. But like I said, my dad and stepmother were busy with babies at that point. My grandfather would sometimes make it to a game if he wasn't working. My childhood was nowhere near as rough as yours, Haley. I feel bad even complaining a little about it."

"It's not a competition, and you don't have to apologize for having a better childhood. You also don't have to pretend it was easy to see your parents split up and start other families. That would have bothered me."

"It was what it was. It upset me for a while, but I couldn't do anything about it. And it certainly doesn't matter now. I don't even think about it."

Despite his strong statement, she had the feeling it wasn't really that black-and-white for him, but she was probably lucky he'd told her as much as he had. "Well, congrats on your big win. You kept your focus, and you did what you knew how to do. I see that same resolute determination in you now, and I find it comforting."

"I'm glad you feel safe with me. I will do everything I can to protect you, Haley."

She met his gaze. "I know you will, Matt. You're a good man, better than I thought when we first met. I assumed you'd be like everyone else I've met in law enforcement, dismissive and cynical, too jaded to even try anymore."

A shadow moved through his expression. "I was beginning to worry that's exactly what I was becoming. When I joined the LA field office, it was run by a really good man, Damon Wolfe, but he left three months ago, transferred to New York, and his replacement, Rebecca Markham, has not been nearly as good. I knew I needed to quit or make a move. Luckily, I ran into Jason one day, and he was raving about his elite task force and said I should join them."

"And your new team is different than your old one?"

"So far, yes. I wasn't even supposed to start until Monday, but Sabrina's death moved up the timeline when my name was found in her pocket. Since I jumped in, everyone else has lined up behind me with enthusiastic support. It's very refreshing."

"I'm glad, and I'm also happy that Sabrina had your name in her pocket. Otherwise, someone else would have shown up at my door, and he or she would not have gone to the lengths that you have." She let out a breath. "So, tell me more about your baseball career. Did you keep playing after the big game?"

"Through high school. That was it. I wasn't good enough to go pro, and when I got to college, I was far more interested in the party scene."

She smiled. "Really? So, you were wild, huh?"

"Just your average eighteen-year-old away at school with no parental restrictions, not that I'd had a lot of restrictions, even during high school. My parents were too busy with the younger kids."

"I have a feeling you didn't go too crazy."

"What about you?"

"I went to community college for two years and then Long Beach State, but I was taking care of Landon, so no party scene for me." She paused. "Did your party scene include a lot of pretty girls? Did you have a college girlfriend?"

"A couple. Nothing serious."

"And more recently?" She knew she should not be asking such personal questions, but she wanted to know everything about him.

He gave her a thoughtful look. "Why so interested?"

"I'm just making conversation. You don't have to answer."

"I had a two-year relationship in my mid-twenties, before I went into the FBI. She was a free-spirited travel photographer, and she wanted to spend a year going around the world. I didn't want to follow her. But I was tired of my financial job, and I was already thinking about the FBI, so it was a natural breaking point for us."

"No broken hearts?"

"Not for either of us. Your turn."

"I hardly dated until Landon went to Westbridge. After that, I moved to Santa Barbara for my first reporting job. It was a young scene, a lot of grad students where I lived, and I had a couple of short-term relationships, nothing serious."

"And in the last six years?"

"I didn't see anyone the first two years after Landon died. I buried myself in my new job and never went out. Eventually, I went on some dates, but there hasn't been anyone I wanted to work less for. I was kind of using that as a barometer. Would I rather be at work, or would I rather go on a date? And, honestly, it probably wasn't any of them who were the problem; it was me. I have been hurt a lot, and I don't like to get too close or too deep. Casual and fun is fine, but intense emotions...those are scary."

He nodded, a gleam of understanding in his eyes. "It's much easier to risk your life than your heart. Or at least, it has been for me."

"Yeah, me, too. Not that I'm in the habit of risking my life, as you are, but I do take professional risks, and I never have a second thought about it. I've written articles that could cost me my job, but I just stormed forward, throwing caution to the wind. I never worried about consequences." She gave a helpless shake of her head. "I don't know why I'm such a coward in my personal life."

"It seems like you just haven't met the right person."

"I guess not. Same for you, huh?" She knew they were treading into dangerous territory, because there was a simmering attraction between them that was getting hotter by the minute. In fact, what was left of her ice cream had already melted. She set her bowl on the coffee table. "We should change the subject."

"Okay," he said, also probably sensing that they were getting too deep. "You've talked a lot about your family, but I wanted to ask you...what happened to your mother? Is she still alive?"

"I think I'd rather go back to talking about my nonexistent dating life," she said dryly.

"We can do that. I was just curious."

"I don't know if she's alive. I haven't seen her since I was eighteen and Landon was thirteen."

"What about when Landon died?"

"I had no way of telling her. I didn't know where she was."

"Did your great-aunt know where she was?"

"She said she didn't. Frankly, I don't think she wanted to know, either. My mother brought a lot of trouble and drama with her."

He gave her a searching look. "Are you telling me you couldn't find her? You, who found Alanna and AJ before I did?"

"I didn't find her because I didn't look. I didn't see the point. It's not like we were going to console each other. But I have to admit that over the years whenever the phone rang in the middle of the night, I thought someone was going to tell me she was dead. But the one call I got was about Landon, and that one I never imagined."

"I'm sorry, Haley."

She shrugged. "It was what it was. I didn't win the lottery with parents, but I did with my brother. He was such a great kid, super smart but also hilarious in a geeky kind of way, and very kind. I loved him so much. I have to find out what happened to him, Matt. I just have to."

"We will. He doesn't just have you anymore; he also has me."

The simple sincerity in his voice made her chest tighten. She looked up to find him watching her with an intensity that made her breath catch. "Matt...thank you."

"I haven't done anything yet."

"Yes, you have. You've protected me, and you've given me a reason to hope again."

He sucked in a quick breath. "I just hope you don't end up disappointed."

"Me, too." She licked her lips. "Matt..."

His gaze darkened at her tone. "I don't think you should say whatever you're thinking about saying."

She slid down the couch, breaching the distance between them as she put her hand on his leg. "How do you know what I'm thinking?"

"Because you have a very expressive face."

"It doesn't have to mean anything. I just said I like casual and fun. Don't you?"

He smiled. "I do. But this wouldn't be that. You're under my protection. You're scared and vulnerable. I won't take advantage of you."

"You can't take advantage of me when I'm the one offering. There's something between us that's unrelated to the case. We have chemistry." She paused, giving him a long look. His face was guarded, but there was a gleam in his dark-brown eyes. "You feel it, too, don't you?"

"I don't want to. I need to maintain a professional distance."

"Now you sound like an FBI agent."

"That's what I am, Haley."

"It's what you do. It's not who you are."

"It is who I am," he said forcefully. "This is a job for me, Haley. And I can't allow it to be anything else. It wouldn't be smart. It would complicate things." He removed her hand from his leg, although his fingers lingered for a moment before he put her hand on the couch.

"Okay," she said. "That was embarrassing. So much for taking risks..."

His expression shifted. "I feel it, too. I just don't think we should act on what we're feeling. We might have regrets."

"Or we might have an incredible night together."

His gaze weakened. "You are not making this easy. I'm trying to do the right thing."

"And you always try to do the right thing, don't you?"

"Yes."

"I like that about you, Matt. I like a lot of things about you."

"I feel the same way about you, Haley, but I think we should call it a night. Regroup in the morning." He got to his feet. "I may not be able to crack the encryption, but I think I'll give it a shot on my computer. Do you need anything?"

"No. I'll do the dishes and then head to the guest room."

"You don't have to clean up."

"It's the least I can do," she said as she got to her feet.

His lips tightened as he gave her a conflicted look. "You may not believe this, but walking away from you is not easy."

She smiled, flattered by the look in his eyes, by the knowledge that no matter how much he wanted their relationship to be professional, it had already crossed the line into personal, and whatever was between them wasn't just going away because he wanted it to.

"It was your choice," she said. "The right choice, according to you. I guess we'll find out if that's true."

———

What a stupid choice he'd made...

Matt regretted everything about his decision to keep Haley at a distance as he spent an unsuccessful few hours trying to decrypt Landon's files and then another five hours trying to sleep without her image floating through his head every few seconds. When he finally got out of bed around eight on Sunday morning, he was in a bad mood, annoyed with himself and also at Haley for being so damned attractive and interesting.

He hadn't connected with any woman the way he'd connected to her. They'd known each other for two days, and it felt like they'd known each other for twenty years. Every moment of being together had been heightened by danger, by the mystery around Landon's death, by sharing their personal histories. He'd told very few people about his life as a kid torn between divorced parents, but after she'd confided in him, he'd found himself revealing more than he normally would.

And now...he didn't know what the hell to do about her. Their conversation, their acknowledgment of the chemistry between them, had changed their boundaries, whether they'd acted on anything or not. He knew he needed to get things back on a more professional level; he just wasn't quite sure how to do that.

As he finished dressing, he could hear her moving around in the kitchen, and he knew he couldn't stall much longer. He'd no sooner stepped into the hallway when he got a text from Jason that he'd be there in ten minutes to pick up Landon's computer drive. He hadn't wanted to take Haley to the office or leave her in his apartment alone, so he was happy to have Jason pick it up.

When he finally made his way into the kitchen, he found Haley standing at the stove in jeans and a soft-blue T-shirt, her hair pulled back in a ponytail. She looked even prettier in the morning light, quickly weakening his resolve to keep things impersonal and professional.

"Good morning," she said, glancing over her shoulder with a smile. "I hope you don't mind. I found pancake mix in your pantry." She flipped a golden pancake with practiced ease. "Also, syrup. In fact, I'm impressed at how much you have in your cupboards."

"Don't be impressed. I have a cleaning lady who stocks my

fridge and cupboards every couple of weeks with the basics. I guess she thought that included pancake mix."

"That's nice. I wish I had someone to do that for me."

Matt poured himself a coffee and leaned against the counter, watching her cook. She was delightfully messy, with pancake mix on the counter and a touch of it on her cheek. He wanted to wipe it off of her face and then kiss her until everything was burning, including themselves.

As his body tightened, he cleared his throat.

She gave him a speculative look. "Are you okay?"

"Fine. How did you sleep?" he asked, trying to distract himself from thinking about what additional lines he wanted to cross.

"Better than I expected." She slid three pancakes onto a plate and handed it to him. "It seemed odd after everything that's happened the past two days. I guess it just all caught up to me."

"You needed the rest. Aren't you eating?" he asked as she turned off the stove.

"I already ate." She refilled her coffee mug, then followed him over to the dining room table. "I was thinking we should talk to Brooke again and show her the video we have. She can tell us who was with her and what she was doing in Landon's room. She has all the information we need."

"Do you think Brooke will tell us everything because you ask nicely?" he asked dryly. "She has had six years to come forward and has not done that. In fact, she's only gotten in deeper with all the people in Landon's fraternity, their families, and their friends."

"How about we don't ask nicely? Can't you bring her in for questioning, interrogate her?"

"We don't have enough evidence to do that. Maybe once the files get decrypted, we will, but right now we don't need to tip Brooke off about what we have uncovered."

She frowned. "We can't just do nothing, Matt."

The doorbell rang, and she jumped. "Who's that?"

"Relax. It's Jason, a fellow agent. He's here to pick up the drive." He got to his feet and went to answer the door while Haley stood up, hovering by the table. After checking to make sure it was Jason, he opened the door.

Jason walked in, wearing gray slacks and a navy-blue polo shirt, looking more like a golf pro than an FBI agent.

"Morning," Jason said, his gaze immediately moving to Haley. "Ms. Kenton. I'm Jason Colter."

"It's nice to meet you," Haley said. "Would you like some coffee? Or pancakes? There's plenty."

"I'm good, thanks. How are you holding up?"

"I'm doing all right. Just eager to get some answers."

"We all are."

"I have the drive in my office," he said, leading the way down the hall. Both Haley and Jason followed. Clearly, Haley did not want to be left out of any conversation.

As he handed over the drive, he said, "The only files we were able to look at were video clips of Brooke Mercer stealing the notebooks out of Landon's desk and handing them to an unidentified male. He also had a camera set up in Drew Sanderson's room at the fraternity where there are a couple of scenes with Drew, Henry, and Jill. The rest of the files are encrypted. I'm guessing that the contents of those files are what got him killed."

"And he's pointing us to a few people in particular," Haley added. "Otherwise, Landon wouldn't have included those clips."

"I'll get Derek on this right away," Jason said as he pocketed the drive. "Are you still interested in going to the golf tournament at Valmont this afternoon?"

"Yes. And Haley will come with us. She makes people nervous, and I want to remind everyone that the FBI has her back."

"I'll meet you both by the valet stand at one o'clock," Jason said. "Most of the golfers will be finishing up then. No jeans, no tank tops, or flip flops, not that you would. Dress code is upscale casual."

"Got it," he said.

"See you then."

After Jason left, Haley said, "I need to go by my apartment and get something to wear before the tournament. I didn't bring anything appropriate for upscale casual."

"Let's do that now."

CHAPTER SEVENTEEN

The valet at Valmont Country Club moved with the practiced efficiency of someone accustomed to handling cars worth more than most people's homes. Matt watched a gleaming Bentley disappear around the corner as he and Haley got out of his SUV.

Jason was waiting for them as promised and escorted them into the club. It felt very much like old money, with wood-paneled walls in the lobby filled with oil paintings of men in golf attire.

"The founding members," Jason murmured, catching his gaze.

"Is your father on this wall?"

"No, he came in later."

"I didn't realize you were a member," Haley said.

"I inherited the membership. Sometimes it's helpful when I need to speak to rich and powerful people in a more casual atmosphere," Jason replied as he led them to the check-in desk, which was manned by a busty blonde with a fixed smile, who looked like she'd spent a lot of time at the plastic surgeon.

"Good afternoon, Mr. Colter," she said with a warm smile.

"Hello, Deb. How are you?"

"Quite well. I haven't seen you in a long time. No golf for you today?"

"Too busy with work."

"Saving the world," she said.

"Trying to."

"And these are your guests?" Deb asked.

"Yes. Matt Lawson and Haley Kenton," Jason replied smoothly.

Deb's smile never wavered as she handed them temporary membership cards. "Welcome. The tournament just concluded. Cocktails and canapés are now being served on the main terrace. The awards ceremony will take place in about thirty minutes, with a buffet lunch to follow. Enjoy yourselves."

"Thank you," Jason replied.

They followed him through the clubhouse, past a dining room where white-jacketed servers were setting tables with crystal and silver, toward the sound of conversation and clinking glasses. The main terrace opened onto a spectacular view of the golf course, with the San Gabriel Mountains rising in the distance.

Matt accepted a club soda from a passing server as Jason and Haley did the same, each of them pausing to sip and survey the scene. It felt very much like the event they'd attended yesterday. There was no art, but the people were very much the same.

"I wonder if this is what these people do every weekend," Haley murmured. "Do they go from one party to another, one tray of rich, decadent canapés to another filled with glasses of the most expensive champagne? It seems so...pointless."

"There's more happening here than champagne and canapés," Jason said. "These events are where a lot of deals are made."

"I'm surprised they would let you be a member since you work for the FBI," she commented. "Aren't they worried about you seeing something or overhearing something?"

"They like having a law enforcement presence. It makes them look legitimate, as if they have nothing to hide."

"Or maybe it's a good place for them to convince law enforcement to act on their behalf," she suggested. "Like shutting down a police investigation. No offense."

Jason smiled. "I'm fairly sure you meant that to be offensive, but I understand where you're coming from. The investigation into your brother's death was shoddy at best, criminal at worst."

"I'm sorry. You're trying to help me get to the truth. I didn't mean to insult you."

"You didn't. This isn't my scene any more than it's yours," Jason said. "But my father liked it. He was politically ambitious, and memberships like this helped him become the deputy director of the FBI. I have no such ambition. But sometimes, the membership proves useful, like today."

"There's Brooke," Haley said suddenly, tipping her head toward the brunette moving toward the women's lounge in a pale-yellow sundress that certainly didn't disguise her beauty. "I'm going to see if I can talk to her."

He didn't like that idea at all. "You can't confront her," he warned. "Not with so many people around."

"She might be alone in the locker room."

"I highly doubt that. We're here to observe, not act...not until it's the right time," he said. "And Brooke won't tell you anything with her friends around."

"I understand, Matt. I'm just going to observe her a little more closely, and if she sees me, I'll simply say hello. If she's alone, I'll see what else I can find out."

He didn't want her to go, but she was already gone, and he couldn't follow her into the women's locker room.

"She'll be fine. This place is crawling with people," Jason said, catching his eye.

"And at least a half dozen of them might have killed her brother."

"Well, I don't think they're going to kill her here, and you wanted to make people nervous, right?"

"By our presence as a group, not by hers alone."

"She's doing her part; let's do ours," Jason said. "Time to mingle."

———

Haley made her way into the women's locker room, which was as posh as the rest of the club. There was plush carpeting under her feet, alcoves of lockers with comfortable ottomans, mirrors for hair and makeup, a spa with a steam room and hot tub, as well as a large bathroom. There were several women washing their hands and reapplying makeup, but none of them were Brooke. As she moved around a corner past a sign pointing to the massage rooms, she heard voices coming from one of those rooms, where the door was slightly ajar. She paused next to a tall potted plant, pretending to be looking at her phone while she eavesdropped.

"You need to pull yourself together, Brooke."

"I'm trying, Jill, but Haley just walked in with that FBI guy and probably another agent. What are they doing here?"

Haley tensed at the mention of her name.

"They're just fishing," Jill said. "You need to get a grip. People are starting to worry about you."

"I can't help being nervous," Brooke replied, and Haley could hear the strain in her voice. "They keep asking me questions and looking at me with suspicion."

"Get past it," Jill said coolly. "You did what you had to do. We all did. This is almost over. Just keep it together for a few more weeks."

Her pulse quickened at Jill's words. *A few more weeks until what?*

"I don't know if I can," Brooke said. "I think I should take a vacation, go away for a few days."

"You can't do that. We have an event next weekend, and I need you in the office. It will also look suspicious if you leave. Just take a breath. They don't know anything. They can't prove anything. You need to act normal."

"What if they find out about—"

"They won't." Jill's voice carried a warning edge.

"How can you be so sure after what happened to that woman?"

"I don't know what happened to her. I don't want to know. And neither do you. We can't look back, Brooke. We have to look to the future. It's going to be good. We're all going to be rich. That's all that matters."

Haley heard voices approaching and slid out from behind the plant, her heart racing, as she put a smile on her face and walked back down the hall, passing two older women who were chatting about someone's husband cheating on his wife. They didn't give her a second look, and she quickly made her way out of the locker room.

She wanted to talk to Brooke even more now that she knew Brooke was scared. She could be the weak link in the group, someone they could exploit, but not here, not where all the others were.

Matt was right. They needed to talk to Brooke when she was alone. But it had been worth the risk to follow her, because now she knew that Brooke was having second thoughts and that there was something about to happen soon. She couldn't begin to imagine what that was, but Brooke knew, and they had to get her to talk. ✗

————

"Jason, Agent Lawson, I didn't expect to see you here," Graham Adler said as he joined them by the bar.

"I understand congratulations are in order," Jason said.

A broad smile flashed across Graham's face as he waved his

hand toward the rest of his foursome. "Henry and I have bragging rights for another year, don't we, son?"

"That's right," Henry said. "Jason, have you met Drew Sanderson and his father, Kent, our more than worthy opponents?"

"We haven't met," Jason replied. "This is my associate, Special Agent Matt Lawson."

He extended his hand to Kent and then Drew, happy to meet Landon's big brother. Drew had brown hair and fair, freckled skin. He was a little softer in the middle than Henry or the older men, including his father, Kent Sanderson, who had white hair, dark eyes, and very tan skin.

"Are you a golfer, Agent Lawson?" Drew asked.

"More of a hacker. But I understand you all finished at the top."

"The Adlers won, not us," Kent interrupted, anger in his gaze. "My son has yet to learn how to keep himself out of the rough. Isn't that right, Drew?"

Drew's jaw tightened almost imperceptibly. "Just wasn't my day, Dad." He gave a careless shrug.

"Seems like it is never your day," Kent said with a sarcastic smile. "I keep hoping you'll start living up to all those golf lessons and that expensive education I gave you."

The silence that followed that comment was thick with tension. Drew's face flushed, and Henry shot Drew a sympathetic look, while Graham's expression grew uncomfortable.

"Now, now, it's just golf, Kent," Graham said. "And you and Drew smoked poor Trent and Charles. They ended up in fourth."

"Trent can barely hold a club," Kent said. "Hardly a victory."

"Kent," Henry said. "Megan was looking for you earlier. She was looking attractive as always."

Kent's face went still, then he cleared his throat. "Excuse me."

"Careful, son," Graham said quietly, but his voice carried a clear threat. "When you poke the bear, sometimes you get bit."

Henry's smile was all innocence, but his eyes glittered with something that looked like malice. "Just making conversation, Dad."

"Sure, you were," Graham said. "I'm going to get a drink."

As Graham left, Henry said, "So what are you two really doing here? Have you found any leads on who might have killed Sabrina?"

"Still looking," Matt replied. "We were hoping to talk to you, Drew."

"I heard you've been asking questions about Landon's death," Drew said. "And that it might be tied to the death of one of Henry's associates, which seems shocking. Of course, I'm happy to help if I can. Landon was my little brother in the frat. I have felt guilty every day that I didn't protect him. I should have seen he was drinking too much that night."

"So, you saw him that night?" Matt asked.

"I did. We talked when he first got there. He was upset about a bad grade on a paper. Of course, his idea of a bad grade was a B plus. He hated to get anything less than an A. I told him to have a drink and relax. I guess that was a mistake, but I never thought he'd get wasted. He'd never done that before."

"Landon wasn't much of a drinker," Henry confirmed. "But what I don't understand is why you aren't spending more time on figuring out who killed Sabrina? That was an actual confirmed murder. Landon's death was an accident."

"Sabrina was killed because she knew something about Landon's death," he said, deciding to make that connection clear.

"What did she know?" Drew asked, surprise in his gaze. "Because if it wasn't an accident, then that means someone got away with murder. And that's not right. If someone killed Landon, then they should pay for it."

"We're going to make sure that happens," he said.

"I can't imagine how Sabrina would know anything about that," Henry said. "She was in law school when Landon died. She wasn't part of our scene. Why do you believe she knew something?"

"Because she said she did," he replied, watching their reactions, but neither one gave anything away.

"To whom?" Henry asked.

"I can't say."

Henry frowned. "It doesn't make sense. If Sabrina knew something, she would have told me. We worked together. I saw her every day."

"Maybe she thought you were involved," he suggested, seeing a glint of anger enter Henry's eyes.

"Whoa," Drew said, putting up a hand. "What are you talking about? Henry didn't do anything. You two should leave. And maybe you should stop talking, Henry."

"It's fine," Henry said, his gaze already returning to calm. "I don't have anything to hide. I liked Landon. I had no reason to kill him."

"Why did you like him?" he asked.

"What do you mean, why?" Henry asked warily as if it were a trick question.

"Landon was a scholarship kid. He didn't come from money. He didn't understand your world. How did he fit in with your group of friends?"

"He fit in well," Drew said, answering for Henry. "Landon was smart and funny, and he could play video games better than anyone. We didn't care that he didn't have money. The rest of us did. And he was one of us."

Drew's impassioned defense of Landon felt genuine, especially the mention of the video games. Haley had told him her brother was obsessed with video games.

"We're not as elitist as you seem to think," Henry added.

"Maybe our fathers were, but we're a different generation. We don't judge everyone by their bank balance."

He didn't believe that for one second.

Drew straightened his shoulders. "I think the awards ceremony is about to start. I'm going to use the restroom. If you want to talk to me again, here's my card." Drew pulled out a business card and handed it to him. "I'm happy to help if I can. I felt so bad for Haley after Landon died. I knew she was pretty much alone in the world." He looked around. "I thought I heard she was here with you."

"She's around."

"I'll see if I can find her to say hello." Drew tipped his head, then walked away.

"I should go, too," Henry said.

"One second. What was that dig you gave to Kent?" Jason asked Henry. "About a woman named Megan?"

"His latest fling," Henry replied. "Kent is so smug and always acts like he's the smartest one in the room. I personally can't stand him or the way he treats Drew, always putting him down. I decided to let him know his indiscretions are not a secret." He paused. "I felt bad for beating Drew today, but it was more than a little satisfying to stop Kent from getting the trophy. Anyway, I suspect I will see you around, since you seem to keep showing up wherever I am."

As Henry strolled away in his usual cocky fashion, Jason said, "That wasn't worth much."

"It wasn't nothing. I'm starting to get a better idea of who the guys are. Henry likes to stir the pot and push the envelope. Drew is under the thumb of his overpowering father."

"What does that prove?"

"I don't know yet, but Henry has ambition and confidence. He wanted to make sure we didn't see fear in his eyes. He could be innocent or guilty as hell."

"And Drew?" Jason asked. "He gave you his card and acted like he didn't have anything to hide."

"He did. I'd like to speak to him again when he's not with Henry. He's one of the few people who has actually gone on record saying he spoke to Landon that night." He paused as Haley suddenly joined them, her face flushed with excitement.

"We need to talk," she said. "Something big is coming. This isn't just about the past; it's about the future."

CHAPTER EIGHTEEN

Matt steered Haley and Jason toward a quieter corner of the terrace, away from the crowd gathering for the awards ceremony. The mountain view provided perfect cover for their conversation, making it look like they were simply admiring the scenery.

"What did you hear?" he asked.

"Jill and Brooke were arguing in the locker room. Jill told Brooke to pull herself together, that people are starting to worry about her," Haley said, keeping her voice low. "Brooke is scared, Matt. She wants to leave town, but Jill told Brooke all she had to do was hang on for a few more weeks."

"A few more weeks until what?" he asked.

"She didn't say. She just reminded Brooke it wasn't about the past but the future, that it was all going to be worth it."

His pulse quickened. "Anything else?"

"Nothing specific. But whatever is happening now is about more than protecting secrets; it's about some big plan that's going to make them all rich."

"I don't like the sound of that," he murmured. "Brooke is clearly the weakest link. We need to put some pressure on her, see if we can break her."

"That needs to be done soon," Jason said. "They have a habit of getting rid of anyone who makes them nervous. And it sounds like that's what she's doing."

"We'll follow her home, get her alone," he said.

"Good idea," Jason replied. "Since you don't need me here, I'm going to head back to the office now and see if I can help Derek open that drive."

"Thanks," he said as Jason walked away.

"We need to stay close to Brooke, make sure she doesn't leave without us noticing," Haley said.

"Agreed, but it looks like that might have to wait," he said as Trent Adler approached them.

"Haley, Agent Lawson," Trent said. "Since I saw you yesterday, I've been thinking a lot about our conversation." He cast a quick look over his shoulder, then said, "I spoke to Landon the day before the party. And you were right when you suggested there was some sort of grading scheme in play. I didn't want to acknowledge that in front of Henry."

"Because he was involved in the scheme?" he asked.

"Because a bunch of us were, including me, and I didn't want to betray anyone."

"But you're willing to do that now?" Haley challenged.

"I couldn't sleep all night. I never thought the grading issue had anything to do with Landon's death because I believed that it was an accident. Now you're saying it's not, and I can't keep quiet anymore."

"What was the scheme?" Matt asked.

"Landon told me the professor he worked for was pressuring him to bump up grades for certain students. Landon didn't want to do it, but after he refused, he found out that Professor Harrington did it himself. But when Harrington changed the grades, he used Landon's access code for the computer. That way, if anyone went looking, they would think Landon had done it."

"What?" Haley asked in shock. "Why didn't you say this before? The police could have talked to Professor Harrington. Maybe he's the one who killed Landon."

"I'm sorry. Like I said, I didn't think it was relevant, but I didn't know that Landon's death was anything but an accident."

"But now you believe it was murder?" he asked.

"I think you both believe it was murder, and I don't know anymore. Maybe what I told you doesn't matter, but I had to say it." He blew out a breath. "I have to go. They're about to announce the awards."

"Are you going to let him walk away?" Haley demanded, turning to him with fire in her blue eyes.

"For the moment. He said what he wanted to say. We need to confirm it through other sources, like Brooke."

She slowly nodded, her gaze still a bit uncertain. "Okay, but why do you think Trent suddenly decided to open up? Was it genuine remorse? A sudden realization that Landon was killed, or..."

"Or he could have been trying to point us in the wrong direction," he finished. "Every one of these conversations could be orchestrated. That's why I'm not going to jump at every ball they throw in my direction."

"You're right. But the conversation I overheard in the locker room was not orchestrated. That one was real. They didn't know I was there."

"Then let's find Brooke. We need to keep our eyes on her so we're ready to follow her when she leaves."

―――――

Brooke left the club around three, and they quickly followed. As Matt drove, Haley thought about the conversation with Brooke and Jill and Trent's admission about the cheating scheme.

"You're quiet," Matt commented, giving her a quick look.

"Thinking about what Trent said. His version of the cheating scheme felt true because Landon wouldn't have gone along with it, but maybe his professor would have. And if Landon was going to be the scapegoat, that would have been very upsetting. He would have felt betrayed by his friends and his professor." She paused. "But he still wouldn't have gotten blackout drunk. No way."

"Agreed. And we can't take anything these people say at face value."

"It's especially odd that Trent wanted to share that at the tournament. He didn't want to say anything in front of Henry, but our conversation was still very public. Anyone could have seen him talking to us, and he wasn't afraid of that."

"Another reason not to believe him."

"Hopefully, we can get Brooke to open up. She's our best hope."

"Well, it looks like she's home."

Home was a U-shaped apartment building near the freeway with an open-air parking area serving as the first floor, the apartment building rising up two stories above it. Brooke pulled into a spot while Matt parked on the street.

They got out of the car and moved into the parking area before Brooke could get to her front door. When she saw them, she froze, panic running through her eyes. "What are you doing here? Did you follow me?"

"Yes," Matt said. "We followed you because we want to talk to you alone, without your friends around you."

"I've told you everything I know," she said, a desperate note in her voice.

"No, you haven't, Brooke," she cut in, drawing Brooke's attention to her. "We know you went into Landon's room in his apartment and that you stole his notebooks."

Brooke's face paled. "That's crazy. I didn't steal anything from Landon."

"It's on video," Matt said shortly. "Do you want to change your answer?"

"Video?" she echoed in shock. "How?"

"Landon had set up a camera in his room," she said. "He obviously didn't trust you. And he was right, wasn't he? You went into his desk, took his notebooks, and gave them to someone. Who was that?"

Brooke licked her lips. "I want to speak to a lawyer before I say anything else."

She ignored Brooke's comment. "Did you love my brother? Or was it all an act? Were you trying to get close to him so you could take something from him? Please, I have to know," she begged. "Landon was all I had left of my family, and he's gone. I have to know the truth."

"I don't know how he died," Brooke said. "I don't. I swear."

"What about your relationship? And the notebooks?"

"I liked Landon. I did," Brooke said, staring directly at Haley. "It didn't start out that way. Henry asked me to flirt with Landon, to get close to him, because he could be helpful to me, to everyone. He was super smart, and the fraternity's grade point average was getting close to putting the house on probation. There would be no parties, no rush, none of that. But if Landon could help change some grades in the class where he was the teaching assistant, then that could help me, too, because I was also in that class."

"You used him," she accused, beginning to see at least some part of the truth.

"We had fun together. It wasn't like I was hurting him. It was just casual."

"You told me it was serious, that you were moving in together after graduation."

"That might have been an exaggeration. We only went out a few times, just enough for me to get a key to his apartment so I could access his computer and his notebooks."

She was blown away by the truth. "You stole his phone and computer, too, didn't you?"

"No. Just the notebooks. I don't know what happened to the other stuff. And I only took the notebooks because Henry made me."

"How did he do that?" Matt asked.

"Henry is the kind of guy who helps you get into trouble and then blackmails you about what you did," Brooke said. "That's what he did to me. That's why I had to flirt with Landon, try to get him to change their grades, and then steal his notebooks. I don't know what was in them. I just know that Landon was working on something that he was excited about, but he told me he couldn't share it because it could be really important."

"What's happening now?" Matt asked. "Landon died six years ago. But more people are dying now. Why?"

Brooke hesitated. "I can't say anything else. I don't know why that woman in Henry's office died. I don't know why she told you she knew who killed Landon or that Landon had even been murdered. I really did believe it was an accident."

"Did you, Brooke?" she challenged. "You knew the frat was trying to use Landon to change grades, and he didn't want to do it. Why didn't you tell me that after he died?"

"Because Henry had dirt on me, and I couldn't say anything, not that I actually knew anything to say."

"You knew what Henry was doing."

"I only knew he wanted the notebooks; I didn't know why."

"What are they plotting to do now, Brooke?" Matt asked.

"I'm not sure."

"Stop lying," she said forcefully. "I heard you talking to Jill in the locker room. She told you to hang on, that everything will be good, that you're all going to be rich. You have to talk now."

Brooke's lips tightened, then she said, "I gave Jill some money to invest for me. She said it was some kind of secret deal, and we were all going to get rich. But then you showed up asking about Landon, and that woman in Henry's office died, and everyone started acting strangely."

"Who's everyone?" Matt asked.

"Henry, Trent, Drew, Jill...others... Look, I'm not like them. I'm not as rich or as powerful as they are. Jill is my employer. I get paid a salary. I don't have access to the company's finances or Jill's private plans. I just plan events, that's it."

"That's not it," she said. "You stole something from my brother, and you played a part of his death, even if you don't want to say it."

Brooke's face paled. "I can't do this. I have a lawyer. If you want to speak to me again, you'll have to go through him." As soon as she finished speaking, she ran toward her door and slipped inside, disappearing into the stairwell.

"I think we should go after her, make her keep talking," she told Matt, starting toward the door.

"Hang on," he said, putting a hand on her arm. "You know when a subject is done talking, Haley. You're a journalist. You've hit this wall before."

"And it pisses me off every time," she said hotly. She stopped abruptly as a scream pierced the air. "Oh, my God. Is that Brooke?"

They ran into the building and up the stairs, taking them two at a time. Another scream echoed through the stairwell, cut short by what sounded like a crash. Matt pulled his gun as they reached the second-floor landing.

The door to apartment 2B was ajar, hanging off one hinge. Through the opening, she could see overturned furniture and Brooke on the floor, blood pooling beneath her.

A figure in dark clothing and a ski mask was rifling through Brooke's purse when Matt pushed the door fully open, his gun drawn.

"Drop the weapon!" Matt ordered.

The man spun around, a bloody knife in his hand. Instead of complying, he lunged toward Matt with surprising speed. Matt fired once as the man charged, but the attacker was already diving low, and the bullet went high, punching into the wall behind him.

The attacker crashed into Matt before he could fire again, driving him backward into the wall. The impact knocked the gun from Matt's hand, sending it skittering across the floor as both men went down hard. The attacker kept hold of his knife, slashing wildly as they wrestled.

She could see Matt grabbing for the man's wrist, trying to control the blade while the attacker fought to drive it toward his throat. They rolled across the floor, crashing into furniture, both grunting with effort.

The gun. She spotted it near the overturned coffee table, maybe ten feet away. *If the attacker broke free from Matt...*

She ran for it, dropping to her knees and snatching up the weapon just as the two men barreled into the dining table, sending a lamp and picture frames crashing to the ground. The gun was heavier than she'd expected, and her hands were shaking.

"Haley, get out!" Matt shouted between gritted teeth as he blocked the knife from coming down toward his chest.

But she couldn't leave. Matt was losing ground—the attacker was on top of him now, pressing the blade down with both hands while Matt strained to hold it back. She could see the knife inching closer to Matt's throat.

She sprang up, gripping the gun tight, heart pounding like a drum. She'd never fired a weapon before, and they were moving fast, rolling and struggling. She couldn't pull the trigger. *What if she hit Matt?*

Matt managed to get his knee up and kicked the attacker off him. The man rolled away and then bolted toward the door.

Matt staggered to his feet and gave chase, blood trickling from where his head had hit the table. "Call 911!" he shouted over his shoulder as he ran after the attacker.

Her fingers shook as she dialed 911. "I need an ambulance at 1247 Westwood Avenue, apartment 2B. A woman's been stabbed. She's bleeding really badly. Please hurry."

The dispatcher told her help was on the way, and she left her phone on as she ran to the kitchen, grabbed dish towels, and then came back to kneel beside Brooke. There were at least two wounds she could see—one in the abdomen, one in her shoulder.

"Brooke, can you hear me?" She pressed the towel against the worst wound, the one in her abdomen. Blood immediately soaked through the fabric. "Help is coming."

Brooke's eyes flickered open, glossy with pain. "I—I don't want to die," she whispered.

"You're not going to die. Just stay with me." She applied more pressure to the wound, trying to remember basic first aid. "Do you know who attacked you?"

Brooke's head moved slightly—maybe a shake, maybe just a spasm. "Why did this happen? I did everything they asked."

"If you tell me what you know, maybe I can help. The FBI can protect you."

"They're going to..." Brooke's eyes rolled back, then refocused again with effort. "Make so much money. Change...change the world."

"How? How are they going to do that? Brooke, stay with me."

"I wish..." Her voice faded to nothing, her eyes closing.

"Brooke! What do you wish?" She checked for a pulse at Brooke's neck. It was weak but still there. "Don't you dare die on me," she said forcefully.

But Brooke had lost consciousness, her breathing shallow and irregular.

Matt stumbled back through the doorway just as sirens became audible in the distance. His face was pale, blood trickling from a cut on his head.

"Are you okay? Did you get him?" she asked.

"No. He got away," he said in frustration. His gaze moved to Brooke. "How is she doing?"

"It's bad. But she's still breathing." She paused. "You need medical attention, too."

"I'm fine. Just a scratch."

The paramedics burst into the apartment, followed quickly by police. While Matt explained to the officers what was happening, she moved into the kitchen to wash the blood off her hands, the sight of it making her want to vomit.

Within minutes, the medics had loaded Brooke onto a stretcher, her face gray and still. She really hoped Brooke would survive, but she didn't know if she'd lost too much blood. "Let me at least clean your cut," she said, grabbing another towel and wetting it before dabbing at the blood on Matt's face. Luckily, the cut wasn't very deep, and as soon as it stopped dripping blood, he waved her hand away.

"It's fine," he said. "The police will secure and process the scene, so we can go."

She was more than happy to get out of the apartment and away from the blood on the floor, a reminder of what had just happened. After they got into Matt's car, they just sat there for a moment.

"Do you think Jill did this?" she asked. "Brooke told her she was nervous about us. Did we cause that to happen? Did we put a target on Brooke?"

"Brooke put a target on herself when she expressed concern and asked too many questions. I don't know if Jill is behind the attack or if she told someone else who decided Brooke was a liability." He paused. "Did Brooke say anything to you before she passed out?"

"She said they were going to change the world and make a lot of money. She started to say something else, but she couldn't get the words out before she lost consciousness. I want to go to the hospital. I know Brooke might be responsible for Landon's death, but she's my last connection to him, and she wanted to say something to me. If she has more to tell, I need to hear it."

"Then that's where we'll go," he said as he started the engine and pulled away from the curb.

CHAPTER NINETEEN

Matt stood in the surgical waiting room of Cedars-Sinai Medical Center, watching Haley pace. Her restless energy was still as high as it had been when they'd arrived an hour earlier. It was now almost six in the evening, and Brooke was still in the operating room. "Do you want to go down to the cafeteria and get something to eat or drink, maybe something decaffeinated?" he suggested.

"I can't eat or drink. I'm too wound up," she said, her voice tense.

"I can see that. Let's get out of here. If you're going to pace, you need more space."

"I wish I could be as calm as you are," she said as they moved down a quiet hallway that led toward the main lobby. "I'm afraid Brooke isn't going to make it, and everything she knew will die with her."

"That could happen," he said quietly. "But I'm sure the doctors are doing everything they can. As for talking to her again, I don't think that will be possible tonight. With the length of the surgery, she'll be in recovery for hours. We should probably go back to my place. We can come back when she wakes up, when she's able to talk."

She frowned. "Let's give it a little more time. I'd rather not leave until I know she's at least survived the surgery. Have you heard any more from Jason? I saw you texting a few minutes ago."

"He was just asking if there was an update on Brooke. Derek is still working on the drive, but no luck yet. He's an expert hacker, so I'm a little surprised, but apparently your brother was very good at securing his work."

"Except for his black notebooks and whatever they contained." Shadows filled her eyes. "Brooke admitted to stealing them. I'm not sure I believe she didn't know anything about what was in them."

"She may be more willing to talk now that someone has tried to kill her. Joining forces with us will be the best way for her to stay safe."

They had just entered the lobby when he saw a young man rush toward the reception desk. He was tall, athletic, wearing expensive jeans and a worried expression. "That's Kyle, Brooke's boyfriend," he muttered. "I know her parents are out of town, but I wondered when one of her friends was going to show up."

Kyle Vance spoke briefly to the person at the desk, then walked a few feet away, pulling out his phone to make a call.

"He looks upset," Haley commented. "I wonder who he's calling. Should we talk to him?"

Before he could answer, another man entered the lobby, heading straight for Kyle. He was dressed in a designer suit and appeared to be in his late thirties or early forties.

As the two men conversed, he opened the camera app on his phone and snapped a photo. Then he sent it to Derek to get an ID. As their conversation intensified, they moved toward the hospital gift shop. Curious as to what they were talking about, he said, "Stay here. I'm going to get closer."

"I'm coming with you."

He didn't bother to argue, since Haley rarely gave in without a fight. They moved across the lobby, standing behind a tall potted plant near the gift shop, so they could hear Kyle's conversation.

"What the hell is going on?" Kyle demanded.

"Your girlfriend will be fine," the man replied. "You need to keep your eye on the bigger picture."

"She's not fine. She's still in surgery, and her condition is critical."

He could hear the fear in Kyle's voice. He genuinely cared about Brooke.

"I don't understand what happened," Kyle continued.

"She walked in on a burglary in progress, and she was stabbed. That's what happened," the man said.

"I don't believe that," Kyle snapped.

"You need to calm down and keep it together."

"Where's everyone else? Why aren't they here?" Kyle demanded.

"Jill is on her way. Have you spoken to the police or the FBI yet? I'm sure someone will have questions for you," the man said.

"Not yet. I'm going upstairs now. I need to see Brooke when she gets out of surgery."

"I'll go with you."

As the men moved down the hall, Matt turned to Haley. "Let's go."

"We can't leave," she protested. "We need to talk to Brooke before they do."

"No one is talking to Brooke tonight. There will be security on her room as soon as she gets out of surgery. There is nothing more we can do here," he added as he urged her toward the exit. "Did you recognize the man talking to Kyle?"

"No. I've never seen him before," she said as they got outside. "He sounded like he was involved. Kyle didn't seem to believe the burglar theory."

He met her gaze. "Yes, they sounded very much involved. But Kyle was shocked by Brooke's attack, which means he's not at the top. I'm not so sure about the other guy."

"We need to find out who he is."

"We will. I sent his photo to my team. We should have his identity shortly."

———

Haley was still thinking about the man with Kyle when they got back to Matt's apartment. She kicked off her heels and dropped onto the couch in exhaustion. Her adrenaline rush had finally worn off, and now she was just tired.

Matt grabbed two sparkling waters out of the fridge and handed her one as he sat down next to her.

"Thanks," she said, taking a grateful sip of the cool, bubbly liquid. "So, what now?"

Before he could reply, he got a text.

"What does it say?" she asked impatiently.

"Kyle's friend at the hospital is Viktor Danilovich. He's an importer/exporter and real estate investor. Worked alongside his father until his parents died in a carbon monoxide poisoning at a resort in Fiji while on vacation last year."

She raised an eyebrow. "That sounds weird."

"It appears to have been a tragic accident. His parents were from Belarus, but he was born in the US."

"Now he's running his family business."

"Yes." He looked back at his phone. "Here's the link we're looking for. Viktor's younger brother, Alexei, went to West-bridge with Henry, Drew, Trent, and, presumably, your brother. Do you remember that name?"

She shook her head. "No." She wanted to feel excited about the new information, but she just felt overwhelmed. "How are we ever going to figure this out, Matt? We're adding suspects instead of eliminating them."

"That isn't defeat in your voice, is it? You, the intrepid reporter who never gives up?"

She frowned at his words. "I'm frustrated."

"Of course you are. But we are making progress. It might be small steps, but we're moving forward."

"I'm a little surprised by your upbeat attitude, Matt. If I had had to guess who was the most optimistic of the two of us, I would have picked me."

A grin lifted his lips. "I would have, too. But I have more perspective on this case than you do." He paused. "I'm starving. How do you feel about turkey chili?"

She was taken aback by the abrupt change in subject, but also hungry and somewhat intrigued by his suggestion. "Turkey chili?"

"Are you a fan?"

"I am, but doesn't that take a long time to cook?"

"Not when I can just defrost it. I made a big batch last week."

She was continually surprised by the man next to her. "Then I'm in," she said as she got up and followed him into the kitchen.

While Matt was heating the chili, she made herself useful by fixing a salad with the lettuce, cucumbers, and tomatoes he had in the fridge.

As she finished the bowl and set it aside, she watched him stir the chili and said, "This is strange, isn't it? Friday morning, you wanted to arrest me, and look at us now, cooking together, living together..." Her voice drifted away as he gave her a look that was a mix of amusement and something else she couldn't define.

"Making a salad doesn't count as cooking, and as for living together, you are in the guest room."

"I know, but you have to admit, this feels oddly domestic but also nice. I've never had a man cook for me before."

"Never?"

"No. Dates are usually out somewhere...drinks, dinner, that kind of thing. And I don't offer to cook, because, well...a restaurant is always a better idea than me cooking. I don't know much beyond the basics, certainly nothing to impress anyone." She paused. "What about you? Do you cook for your dates?"

"I have made dinner for other women. Sorry to say you're not the first."

"I figured as much," she said dryly.

"With the work I do, sometimes I just prefer to be home."

"It's interesting you say that, because your apartment isn't homey. It's beautifully decorated, but the only room that really feels lived-in is this one. The rest of your place could use a more personal touch. I could help you warm it up."

"I'll keep that in mind."

She slid onto the stool at the kitchen island. "You're just telling me what I want to hear, aren't you? Is that a tried-and-true FBI technique?"

"Sometimes. People are generally more agreeable when you tell them what they want to hear. But I learned that when I was a kid, not when I got to the FBI," he said with a smile. "After the divorce, my parents competed for a while to be the best parent, but not really in my eyes, rather in their rival's eyes. When my mom would make me dinner, she'd ask me if it was better than what my dad fed me. I would say yes. And when my dad asked me if I liked living with him better than with my mom, I'd say yes."

"So, you never got to have your own opinion."

"I had my own opinions; I just didn't share them. What was the point? It wasn't like making one of them unhappy would make me happier."

"You became cynical at a very young age."

"And you didn't?" he challenged.

"No, I did," she admitted. "But Landon kept me from going too dark. He was always looking up, always believing that some kind of magic was out there, that people were inherently good, we just couldn't always see it. We used to go up on the roof of our apartment building after my dad died. We'd lie on our backs and look up at the stars, and Landon would point out constellations. He'd tell me about all the other worlds that could be out there, how we were just one small grain of sand in the universe. He wanted me to look up, look forward, believe in tomorrow." She gave Matt a tired, sad smile. "Now all I do is look down and backward, trying to find answers in the past. It's ironic, isn't it?"

"Maybe finding those answers will let you look forward again."

"What about you? What made you look forward when you were a kid?"

Matt was quiet for a moment as he stirred the chili. Then he said, "Birthdays."

"Really? Because you got two celebrations?"

"No, because I wanted to get old enough to control my own life. I hated flying back and forth between San Francisco and San Diego, never knowing which parent actually wanted me there. I always felt like I was interrupting their new lives, their new families. I couldn't wait to be eighteen, so no court could tell me where I had to be."

"That makes sense."

"I envy your relationship with Landon, the closeness you shared," he said, glancing back at her. "My siblings are so much younger; we never had that kind of bond. I have certainly never had anyone in my life who would fight for me the way you fight for Landon."

"Landon and I fought for each other," she said quietly. "It was the only way we survived. It's a habit I can't break now, even though he's gone."

As the chili began to boil, Matt lowered the heat, and she got up to get some salad dressing from the fridge. As she turned around, she collided with Matt, who was reaching for a spoon. She stumbled as she set the dressing on the island, and Matt's hands landed on her waist to steady her.

He was suddenly so close, his face just inches away from her; his lips parted, his breath mixing with hers. For a moment, they just stared at each other.

"Haley," he said, his voice rough and sexy.

She knew he wanted her to move away, but all she wanted to do was get closer, and she couldn't stop herself from putting her hands on his shoulders. She licked her lips as she gazed into his eyes. "I know this is complicated, but—"

"I don't care anymore," he interrupted. And then he kissed her.

She responded immediately, her fingers curling into the fabric of his shirt as the sparks ignited between them, creating fiery kisses that were hungry, desperate, full of a need they'd both been denying. But now they'd surrendered.

Matt's hands tangled in her hair, holding her close as he deepened the kiss, sending heat shooting through her body. The closer they got, the more she realized it wasn't close enough. She wanted to lose herself in him and for him to lose himself in her. She wanted to put away all the questions and fears and just savor what was happening right this second.

And then a buzzing phone jolted them apart.

Matt's phone was vibrating on the nearby counter. He looked at it, then back at her. "I should—"

"Get it," she finished. "It could be important."

As he stepped away, she let out a breath and pushed her messy hair behind her ears as she moved around to the other side of the island.

"Hello?" Matt said, a question in his voice. "Who is this?" He paused. "Anthony?"

Her pulse jumped. Anthony was the name of his whistleblower, the one whose phone had been disconnected, who'd given Matt's name to Sabrina. She motioned for him to put the phone on speaker.

"Anthony?" he repeated as he did as she requested. "Where the hell are you? I've been looking for you."

"You're not the only one. Someone broke into my apartment on Saturday. I think it had something to do with Sabrina Lin's murder."

"You heard about that?"

"Hell, yeah, and I can't believe she's dead."

"You sent her to me. Why?"

"Because she needed to get help from someone in law enforcement she could trust. And the only person I knew was you."

"Why did she need help?"

"She was looking at a corporate fraud case and thought it tied into a murder at Westbridge University. She was killed the day after she went there to talk to Professor Harrington. She thought he had information she needed."

"What information?"

"It's a long story. I told her to stay away from Westbridge, that it was too dangerous. She needed to get your help before she did anything else. Obviously, that didn't happen."

"We need to talk, Anthony. You need to tell me everything, so I can help."

"I want to meet, but I don't have a good feeling. I spent a lot of time reinventing myself, getting a place to live under a new name, starting over in a new job as someone else, but I made a mistake. I gave Sabrina my real name so that she could give it to you, and now, dammit, someone is after me—"

Silence followed his abbreviated sentence. "Anthony? Are you there? Talk to me," Matt said.

"I think someone is here. I'll be in touch," Anthony said in a hushed tone. And then the call disconnected.

Matt swore as he set down the phone.

"Do you think he's okay?" she asked with concern. "He sounded scared."

"I don't know. I hope so."

"He said Sabrina went to Westbridge to talk to Professor Harrington. We need to talk to Harrington, too." She was surprised when Matt didn't instantly agree. "You don't think that's a good idea?"

"I don't like that we just got a clue dropped into our laps. It could be a trap."

"But Anthony is the whistleblower you worked with, the one who recommended you to Sabrina. Would he try to entrap you?"

"I don't think so, but I can't completely discount the possibility."

"We were going to talk to the professor anyway. We need to find out what he knows about the grade-changing scheme, and now we can ask him what he said to Sabrina."

Matt's lips tightened. "I can't keep taking you into dangerous situations, Haley. I need to get you into a safehouse with guards at the door."

She saw the determination in his eyes, but she couldn't let him lock her away. "I'm not going to hide. You just said you admired the way I fight for my brother. Let me fight."

"I don't want anything to happen to you. In case you haven't noticed, I'm starting to like you quite a bit."

"I feel the same way, and I also feel the safest when I'm with you. I can't trust anyone else. Please, don't leave me behind, Matt."

He drew in a deep breath and let it out. "I'll think about it. As for what happened before Anthony called—"

"Let's not talk about that," she interrupted. "It was great. Can we leave it at that?"

"Can we?" he queried, giving her a searching look.

"Yes. Let's just have dinner and put everything else aside." She could see Matt putting up his professional walls, and she didn't think a conversation about the way they'd just kissed each other would be helpful. "Is the chili ready?"

"It is," he said, a conflicted gleam in his eyes. "I still feel like we should talk, Haley."

"We've done enough talking," she said decisively. "Let's eat. We'll figure out tomorrow...tomorrow."

CHAPTER TWENTY

Monday morning, on the drive to Westbridge University, Matt was still wondering if he'd made the right decision in allowing Haley to go with him. But unless he arrested her, she was going to leave whatever safehouse he put her in and talk to whoever she wanted to talk to.

She'd also argued that as Landon's sister, she might be able to get more out of Professor Harrington than he could, and it was a valid point. He just hoped he wasn't making a huge mistake. Although his biggest mistake so far had probably been kissing Haley in his kitchen last night. He'd been fighting his attraction to her, and he'd slipped up. It had been one hell of a kiss, too, and it was probably fortunate that Anthony had called just in time to derail whatever runaway train they'd gotten on.

After that, they'd eaten dinner in relative silence. Then Haley had said she was going to bed, and he'd gone into his office to write down his thoughts on the investigation. He'd spent a couple of hours going over everything they'd learned so far, and while there were a lot of pieces on the game board, he couldn't connect any of them directly to a crime. But whatever was happening now had started at Westbridge, and it was time to go back to the beginning.

His phone buzzed, and he put it on speaker, eager to hear how Jason's visit to the hospital this morning had gone. "Jason, how's Brooke? Were you able to question her?"

"Yes. But she was still out of it. The doctor said she lost a lot of blood, and she's very weak. She could barely keep her eyes open. He told me to come back later today."

"Did she say anything at all?"

"She told me she was scared. I asked who she was scared of, and she said everyone. I told her there were guards outside her door, and I was going to restrict visitors, including her boyfriend, until she was feeling better. She was fine with that. She didn't fight to get Kyle in or anyone else."

"That's interesting."

"Jill Adler, Trent Adler, and Kyle Vance were in the waiting room. They all displayed the appropriate amount of shock, concern, and ignorance."

"What about the Russian man who was there last night?"

"Wasn't there this morning, and we haven't dug up any information on Viktor Danilovich other than what I sent you last night. I'm heading back to the office now. Derek thinks he might be close to a breakthrough on the drive, so I'll let you know as soon as that happens."

"Thanks."

"I'm glad Brooke is still alive," Haley said. "I just hope she has more to say."

"We'll give her time to recover and then press harder."

He turned his focus back to the road as he drove down the Pacific Coast Highway to the hills of the Palos Verdes Peninsula, where the campus was located. As he got closer to Westbridge, he left the highway, entering the winding roads of the peninsula where the woods thickened, and city living quickly dropped away. He slowed as the campus gates came into view: smooth stone walls, an engraved sign that said Westbridge, and a security kiosk.

He showed his badge at the kiosk, and they were waved on.

The road curved upward, and then the campus suddenly opened in front of them—a breathtaking vista of red-tiled roofs and cream-colored stone buildings set on terraced hills above the Pacific Ocean. Tall oak trees created natural boundaries between academic quads, while perfectly manicured lawns stretched between Spanish colonial buildings that looked like they'd been transplanted from a European monastery.

"It's beautiful," he murmured.

"It's supposed to be," Haley said. "Everything here is designed to look perfect. To make you believe that nothing bad could ever happen in a place this pristine. But, of course, that isn't true."

He drove down the main road past the library—a massive stone structure with Gothic windows—and the student center, where clusters of young people sat at outdoor tables under umbrellas. The cars in the parking lots were BMWs, Mercedes, and a few Teslas. This wasn't a place where scholarship kids blended in easily.

"Turn left here," Haley said suddenly, pointing to a smaller road that led away from the main campus. "Fraternity row is down that way. I want to show you the fraternity house before we go to faculty housing."

The road curved through a grove of pine trees before opening onto a street lined with large houses, each one displaying Greek letters and surrounded by well-maintained landscaping. They looked more like expensive suburban homes than college housing.

"Stop," Haley said as they approached a large Tudor-style house. "That's it. That was Landon's fraternity."

Matt pulled over, studying the imposing structure. Behind the house, the manicured lawn gave way to a wooded area.

"The pond is back there, behind the house," she said, her voice barely above a whisper. "Through those trees. I need to see it again."

"Haley, wait."

She gave him a tense look. "Why?"

"It's going to be upsetting."

"Everything is upsetting. I need to see it again. I need to go back to the beginning."

Her words echoed his earlier thoughts, and he got out of the car. He couldn't let her go back to the beginning alone.

They walked around the side of the fraternity house, past a patio with expensive outdoor furniture and a barbecue area. Beyond that was a thick wooded area with a narrow dirt path leading through the trees. The air grew cooler as they descended, the sounds of campus life fading behind them.

The pond was smaller than Matt had expected, maybe thirty feet across, fed by a creek that meandered through the woods. The water was dark and still, reflecting the overhanging branches. Someone had built a small wooden dock that extended a few feet into the water.

Haley stopped at the edge of the water, her hands clenched into fists at her sides.

"When I got here that morning," she said, her voice hollow, "his body was still on the ground. Right there." She pointed to a spot not far away. "In a black bag. I couldn't believe it was him. I thought there had to be some terrible mistake. They told me I didn't have to look, that his fraternity brothers had already identified him, but I had to see."

He stayed quiet, letting her process the memories, knowing how horrendously painful that moment must have been for her. Landon had been an extension of herself—not just her brother—her best friend, her whole family.

"There were people everywhere," she continued. "Police, paramedics, campus security. They had yellow tape around the whole area. But I couldn't hear anything but the pounding of my heart and the unzipping of the bag. And then I saw his face." Her voice caught in her throat as she looked away from him to some point on the ground near the water. "It was him. But I still didn't want to believe it. His face was blue. His hair was wet. He looked frozen. It was the most horrible image I've ever seen, and I'll never forget it. I fell to the ground, and I couldn't stop crying. I don't know how long I was there until the police detective—Julia—helped me up. She gave me a hug and said she was going to find out what had happened. She was like an anchor for me in a storm of emotions. The only one who seemed able to look me in the eye. Because when I turned to the fraternity brothers, they all glanced away. No one wanted to see me. No one wanted me to see them." She drew in a breath and looked back at him. "I think his killer might have been standing right there, behind the tape, in the crowd of onlookers."

He didn't say anything, sensing she needed to talk through the memories.

"I started screaming at them. 'How did this happen? Why didn't anyone help him?' They just stared at me. Henry, Trent, Drew—they were all there that morning. And no one had anything to say. Julia pulled me away and asked me if I had someone I could call to come and be with me. I said, no. Landon was the only person I could have called, and he was gone. She had another officer take me down to the station, and after a while, I was calm enough to talk to them, and we went over everything I knew, which was very little. After that, I went to Landon's apartment, and that's when I ran into Brooke."

"When did you first talk to the frat guys?"

"The next day. But they told me nothing. I stayed in a motel for almost two weeks after that, talking to Julia every day, until she told me I needed to go home, return to my life, my work, and let them do their job. So, I did. But it was less than a week later when she informed me the investigation had concluded. Landon's death was deemed an accidental drowning, a result of the high level of alcohol in his body. They did next to nothing to really investigate. I pleaded for them to keep looking for answers. Julia told me there was nothing more that could be done officially, but she'd keep asking around. She stayed in touch with me for a while, but nothing new ever came up. It took me a long time to stop asking for updates. When she left the force, that was the end of it." Her chest heaved with another ragged breath. "I can't believe I'm back here." She surveyed the scene once more. "It's such a pretty area, so calm and quiet. How could Landon die here in this pond that isn't even very deep?"

"We're going to find out, Haley."

"I've heard that before. It never happens."

He hated the edge of defeat in her voice, not that he couldn't understand it. "It's different now. You know that. You needed to go back into the past, and I'm glad you brought me here. But now you need to return to the present. You're not helpless and alone, not this time."

She squared her shoulders and lifted her chin. "You're right. I'm ready to go. Let's talk to Professor Harrington."

As they walked up the path, Matt noticed how isolated this area was. On a dark night, with music playing from the fraternity house, and hundreds of kids partying, no one would hear someone calling for help down here. The perfect place for murder disguised as an accident.

———

After returning to the car, he drove back through the main campus and up into the hills where faculty housing was located. The houses here were scattered among the trees, each one carefully positioned to maximize privacy while taking advantage of the dramatic Pacific coastline views.

Professor Harrington's address led them to a modern glass and steel house that seemed to float among the trees, its clean lines a stark contrast to the Spanish colonial architecture of the main campus below. The home was perched on a ridge with an unobstructed view of the ocean.

"They provide incredible housing for their faculty," he commented.

"One of the perks of teaching here. The university has very

little in the way of faculty turnover because they take good care of their professors."

"That probably makes them extremely loyal."

"I know. I'm mentally preparing for Professor Harrington to plead ignorance and tell us nothing."

He nodded, unable to disagree. But he hoped they might catch a break. According to the research he'd done last night, Professor Justin Harrington was in his late forties and had divorced his wife five years ago, the year after Landon's death. Harrington was a popular professor with silver-threaded brown hair, blue eyes, and an apparently sexy scholarly look that had put him on the informal *hottest professor* list that circulated in social media from current and past Westbridge students. Harrington taught advanced-level programming, data structures and algorithms, financial computing, and a basic economics class. Landon had served as his TA in two of those classes.

He pulled into the circular driveway, right behind a car with an open trunk and several suitcases inside. "Looks like Harrington is taking a trip."

"Hopefully, he's still here," Haley said as they got out of the car and moved up the steps to the front door, which was ajar.

He knocked on the door and then stepped inside. Harrington, dressed in jeans and a button-down shirt, came into the entry, carrying a large box, which he dropped in alarm when he saw them.

"Who the hell are you?" he asked.

"Agent Lawson, FBI," he said, showing his badge. "And this is Haley Kenton."

Harrington's jaw dropped, panic flaring in his eyes. His gaze darted past them, as if he was judging whether or not he could run.

"We need to talk to you, Professor," he added.

"I was just...I'm on my way to visit my sister in Portland. Family emergency."

"Are you taking your entire house with you?" Haley asked,

waving her hand toward the stacked boxes visible in the living room behind Harrington.

"I'm taking a sabbatical," Harrington said. "To care for my sister. I can't miss my plane."

"I don't believe you're leaving because of your sister," he said. "You're scared. And you're on the run because Sabrina Lin was killed the day after she came to see you, and because you know we want to talk to you about Landon's death. You probably also know that Haley is Landon's sister."

"Yes. I remember you," Harrington said, his gaze moving to Haley. "I'm still very sorry about what happened to your brother."

"I don't need your compassion; I need answers," Haley said, shutting the front door behind her. "And you're not going anywhere until I get them."

"I can't imagine what I could tell you."

"Let's start with what you told Sabrina Lin," he said, drawing Harrington's attention. "You didn't act surprised when I said she was killed after seeing you."

"It was in the news. It was a terrible thing."

"Why did she come here to talk to you? And what did you discuss?"

"I taught a class in the law school on legal issues regarding cyber software. She was one of my students."

"But she didn't come here to talk to you about that class," Haley said. "She came to speak to you about my brother. She found out something that led her to believe Landon's death was not an accident. What was it?"

Harrington inclined his head. "She wanted to know about Landon's research, what he was working on that had to do with forecasting financial market fluctuations."

"What did you tell her?"

"That that subject matter was not part of the curriculum in my classes."

"But?" Haley pressed.

"But I knew Landon was working on something that would help investors with their strategies," he conceded. "Landon told me about his father losing all his money in a stock market crash and his subsequent suicide. He wanted to change the system."

"He told you about our father's suicide?" Haley said with surprise. "He never talked about that."

"It slipped out one night. We were working late. He was tired. But he was driven. He thought he was on to something that could be useful in preventing others from going through what his father and his family had gone through."

"After he told you about it, who did you tell?" Matt asked.

"No one," Harrington replied.

"You're lying," he said, noting the way Harrington's gaze averted with his answer. "You can't look at me or Haley now, because you're not telling the truth."

"I'm sorry your brother is gone, but you can't bring him back. You need to let this go. Look at what happened to Sabrina," the professor said. "She asked questions, and she's dead."

"Is that why you're running?" Haley asked. "You're afraid you're next? Why?"

"I can't say any more. I owe...too much."

"Money?" he asked sharply.

"Loyalty," Harrington said, meeting his gaze. "I was bailed out of a sticky situation by some powerful people, and if I were to talk, that situation would be revealed, and that would be the end of my career. That's what I told Sabrina when she asked."

"It looks like you're already at the end of your career," he said bluntly. "You're not taking a sabbatical, you're done here. It's over. Why?"

Before Harrington could answer, Haley said, "Would the career-ending issue be about changing grades for the guys in Landon's fraternity?"

Harrington's face tightened. "You know about that?"

"My brother didn't want to do it, so you did it for him. You overrode him, right?"

"I had to. Like I said, I owed a debt that had to be paid. I couldn't risk losing my job over raising a few grades for a couple of kids."

"Landon was angry with you. Was he going to turn you in?" Haley asked. "Did you kill him before he could do that?"

Matt wasn't surprised at Haley's direct question, because he'd been one second away from asking the same thing.

"No! God, no!" Harrington said forcefully. "I could never kill anyone. Never. I actually felt deeply ashamed in the face of Landon's strong ethical stance. He was barely out of his teens, but he knew what was right and what was wrong."

"He did know right from wrong. You, apparently, did not," Haley said harshly.

"What were they holding over you?" he asked Harrington.

Harrington hesitated, then said, "I had an inappropriate sexual relationship with a student. It was a setup, but I didn't know that at the time. Once they had me, they had me. I couldn't lose my job. I made a bad decision; I never thought it would lead me here. And I swear I don't know what happened to Landon."

Matt thought about that as Haley's questioning gaze met his. He turned back to Harrington. "You said you don't know what happened, but you were suspicious, weren't you?"

Harrington tipped his head in acknowledgment. "The story didn't ring true, and it occurred to me that one of Landon's frat brothers might have found out about his work and wanted to get access to it. There are many Westbridge families with ties to the financial industry, including several in Landon's fraternity, Trent Adler and Drew Sanderson, to name two of them."

"Were they the ones blackmailing you?"

"I don't know. My tormentor was disguised, but the girl in question was very good friends with Henry Adler, so I suspect he was involved."

"Henry did the same thing to Landon," Haley said. "He sent

a woman to him, someone who would flirt and pretend to like him so she could get her hands on his work."

"You're talking about Brooke Mercer?"

"Yes."

"Brooke was struggling in my economics class. She was one of the ones whose grades I changed. I believe she was in trouble in other classes as well, but this one grade would keep her from getting kicked out of school."

"But Henry is a lawyer," Matt said. "He's not in the financial industry. What was his stake?"

"He could still get rich off of whatever Landon had, especially if his friends knew how to use it," Harrington said.

"Who would have known or foreseen how valuable Landon's work might be?" he asked.

Harrington thought for a moment. "I don't know. Any one of them. They all come from wealthy families with significantly large portfolios. Some work in the financial industry, others don't, but that doesn't mean they couldn't benefit from stock manipulation."

"How did the algorithm work?" he asked. "Was it a software program?"

"Landon was going to show me when it was finished. He didn't want to get into it before then, so I don't know the details."

"Was it finished when he died?"

"I'm not sure. By then, we were not in accord. He was unhappy with the grade situation, and we were barely speaking."

"What exactly did you tell Sabrina?" Haley asked.

"What I just told you."

"Why was she looking into this now?" Haley asked. "My brother died six years ago."

"She was doing pro bono work for a company that had been crushed in a recent financial drop; their stock shorted. They suspected market manipulation but needed help trying to figure it out. She ran into an accountant there who also believed there was fraud, and that fraud might tie back to her law firm and its connection to Westbridge. Apparently, that individual had seen similarly unusual market drops and stock shorting on two occasions in the past with another company tied to Westbridge. As she was digging into it, she remembered talking to someone at Westbridge after Landon died, who thought Landon had been killed because of a financial forecasting model he was working on. She wanted to know if I knew about Landon's research project."

Harrington's explanation finally connected Sabrina in the present to Landon in the past.

"What did you tell her?"

"What I just told you, that I only knew it had something to do with financial forecasting. That's all I know," Harrington added. "Now, I need to get out of here. If you know Sabrina talked to me, they probably do, too."

"And you think Henry Adler is running everything?"

"Actually, I don't. To be frank, I'm not sure any of those students were capable of murder. Blackmail, yes, but killing someone...that's hard to fathom. I think it's more likely one of the parents hired someone to take care of whatever problem they saw and are probably still doing that."

"They're not kids anymore. They're adults," Haley pointed out.

"You're right. I just think of them as kids. But they're not. And maybe one or more of them is a killer. I don't know. But I'm not waiting around to find out."

Harrington was about to grab the box at his feet when the sound of shattering glass filled the air. The front door exploded inward in a shower of crystal shards, and a figure in black tactical gear stepped through the opening, assault rifle raised.

His first shot caught Harrington in the shoulder, spinning him around. Matt drew his weapon as Haley grabbed the wounded professor and dragged him around the corner into the hallway.

Matt fired twice, forcing the attacker to take cover behind the stone entryway pillar. He backed up to where Haley was helping Harrington stay upright.

"Back door?" Matt asked quickly.

"Kitchen," Harrington gasped, blood seeping through his fingers as he clutched his shoulder.

"Get out of here, both of you," Matt ordered. "Go now."

The gunman advanced, unleashing a burst of automatic fire that chewed up the doorframe and forced Matt to retreat deeper into the hallway. He ducked into a bedroom as bullets sparked off the walls behind him.

Waiting a beat, he leaned out and fired three quick shots. One caught the gunman center mass, but the tactical vest absorbed the impact. The man stumbled but kept coming.

Another spray of bullets forced Matt back into the bedroom. His mind raced—he was outgunned, with limited cover, and he had no idea if Haley and Harrington had escaped.

The footsteps in the hall were getting closer. Matt spotted a bathroom connected to his room that led to another bedroom. He moved quickly through the connecting rooms, circling around to come up behind the attacker.

He emerged in the hallway just as the gunman entered the first bedroom, looking for him. Matt fired, catching the man in the arm. The attacker spun and returned fire, but his aim was off, bullets going wide. Still, the gunman unleashed another burst of automatic fire, forcing Matt back behind the doorframe. In those crucial seconds of cover fire, Matt heard the crash of breaking glass from inside the bedroom.

When the shooting stopped and Matt looked around the corner, he saw the shattered window in the bedroom. The attacker had bought himself time to escape.

He rushed to the window. Outside, the attacker was limping toward a motorcycle parked on the street. Before Matt could get a clear shot, the man was speeding away, disappearing into the tree line beyond the main road.

"Haley!" Matt called out as he moved back into the hallway.

"In here!" she yelled from the direction of the kitchen.

He found them in the pantry—Haley kneeling beside Harrington, pressing a towel against his shoulder wound. Blood had soaked through the makeshift bandage and was spreading across his shirt.

"He's gone," Matt said, pulling out his phone. "I'm calling for an ambulance. You're going to be okay, Professor."

Harrington's face was pale, his breathing shallow. "None of us are going to be okay if you keep asking questions. We're all going to end up dead." Harrington sent Haley an imploring look. "Landon wouldn't want you to die trying to get justice for him. He loved you so much. He told me you raised him, that all he wanted was to make you proud of him."

"He did that," she whispered, her voice breaking. "Every day."

"He was one of my best teaching assistants," Harrington said, his voice growing weaker. "Brilliant mind. I just wish I could have protected him."

"So do I," Haley said, applying more pressure to his wound as sirens wailed in the distance.

As the sirens grew louder and campus security vehicles appeared in the driveway, Matt went out to update them. This attack had been more aggressive than the last, more professional in nature, and if he hadn't been able to fight back, they might all be dead. They weren't just dealing with spoiled rich kids. They were at war, and they still didn't know exactly who they were fighting.

CHAPTER TWENTY-ONE

It was after four on Monday afternoon by the time they left the Westbridge campus, and Haley's nerves were tighter than they'd ever been. Every car behind them seemed like a possible threat. Every turn could hold some unexpected new horror. She twisted her fingers, not sure where they should go next. They had learned a lot from Justin Harrington but had almost lost their lives in the process.

After Harrington had been taken to the hospital, they'd talked to the local police as well as the campus police. Two of Matt's team members, Jason Colter and a woman named Andi Hart, had shown up at the house, and Matt had given them the update on everything that had transpired.

The intensity of the attack had definitely ratcheted up the danger of the investigation, and before they'd left the university grounds, Jason had given Matt the address and directions to a safehouse, where they were headed now. She wasn't sure why Matt's apartment was no longer safe, but she hadn't had the energy to ask questions. She felt overwhelmed and numb.

Her phone buzzed, and she saw a text from Julia, asking her what the hell was going on. She'd just heard about the shooting at Professor Harrington's house. Julia wanted to know if she was there, if she was okay, and if she had learned anything new. She couldn't begin to answer that question in a text, and since Matt didn't want her to talk to Julia anyway, she just said she was okay, and she'd be in touch.

As she sent that text, she realized she had another one from her editor at the *Sentinel*, checking in on her, wondering if she knew when she'd be back to work. She texted her back as well, saying that she needed at least the rest of the week to figure things out.

"Who are you talking to?" Matt asked.

"Julia. She heard about the shooting, wanted to know if I was there, if I was okay. I told her I'd fill her in later. I can't get into it now."

He frowned, his gaze narrowing. "How did she hear about that?"

"I don't know. Maybe it was on the news. Or maybe she has access to a police scanner. Does it matter?" She paused. "I'm not going to tell her anything, but I couldn't just blow her off."

"I understand. Was that the only text you got?"

"My editor checked in. She knows I'm looking into my brother's death. I told her I'll need a few more days off."

"Good. Now that you've done that, I want you to turn off your phone. Power it all the way off."

"Why? What if someone tries to call me?"

"They can still text you. We'll be able to retrieve your messages at the safehouse, but I don't want anyone tracking your phone."

"What about your phone?"

"I shut it down before we left Westbridge and have forwarded my calls to a secure landline at the safehouse. I meant to tell you to turn it off earlier, but I forgot." He shook his head, irritated with himself over that mistake.

"Well, you've had a lot to deal with," she said as she powered down her phone and put it back in her bag. "Do you want to talk about what we learned?"

"If you want to talk, I'll listen. I'm also happy to be quiet. Your choice."

She stared down at her hands, which she'd scrubbed a half-dozen times but were still tinged with pink from Harrington's blood. "I've had the blood of two people on my hands in two days. And all I can think is that at some point I'm going to be the one bleeding out on the floor." She gave him an anxious look. "I feel overwhelmed, Matt."

"I know. I'm going to do everything I can to protect you."

"The attacks are getting worse and worse. I wonder if we'll be safe anywhere."

"This will be a safe space for us," he assured her. "Trust me."

"You're the only one I can trust," she said, meeting his gaze. "Don't let me down."

"I won't."

Twenty minutes later, Matt pulled into the parking garage of a two-story townhouse that appeared to be part of a duplex. It had taken two codes to get into the garage and then the house, but once inside, she was pleasantly surprised by how modern, up-to-date, and nicely decorated the house was. "This is better than I expected."

"It apparently used to be the home of the head of my task force. He turned it into a safehouse after he got married."

She followed Matt through the kitchen and into the living room/dining room area. There was an office and bath downstairs, and two bedrooms upstairs.

"You can have this room," he said as they entered the primary bedroom, which had a king bed and en suite bathroom.

"That's very generous."

"You've had a rough day."

"They all seem to be rough. I'm just glad we made it through. Who knows what tomorrow will bring?"

"Hopefully answers."

"I'm having a hard time believing that anymore. Answers

always seem to be just out of reach," she said, sinking onto the edge of the bed.

He sat down next to her. "We're going to figure this out, Haley. I know it doesn't seem that way, but we know a lot more now than we did yesterday. We have a better idea about what Landon was trying to do. We know what Sabrina was looking into and how she got my name, and we know that Harrington had nothing to do with Landon's death. That he was also a pawn."

"But we don't know who killed my brother and what they're up to now," she said in frustration. "And today, when the front door shattered, and that man walked in with that enormous gun, I really thought we were going to die. I've never been so scared in my life. I keep hearing the sound of the gun going off. I don't know how we escaped, but I do know it's because of you."

"I just did my job."

"You did it very well, and I'm grateful. But I don't want you to feel responsible for me."

"I am responsible for you," he said firmly. "You're under my protection."

"It's your job to catch the criminals, not to protect me."

"At this moment, it's both."

"It doesn't have to be. If you need to be at your office, then you should go. I'll be fine here on my own, right? No one knows where I am. My phone is off. I'm safe. And I don't want to hold you back."

"You're not doing that. I gave Jason and Andi all the information we had. They're at the office, along with other members of my team."

Despite his words, she could see the conflict in his gaze. He wanted to be in two places at the same time. "Are you sure, Matt? I really will be okay on my own."

"I'm sure."

A heavy silence followed, thick with everything they hadn't

said aloud... "Matt?" she asked, giving him a questioning look. "What are you thinking?"

"You don't want to know, Haley," he said roughly.

"Are you really worrying that much about leaving me alone?"

"Yes. Not just because you're in danger, but because I want..."

Her heart pounded against her chest as she suddenly realized what all that unspoken tension was really about. "I feel the same way," she murmured.

"I didn't tell you how I feel."

"Yes, you did. I can see it in your eyes. Hear it in your voice." She held his gaze to hers. "You want me. And I want you. So, don't leave me. Stay here. With me. For just a little while."

"It won't be a little while," he said.

"That's fine, too," she said, pressing her body against his, putting her hand to his face. "All I need right now is to be with you." As the words left her mouth, she realized how absolutely true they were. "I don't want to think anymore. I just want us to be together. Don't say no."

Her words unleashed the last of his restraint. He leaned forward, his mouth finding hers in a kiss that was desperate and hungry. She wrapped her arms around his neck as she took everything he had to give. And that only made her want him more.

They broke apart just long enough to pull off their clothes with shaking hands, their movements urgent and clumsy with need. He made a quick trip into the bathroom to get protection before coming back to her, before pressing her back against the mattress.

Skin met skin, she let out a gasp of pure pleasure as his kiss, his touch, drove everything else out of her mind. All she needed was him. All he needed was her. The rest of the world could wait.

———

They'd made love until the sun went down, the stars came out, and Haley's stomach rumbled. Matt smiled as they lay face-to-face, tangled in the sheets. "You're hungry."

"And embarrassed," she said. "My stomach is too loud."

He laughed at her sheepish smile. "I'm hungry, too. I'm sure there's food in the freezer downstairs. Why don't we go downstairs and check it out?"

"That sounds like a good idea, although I hate to leave this beautiful little bubble we've been in. This was...nice."

"Nice? That's the best you've got?" he scoffed.

"Okay, it was amazing. You were incredible."

"Now, you've gone too far. It was all you," he said, feeling more relaxed than he had in a very long time. He'd crossed a line that he shouldn't have crossed, but it had been more than worth it.

"It was us," she corrected, giving him a warm smile that made his gut clench. "I have to say I never thought I'd sleep with an FBI agent."

"Technically, you haven't slept with me," he teased.

"Good point. But I think we should share this room tonight. No point in messing up another one, right?"

"Absolutely right."

Relief ran through her eyes. "Good. I was afraid you were going to say this was a mistake."

"It probably was a mistake, but I feel too happy to care."

She laughed. "How could anything that felt that good be wrong?"

He grinned back at her. "I certainly can't answer that question. But what I can do is check out the freezer downstairs and see what I can heat up."

"I'll meet you in the kitchen."

After throwing on some clothes, he went downstairs and opened the freezer, finding quite a few options. He turned on the oven to preheat, then pulled out a large pizza. He was just putting it in the oven when Haley walked in, looking sweetly sexy, her face flushed, her eyes bright, her hair tangled from his fingers, sending all kinds of images through his head and feelings through his body. It took all his willpower not to grab her and steal another kiss, maybe more.

"What did you find to eat?" she asked.

"Pizza. Just put it in."

"That sounds perfect."

"There are some snacks in the cupboard: chips, crackers, cookies."

"I'll just take a drink," she said, grabbing a bottle of water from the fridge. "Are you going to check in with your team?"

"Jason said he'd call me if there were any updates; otherwise, I'll touch base with him in the morning." He felt a little guilty that he'd spent the past few hours in bed with Haley instead of working, but they'd both needed time to regroup after the attack at Harrington's house, coming so soon after the attack on Brooke.

"I wonder how Brooke is doing," Haley said, as if reading his mind.

"When I spoke to Jason at Harrington's house, he said she was improving but still too weak to talk. He has kept the no-visitor rule in place. Hopefully, by tomorrow, she'll be able to speak to us."

"I'm glad she's going to be all right."

"Eventually. And Harrington will be fine, too. His wound was not as bad as Brooke's."

"They're both lucky. You didn't just save me, Matt; you saved them, too."

"Maybe they'll show their appreciation by talking," he said dryly. "Although I think Harrington told us everything he knew."

"Perhaps Brooke did, too."

"We still have your brother's drive. When Derek gets that

open, we'll be able to fill in the rest of the blanks." He paused as the oven timer went off. "Let's table this discussion until after we eat."

CHAPTER TWENTY-TWO

The pizza was perfectly crispy, and as they ate, it was relatively easy to pretend she and Matt were just hanging out, getting to know each other better, satisfying a different kind of hunger than the one they'd recently slayed. But reality was hovering in the back of Haley's mind, a reality she shouldn't ignore, but maybe for a few more minutes...

When she finished eating, she leaned back with a soft sigh. "That was good. Much better than the frozen stuff I usually buy."

"I'm glad," Matt replied, but she could see his mind was already elsewhere.

"You're thinking about the case," she observed.

"I keep going back to what Harrington told us about Sabrina connecting with an accountant at a legal aid office. We know that accountant was Anthony Devray. And we know that Sabrina asked Harrington about your brother's financial forecasting model."

"Okay," she said slowly. "Where are you going with this?"

"Anthony said he told Sabrina to stay away from Westbridge. But I don't think that was because of your brother's death. I believe Anthony saw a connection between Westbridge and the corporate fraud case they were both working on. I wonder if that's because he saw similarities between that fraud case and the case he brought to me, which involved Meridien Developments."

"Was Meridien tied to Westbridge?"

"I don't know. I never looked for a connection because I didn't know about the dangerous Westbridge alumni network at that time. If there was a link, it would make sense why my investigation was shut down. I need to review those case files."

"Can you do that from here? And can I help?" she asked eagerly.

"I can't let you look at an FBI file."

"Haven't we moved past the rules?" she said, rolling her eyes. "What if I just happened to see information on your computer screen when you weren't looking?"

"I don't think so, Haley."

"I want to help, Matt. And perhaps you could benefit from a fresh perspective."

She made a good point, but still... There were some lines he really shouldn't cross. "I hear you, but this is something I need to do myself. I will tell you if I learn anything new."

"Okay. I get it. And if you need to go down to your real office where you have more resources, I'm sure I'll be fine here on my own."

"I'm not leaving you now." He paused. "I should have put you into protective custody earlier, or at least after Brooke was attacked, but I didn't. That could have been a fatal mistake."

She could see the guilt in his eyes. "It wasn't a fatal mistake, and you didn't do it, because I wouldn't let you."

"*Because* I didn't trust anyone else to protect you," he corrected. "I care about you, Haley."

"I care about you, too," she said softly. "And I don't just trust you to keep me safe, Matt; I trust you to tell me the truth. I can't live with lies. I have to know where I stand. I have to know what happened to my brother, even if it hurts like hell. I feel like every day, every single person we talk to is lying about something."

"I won't lie to you as long as you promise not to try to protect your brother's name at the expense of stopping this criminal enterprise."

She was surprised by his words. "Why would you think I would do that?"

He gave her a pointed look. "Your love for Landon is fierce. You weren't his mother, but you protected him like a mama bear. And there's a scenario where you might find out something about Landon that you don't believe or don't want to accept."

"I doubt that will happen."

He met her gaze. "I don't. Someone may try to spin whatever Landon was working on into something negative. You can't allow yourself to be conned or to make a rash decision because it looks like Landon is being framed."

"Do you think they'll try to do that?"

"Almost a hundred percent sure that's what they'll do. Who better to blame than someone who is dead?"

"You're right. Okay, I won't bite. I won't jump at a false flag. I'll be smart."

"Good. I need to go into the office here and check my messages on the computer."

"Can I do that, too?" she asked. "Just in case Julia found something. I know I'm not supposed to be talking to her, but she doesn't know that, and she might send me some information."

"Sure."

He led the way into the office and opened up the computer, setting her up to check her text messages, but she had nothing new from anyone, which was disappointing.

After that, he did the same. "This is odd," he said, pointing to a text. "Shari wants to meet tomorrow morning. She says she has information that could help me with the connection between my case and Westbridge."

"That sounds interesting, but also like a possible trap. Do you trust her, Matt?"

"I used to. I'm not sure anymore."

"It seems prudent to be suspicious. But she was spending time with Senator Matson, so maybe she does have information."

"It's possible." He tapped his fingers on the desk, as he thought for a moment. Then he turned to her. "When our investigation into Meridien Developments was abruptly ended, Shari wasn't nearly as upset by that as I was. In fact, she said she could see why Director Markham didn't think we had enough evidence to keep going."

"Did that piss you off?"

"Yes. I was angry and frustrated with everyone." He paused. "I need to go through that file again, but in the meantime, let's see where the executive board of Meridien went to school." He opened the Meridien website and ran down the list of officers as well as the board of directors. "Look at this," he said, pointing to one of the names. "Charles Adler is on the board of directors at Meridien."

"That can't be a coincidence. What about your new FBI director?"

"Good question." He opened another tab.

She peered over his shoulder as he ran the search on Rebecca Markham, her excitement growing when she saw that Rebecca had graduated from Westbridge. "She's one of them."

"She is. But Rebecca is in her early forties, so she's too old to be tied to Landon's grade and too young to be tied to any of the parents, but she is part of the alumni network," he said. "Maybe she shut the case down because Charles Adler asked her to do so."

"And if Shari didn't care about the investigation ending, perhaps she has a connection, too," she suggested.

"Possibly. But I know Shari didn't go to Westbridge. She

graduated from NYU. She didn't even move to California until a few years ago."

"Did Shari ever mention Adler when you were working on the Meridien case?"

"Not that I can recall. We weren't focused on the board, though, more on the top executives and their financials."

"In light of this, what do you think Shari wants to tell you?"

"I have no idea. She mentions both Sabrina and Westbridge, and I told her Sabrina's case might be tied to a death at the university."

"She was with Senator Matson the other day. She might have asked him about Landon's murder after you spoke to her." She paused. "What do you want to do, Matt?"

He thought for another moment, then said, "I want to flip the switch."

"What does that mean?" she asked curiously.

"I'll tell Shari I'll meet her at Café Luna on Third Street at nine a.m.," he said, as he sent the text. "But I'm not actually going to meet her."

"I'm confused."

"I'll plant a tracker on Shari's car so we can see where she goes after I call her and give her some information that will make someone very nervous."

She smiled at the sly expression in his gaze. "Well, don't leave me hanging..."

"I'm going to tell her I got delayed at work because we just found evidence tying Trent Adler to Landon's death, the death Sabrina Lin was looking into when she was killed."

"That's an interesting choice. You're picking Trent because he's Charles's son?"

"Exactly. And Landon's death is connected to Senator Matson, so if she talks to him or to Charles Adler, we'll know what side she's on, and we can use that to our advantage."

"She might not go in person; she might call."

"I don't think she'll want to share this information on the

phone or in text. It's time to go on offense, Haley. The West-bridge conspiracy network is about manipulation. It's time we became the manipulators."

She gave him an approving smile. "I like your devious plan. In fact, I think it's kind of hot."

He rolled his desk chair over to her. "Only kind of?" he teased as he leaned in and gave her a kiss that set her body on fire. "We've done enough for tonight. Let's go to bed."

She wrapped her arms around his neck and pulled him in for another kiss. "I think the bed might be too far. How comfortable is that couch?"

"Let's find out."

———

Tuesday morning, Matt parked in the lot next to Café Luna on Third Street in Santa Monica.

"What if Shari sees you putting the device on her car?" Haley asked.

"She's already inside, and this lot isn't visible once you're in the café. Her car is just over there. Hang tight. I'll be right back."

She watched him walk casually past two other vehicles before dropping to one knee to ostensibly tie his shoe. Before he rose, he attached a tracking device to the underside of the wheel well. When that was done, he got back in the car, pulled out of the lot and drove around to the front of the building. He parked in a spot down the block but where they could see the front door of the café.

Matt's tension was palpable, his enthusiasm contagious, and Haley felt more optimistic than she had in a while. "What now?" she asked.

"Time for the next step." He took out his phone and called Shari, using the speakerphone so she could hear.

"Matt? Where are you?" Shari asked in a stressed voice. "You're never late."

"I got hung up at work. We had a big breakthrough."

"Really? Into the murder of Sabrina Lin?"

"No. The murder she was looking into at Westbridge several years ago."

"What did you find?"

"An eyewitness, who also happens to have physical evidence that will bring down some very important people."

"That's huge."

"What did you want to tell me, Shari? You said you have information on Sabrina?"

"Actually, I wanted to talk to you about the university murder. You mentioned it might be connected to your current case, but I'm not sure my information is relevant anymore."

"Why don't you let me decide if it's relevant or not."

"I heard from a source that the police had a suspect in the death of Landon Kenton, a student who was angry at Kenton for not changing his grade when he was a TA."

"If they had a suspect, why didn't they act on it?"

"Apparently, by the time they heard about this person and went to speak to him, it was four months later, and he had died of an overdose after discovering his grades had made him ineligible to graduate."

"Do you have a name?"

"Jeremy Allen," she said. "Did your eyewitness mention him?"

"No. Our evidence is on Trent Adler."

"Trent Adler?" she echoed. "As in the son of Charles Adler?"

"Yes."

"Your evidence better be good. Trent's father is a powerful person with a lot of connections."

"I'm aware of that, but the evidence is solid, so I'm not worried. I gotta run. Thanks for reaching out."

"Sure. Good luck with everything, Matt."

"Thanks, Shari." He ended the call and looked over at Haley. "What do you think?"

"Shari gave you a name. We don't have evidence on Trent, so maybe Jeremy Allen is a good lead, and Shari is on the right side. Her source could be Senator Matson. Maybe he wants the case to be solved now, although that seems doubtful." She sat up straighter as the café door opened. "There's Shari. She's leaving."

He opened the tracking app on his phone. "Let's see where she goes."

"What if she just goes to work? This whole thing will have been pointless."

"Not entirely. We heard what she wanted to tell me, and maybe Jeremy Allen is a lead we can follow, but we'll see what happens."

Within minutes, Shari's car pulled out of the lot, and Matt set his phone on the console between them so they could both see the red dot on the screen moving north. Then he pulled out of his spot, heading in the same direction. Because of the tracker, Matt was able to keep some distance between them and avoid tipping Shari off to the fact that she had a tail.

For the next thirty minutes, they followed the red dot through the streets of Santa Monica, Century City, and into Beverly Hills, driving past large homes, mansions, and finally estates with iron gates and homes tucked far behind those gates. When Shari's car finally stopped, Matt parked just around the corner and put the address into his phone.

"Who lives there?" she asked impatiently.

He met her gaze. "Charles Adler."

Her stomach flipped over. "She's going to tell Charles that his son might be wanted for murder. He probably won't believe it."

"It will still concern him," Matt said. "And now I know that Shari knows Adler well enough to visit him at his home. Damn. She had to have had something to do with our case against Meridien Developments getting shut down. I blamed it on Markham, but maybe Shari was reporting information that wasn't true up the chain to protect Adler's company."

"Or they were both in on it."

"True."

"Senator Matson could also be part of it," she said. "Shari has a lot of connections with the key players in our investigation." She paused, seeing the betrayal in his gaze. He'd trusted Shari. "I'm sorry, Matt."

He gave a careless shrug, but she'd learned by now that Matt's indifference was often a mask for just how much he did care. He was probably also embarrassed he hadn't seen through Shari before now.

"What do we do next?" she asked.

"We divide and conquer. We continue to sow seeds of distrust within the group. Right now, Charles is wondering if Trent killed Landon and might be in trouble. We need to find ways to throw off the others in the group. They've been working as one unit, completely on the same page, everyone with the same story. If they each start to feel more pressure, they'll begin to wonder if they're being set up as a fall guy."

"I like that, Matt. And I might have an idea..."

CHAPTER TWENTY-THREE

Matt gave her a questioning look. "What's the idea?"

"If we're going to divide and conquer, our next target should be Henry. He blackmailed Brooke and probably Professor Harrington. We need to use the same strategy. Get some dirt on him and use it against him."

"We'd have to find the dirt first."

"Unless we manufacture it. Like you did with the fake evidence connecting Trent to my brother's murder."

"We're going to need more concrete evidence to go directly at Henry. The Trent evidence was a ruse to see which side Shari was on. It won't stand up legally."

"It doesn't have to. It's still going to disrupt the Adler family, if not all their friends." She thought for a moment. "We should talk to Brooke about Henry. If he has a weakness, she probably knows what it is."

He gave her an approving nod. "Good idea. I wanted to check in at the hospital this morning anyway."

As they drove to the hospital, her mind raced with possibilities. If Henry had any kind of addiction: gambling, drugs, or women, that could be a potential goldmine. Or maybe Brooke would know who Henry was sleeping with, and they could create havoc in his personal life. It would also be interesting to see if they could pit Henry against his father, Graham, not just the other people his age. There was a good chance Henry was either the mastermind behind everything or very high up in the chain.

"Have you come up with a plan yet?" Matt asked with a knowing smile as he turned into the hospital lot.

"Working on several," she said, grinning back at him. "You're not the only one with a devious mind. We might have that in common."

"Just remember, we can only go so far. I'm still an FBI agent. There are some lines I can't cross."

Despite his clever mind, he had a strong moral compass, and she liked that about him. But then, she was starting to like everything about him. It was more difficult to find things she didn't like. The closer she got to him, the closer she wanted to be. She just had no idea what was going to happen when all this was over, when they weren't living in each other's pocket, but that was a worry for another day.

―――

After Matt showed his badge to the guard outside of Brooke's room, they were allowed inside. Brooke was sitting up in bed, her phone in her hand, looking pale and weary, but better than the last time she'd seen her.

Her gaze grew wary as they approached. "Do you know who attacked me?" she asked.

Matt shook his head. "Not yet, but we're working on it."

"I'm afraid of what's going to happen when I get discharged. How can I go home? How can I be safe anywhere?"

"You won't be safe until we find out why someone wanted you dead," Matt said. "And we need your help to do that, Brooke."

"I told the other guy everything I knew. I'm not as much on the inside of things as you might believe. And since I almost died, I've had a lot of time to consider the fact that this attack was probably directed by someone I know, maybe someone I think is a friend. I don't know who to trust anymore."

"We believe the same thing," she said. "You told us that Henry blackmailed you into stealing Landon's notebooks. That's right, isn't it?"

Brooke gave her a guilty look. "Yes. Henry was behind my entire relationship with Landon. I couldn't get kicked out of school. I had to do what he asked. But I never imagined Landon would end up dead."

While she still held enormous anger toward Brooke, she pushed those feelings aside so she could get her help. "Let's not talk about Landon right now. Let's talk about Henry."

"Henry is not a nice guy. He uses people."

"Which is why you're going to help us use him," she said.

Brooke's gaze flickered with curiosity. "How so?"

"We need you to tell us anything about Henry that shows his darker side. Is he into gambling, drugs, porn? Does he sleep with married women or hookers? Does he cheat at golf, steal from his friends, or his company?"

"I want to help, but I'm afraid."

"Brooke," Matt said. "When you're discharged, we're going to set you up in a safehouse with two guards watching over you. No one will be able to hurt you again. But the faster we shut down whatever they're doing, the faster your life returns to normal. Until then, you won't be able to go home, go to work, see your fiancé...nothing."

"Okay," she said. "Let's see. Henry likes strippers. But he doesn't go to ordinary strip clubs. He goes to a private club for rich guys where discretion is everything. It's called Sterling's. It's in downtown LA. He also likes cocaine and uses it regularly. Does that help?"

"Yes. Now, are you aware of anyone else Henry blackmailed besides you and Professor Harrington?" Matt asked.

Her eyes widened with surprise. "He blackmailed Professor

Harrington? I did not know that. As for others, I don't know, but Henry has never wanted to put in real work. He's always looking for a shortcut."

"Okay," Matt said. "Talk to us about Kyle."

"What do you want to know?" she asked, her expression turning wary again.

"He works for Drew Sanderson, right? What does he do there?"

"He's a financial analyst."

"What's his relationship to Viktor Danilovich?"

"I'm not sure," Brooke said. "Kyle met Viktor through Drew. Viktor is the older brother of

someone we went to school with, Alexei Danilovich. I liked Alexei, but his brother seems shady, and he gives me the creeps. Kyle told me that Viktor is doing some work with Drew's company but didn't say what."

"So, Viktor could be involved in this money-making scheme as well."

"Kyle had dinner with Henry, Viktor, Drew, and Jill last week," Brooke replied.

"Why weren't you there?"

"I wasn't invited. Kyle said it was business."

"But Jill was there," she said. "Where does she fit in with everyone?"

"Jill and Drew have been dating. They were friends for a long time, but she told me they had a drunken hookup a few months back, and she'd started looking at him differently. I didn't want to ask too many questions about it, because we're all in this group, and it's kind of strange that they're suddenly together. Trent isn't happy about it, either. According to Jill, Trent and Drew are barely speaking."

Brooke paused, then added, "But everyone seems to be acting differently the past few days. Ever since that woman got shot, and you two showed up at the charity event, Jill has been bitchy, Kyle is secretive, and Henry is even more disgustingly smug than usual. I don't know what to think about anyone, not even my fiancé. I feel like they're all suddenly strangers, people I don't recognize anymore."

She exchanged a glance with Matt, thinking it was ironic that Brooke, who had deceived Landon, was now discovering that others, including her fiancé, might be lying to her. "You must know something about their get-rich-quick plan."

"All I know is that they have a plan to make money on the stock market and it's going to happen before the election. Jill convinced me to give her some money to invest, so I did. But I don't know the details. If I could help you more, I would. I want this all to be over. I want to feel safe again and be able to trust people."

"You can't trust any of your friends," Matt told her, not a trace of doubt in his voice. "Not Jill, not Kyle, not Henry, not anyone."

"What am I going to tell Kyle? He's been texting me nonstop that he wants to see me, and that I need to get the guard to let him in. I told him I don't have any say over it, but he keeps grilling me about what the FBI is asking me. Jill has texted, too. She's concerned and wants to bring me comfort food. What am I going to say?"

"You're going to tell them you won't be discharged for a few more days, probably not until Saturday," Matt said. "You'll also tell them that you've asked us to put them on the visitor list, and you're waiting to hear back on when that can happen. Tell them you miss them, and you can't wait to see them again."

"Am I really going to be here until Saturday?"

"We'll try to move you before that, but it will be unexpected. You won't know when, and they won't know when. We are the only people you can trust, Brooke. We want you to be alive. I can't say that for anyone else," Matt said.

She paled as his words sank in. "It's hard to believe any of my friends would want to kill me."

"When a lot of money is at stake, people change," Matt said.

"Before we go, I'm going to ask you to text whoever is concerned about you, your boyfriend, your friends, your parents, and tell them what I just said. You'll also add that the FBI is taking away your phone, so they shouldn't worry if they don't hear from you, but that you were told you'd get it back tomorrow. Do that now."

"You're really going to take my phone?"

"Yes," he said, giving Brooke a hard look. "I can't trust you not to share what we've just discussed. Start texting."

Brooke did as he asked. Then she handed over her phone.

"What's your code?" Matt asked.

She rattled off six numbers. Matt put them into the phone and unlocked it. "Good," he said. "I know you're feeling like you're trading one enemy for another, but we are going to make sure you're safe."

"My parents want me to come and stay with them in Connecticut. I was thinking of going there."

"When this is over," he said.

"I'm not going to get charged with anything, am I?"

"As long as you're telling us the truth about your involvement and you keep helping us, you'll be fine."

Brooke nodded, then said, "I hope you find out who killed Landon and make them pay, Haley."

"Even if that's one of your friends?"

"Yes." Brooke let out a sigh. "One other thing—your brother really loved you, Haley. I had to write a paper once about someone I thought was a hero, and I asked Landon for ideas. It was supposed to be someone famous, and he said he couldn't think of anyone famous who had been more heroic than the sister who had basically raised him. He said you saved his life. You were his second mother, and he was so lucky to have you in his life."

Her eyes filled with moisture. "Thank you for telling me that," she said, then followed Matt out of the room.

"That was more helpful than I expected," Matt said as they

left the hospital and got into his car, which he'd left with the valet right outside the front door.

"It was," she said as she fastened her seatbelt. "Brooke is learning the hard way that the people she loves might not be who she thinks they are." She glanced at him. "It makes me wonder how well we ever really know anyone."

"It probably depends on how much you want to know someone. Or whether the surface stuff looks so good, you don't want to dig deeper. Maybe Landon getting attention from a very pretty girl was just too much to resist. He didn't want to see that she had an ulterior motive. Who would?"

"You're right. But that's not me. I'm always suspicious of motives. I have a hard time trusting anyone after the way I grew up. Love has always looked deceptive, painful, and fleeting."

Understanding filled his gaze. "I've felt the same way. That love is always a risk, maybe one I don't need to take."

As their gazes clung together, she felt the connection between them deepen even more.

"But maybe it is worth the risk," he said, surprising her with his words. "If it's with the right person."

Her heart skipped a beat as they moved into dangerous territory. "Maybe," she agreed. "If it's with the right person."

He smiled as he started the engine. "Let's go home."

It was strange to think of a safehouse as a home, but anywhere with Matt was starting to feel that way. Words ran through her head that she couldn't yet say, because maybe Matt was the right person for her, and she was the right person for him. But she wasn't sure when or if either of them would have the courage to say that out loud.

———

When they entered the safehouse, Matt headed into the office while Haley grabbed drinks from the refrigerator. While Brooke's information about Henry made him eager to see what dirt he could build on him, he wondered if that wouldn't take too long. They were running out of time, and Henry would be a tough nut to crack. Maybe they should focus first on a weaker player.

Haley came back a moment later with two bottles of water and handed him one. "I'm ready to find some dirt on Henry."

"I've been thinking about that. As much as I want to take Henry down, I'm leaning toward squeezing Trent Adler a little tighter. By now, he probably thinks he's being set up, either by the FBI or someone else. Maybe we tighten the screws."

"That's a good point. Brooke said that Trent Adler and Drew are on the outs, so maybe Trent would flip on Drew."

"I'm sure Trent will lawyer up quickly, but maybe we can get him into a more casual setting, take him by surprise." The phone rang, startling them both. "Lawson," he said, putting the phone on speaker.

"It's Jason. I've got good news. Derek opened Landon's drive."

His pulse jumped. "Excellent. What did you find?"

"Hang on a second; I'm going to move us to video so you can hear from Derek directly."

"Haley is also here," he said.

"Good. I'm sure she'd like to hear what her brother created."

"I would," Haley quickly agreed as the call moved to the computer monitor, and Derek's face appeared.

"Hello," Derek said. "I'll get right into it. Landon Kenton developed an algorithm that was originally designed to protect investors. It could identify and counter all the ways markets could be manipulated. But in order to protect against market manipulation, Landon had to map out every possible way to cause it. Every vulnerability, every trigger point, every domino that could be pushed."

"And if someone reversed the algorithm, they could crash the market?" Matt asked.

"Exactly," Derek replied. "Instead of protecting investors, his algorithm could become the perfect weapon to destroy some people while enriching others. It could trigger automated trading systems to create a domino effect that would crash multiple markets simultaneously while positioning certain players to profit massively from the chaos." Derek paused, letting that sink in before adding, "We've been studying market fluctuations over the past two years, and it looks like there have been test runs, four separate incidents, each one perfectly timed, perfectly positioned to maximize profits for those in the know, while devastating others. Unless you knew what you were looking for, you probably wouldn't see anything suspicious to the dips, but when you take into account manufactured news reports or misleading reports, it appears that someone deployed the algorithm to see how it would work or not work and then refined it."

"Can we trace who's doing it?" Matt asked.

"Not so far, but our guess, based on the incidents we've flagged so far, is that they're building toward something bigger, and it might be tied to the upcoming election in three weeks. A market crash before the vote would create massive instability and could influence the outcome of the election, possibly even shutting down the market." Derek paused. "Flynn has contacts at the SEC. We're going to see if we can put our heads together to track down which companies benefited most from the possible test runs."

"This is much, much bigger than we thought," he muttered, exchanging a quick glance with Haley.

"I can't believe my brother designed something so powerful," she said, shaking her head in bemusement. "Or that what he built for something good could be used in such a negative way."

"Unfortunately, that's the story of a lot of tools, weapons, and drugs," Derek said. "If they fall into the wrong hands..."

"Then all hell breaks loose," she finished. "It's hard to believe that Landon's fraternity friends could do something so diabolical."

"I'm going to give you back to Jason," Derek said. "I still have some files to go through."

Jason's face appeared on the screen as Derek disappeared. "Looks like Sabrina Lin's murder was just the tip of the iceberg."

"I agree," Matt said. "And I think my former investigation into Meridien Developments is part of this market manipulation, which probably means Charles Adler is one of the main players. I believe my former partner, Shari Drummond, was working with Charles, maybe the new director as well."

"Speaking of Director Markham, she called me about twenty minutes ago. She wants to know if we have evidence tying Trent Adler to an old murder."

He smiled to himself. "I planted that false flag with my former coworker. Shari was at the museum on Saturday, cozying up to Senator Matson, and I wanted to find out what side she's on. She took my bait and ran straight to Charles Adler. Now, I know she's on their side. Markham probably is, too. The list of people with dirt on their hands is getting longer."

"Well, Markham can't shut us down. Our team operates outside her jurisdiction."

"What did you tell her?"

"That I couldn't get into the details of our investigation. She said she expected a call back from Flynn within the hour. He's in San Diego, so I told her he's unavailable, but I'll pass the message on." He paused. "What's your next play?"

"I want to squeeze Trent, use my false flag to see if I can get him to flip on his friends."

"That won't be easy. He knows a lot of lawyers."

"I'm working on a way to get him into a more casual setting, take him by surprise. I'll let you know what I come up with."

As soon as he put down the phone, Haley said, "I have an idea about Trent. I can ask him to meet me."

"Absolutely not."

"Hang on," she said, sending him an annoyed look. "I'll tell him the FBI thinks he killed my brother, but I don't believe that because Landon said how much he liked him. And I need to talk to him personally. All I have to do is get him somewhere, and then you can take over."

He frowned, not wanting to put her in danger. "It's risky."

"Everything is risky, but we have to try. If they're going to use my brother's brilliant algorithm for evil instead of good, then we have to stop them, and Trent might be the key. I want to take this chance."

"We'd need to think of a place to meet," he said slowly.

"What about something near Westbridge? My brother used to go to a coffeehouse a few blocks off campus. He loved studying there. It was called the Library Café. It would be a place Landon would have told me about, a place Trent might remember from his college days, and maybe where he'd feel comfortable, even a little nostalgic," Haley suggested. "It's not anywhere near where he lives now, or where the others would be spending time. This could work, Matt."

He didn't like the gleam of excitement in her eyes. "It could work, but you're telling Trent exactly where you're going to be at a specific time. If he's in the thick of this, he could send someone to the coffeehouse to get to you."

"Well, it's a public place, and you'll be there, too. We can do it soon. It's three o'clock now. It will take us thirty minutes to get there. We can set it for four thirty just to make sure we have enough time, but not too much time for him to send someone to find us."

"He could do that in an hour and a half."

"It's not perfect, but we have to try, don't we? And when we were talking to Brooke, she never mentioned Trent being part of the inner circle."

"Okay," he said, making a decision. "But I'm going to send an agent to the café ahead of us, and I'll have two more outside as backup."

"Can I call him now?"

He nodded, knowing his desire to protect Haley was overriding his logic, and he couldn't let emotions get in the way. "I have his number." After retrieving Trent's number from the case file, he punched it into the phone, then handed it to her, putting it on speaker.

The phone rang several times before a man answered. "Hello? Who is this?"

"It's Haley Kenton. Is this Trent?"

"What the hell do you want?" Trent demanded, anger in his voice.

"To talk to you," she said in a calm voice. "The FBI told me that they think you killed my brother."

"That's not true. I had nothing to do with Landon's death."

"I actually believe you. Landon told me you were one of his best friends in the house, and after he died, you were one of the only ones who looked upset about it. I can't believe you were faking that kind of emotion. It felt very real to me."

"It was real. Landon was a friend," Trent said.

"Would you be willing to talk to me? I might have information that could clear your name and get us closer to the truth, but I need you to look at it before I show it to anyone else."

"Tell me what it is now."

"It's something you need to see. I'm going to be at the Library Café at four thirty. I think you know it. It's right by Westbridge. It won't take long."

"Why should I trust you?" Trent asked. "Last time I saw you, you were with that FBI agent."

"All I want is justice for my brother, and I don't like the direction the FBI is going. I think they're listening to someone who might be trying to set you up." She paused. "It's up to you. If you don't want to come, we'll see what happens."

There was silence on the other end of the phone. Finally, Trent said, "I'll meet you there."

Haley let out a breath as she met his gaze. "We're on."

He wished he could feel as excited as she looked, but he was thinking like a man who cared for the woman in front of him instead of like an FBI agent, and Haley would never be truly safe and get the answers she deserved unless he started thinking with his head instead of his heart. It wasn't a problem he had ever had before, and he was a little stunned he'd let himself get so deeply involved with her, but it was too late to change that. He just had to make sure she stayed safe. That was all that mattered.

CHAPTER TWENTY-FOUR

Haley arrived at the Library Café fifteen minutes early, picking up a coffee before choosing a table with a clear view of the front door. She'd been to the café twice with Landon, as it was one of his favorite places to eat and study off campus. It was cozy and comfortable, with mismatched furniture, floor-to-ceiling bookshelves with books you could actually take with you if you wanted. The menu featured a full selection of coffees, teas, and spiced ciders with sandwiches, salads, soups, and a glass display case filled with delicious desserts. Students from nearby Westbridge occupied many of the tables, bent over laptops and textbooks, while there were also locals chatting over coffee.

Agent Andi Hart sat nearby, sipping coffee, a newspaper in front of her. Matt had told her that Agent Hart would be in the café. He didn't want her to be alone for even a second, but he didn't want to scare Trent off with his presence, so he wouldn't enter the café until Trent had already taken a seat. Jason was waiting with Matt and would have his eyes fixed on the entrance to the café to ensure there was no trouble.

She hoped it was overkill for this meeting, but she was grateful for the thorough preparation. They'd had too many close calls already.

She felt both nervous and excited about the upcoming meeting. This was what she did every day in her job. She got people
to talk so she could get to the truth. She just hoped Trent would
be cooperative. Despite what she'd told him about seeing real
emotion in his eyes after Landon died, she wasn't at all sure that
hadn't been an act.

She sat up straighter as Trent walked into the café, wearing a
suit and tie. His brown hair was messy, not styled as it had been
the last time she'd seen him, and his tie was loose around his
neck, as if he'd been pulling at it all day. His gaze swept the room
before landing on her. He gave a nod, then walked toward her,
tight lines around his eyes, stress evident in his hard jaw. He
pulled out the chair across from her and sat down.

"I've got five minutes," he said, his voice low but carrying an
edge of panic barely held in check. "Whatever you want to show
me, do it now."

"You're going to need more than five minutes for this, Trent.
Because I'm not just trying to save you from being charged with
Landon's murder, I'm trying to save your life. Whoever killed my
brother is setting you up, and if that doesn't succeed, you're
going to end up exactly like Landon."

Trent's face went pale. "That's ridiculous. Nobody wants to
hurt me."

"I'm sure Brooke thought the same thing."

"That was a burglar. She came home at the wrong time," he
said, clearly desperate to believe that.

"That wasn't what happened."

"Well, I don't know what happened to Brooke or your
brother. I just know I haven't done anything wrong."

"Haven't you?" she challenged.

"No. And since you don't seem to believe that, what do you
want from me?"

She looked up as Matt slid into the chair beside Trent, effec-
tively blocking Trent's escape route.

Trent shot her a dark look. "This was a setup."

"Not exactly," she said. "We want to help you, Trent."

"I seriously doubt that, and I'm not talking to either of you."

"Sit down," Matt said as Trent started to rise, his firm voice giving Trent pause. "Haley is right. We're trying to help you stay alive."

After a moment, Trent took his seat. "What's going on?"

"Did your father tell you we have an eyewitness who says you killed Landon and has evidence to prove it?" Matt asked.

"Yes. And that's a ridiculous story. I wasn't even at the frat party that night. I was at a friend's house. Who is this alleged eyewitness, and if you have evidence against me, why haven't you arrested me?" Trent asked. "Why have Haley set up the meet?"

"Because I didn't believe you'd talk to me without a lawyer."

"And I won't. I'll call my uncle or my cousin right now. They'll be down here in a second."

"I don't think Henry is the one you want to call," she said, giving him a pointed look.

Trent flinched. "Are you saying Henry is the witness? That's impossible. He wouldn't...we're cousins. We're family. And I'm innocent. I liked Landon. I sure as hell didn't kill him."

"But you know that your cousin and your friends wanted Landon's research notes," she said. "Henry orchestrated my brother's entire relationship with Brooke, who stole Landon's notebooks. Now your friends are getting nervous because the FBI is looking into Landon's death, and they're not going to go away at anyone's request. Which means the real killer needs someone to take the fall. That's you, Trent. But I don't think you are the killer. I believe someone else killed Landon and that you might have some idea as to who that is."

He stared back at her, his gaze conflicted. "I'm not part of any of this. I have deliberately put space between myself and all of them, including my own sister."

"That space isn't going to be enough," Matt told Trent. "Don't you get it? It doesn't matter what you do now. You know enough about them to be dangerous. That's why they're setting you up."

"I don't know anything."

"Sure you do," Matt said. "You can't be neutral, Trent. You have to pick a side."

"I can't do that," Trent said stubbornly. "You're asking me to turn against my family."

"It's you or them," Matt said. "If you don't help us, you'll be the one charged with the murder of Landon Kenton and Sabrina Lin and the attacks on Brooke Mercer and Professor Harrington."

"Professor Harrington? What the hell happened to him?"

"He was shot," Matt said. "Yesterday. This whole thing is blowing up. And you are in the worst possible position."

"You don't have anything."

"Come on, Trent. You know that evidence can be manufactured. People can be paid to talk. That's how things run in your world. Anything and anyone can be bought."

Trent's gaze filled with dark shadows as Matt's words sank in. She could see his guard slipping, his fear setting in.

"What are they doing, Trent?" she asked. "What are they doing with Landon's research?"

"I only know that they got hold of an algorithm that Landon created, that has something to do with investments. Jill told me that it's completely legal, just advanced analytics."

"But you know that's not the whole story," she said.

"I don't want to know the whole story," he said candidly. "I can't imagine whatever they're doing is good. I tried to talk to Jill, but since she started dating Drew, she doesn't listen to me at all. She's brainwashed. She keeps talking about the greater good, about needing good people in power."

"They want to mess with the election, don't they?" Matt said. "Who's in charge? Drew? Henry? Kyle? Or is it the fathers? Graham Adler, your dad, or Kent Sanderson? What about Viktor Danilovich? Who's calling the shots?"

As Matt rattled off names, Trent grew more and more distressed.

"I'm not sure," Trent said. "Like I told you before, I haven't asked questions, because I didn't want to know." Trent gave them a pleading look. "I did not kill Landon or do any of those other things. You can't let them frame me. I won't be the fall guy."

"What did your father suggest you do when he told you that you were a suspect?" Matt asked.

"My father? How do you know he knows?"

"Because I do, and I believe he's involved in the stock manipulation."

Trent gave Matt a long look, then said, "He told me his plane would be ready to go at eight o'clock tonight. He wants me to go to the Maldives."

"Where there's no extradition treaty," Matt said. "We're not going to let you run, Trent."

"I don't want to run. I have a legitimate business and someone I just started seeing, whom I'd like to get to know better. I have a life I want to live. What do I need to do?"

"I'd like to take you down to my office," he said. "It's not at FBI headquarters; it's a separate building. No one will know you're there. We'll sit down and go over everything you know in great detail, including your college days, and what happened with Landon, and then we'll get to what the plan is for Landon's algorithm. When we're done, we'll put you in a safehouse with a security detail to make sure no one gets to you. But you'll need to hand over your phone now and give us your password. You have to be completely transparent. If you're not, you're going to get swept up with everyone else, because we are going to take this group down. You can count on that."

Matt's words were convincing, and in the end, Trent inclined his head. "All right. But I want you to protect my sister, too. Jill is not a criminal mastermind. She's been brainwashed by Drew and is eager to prove herself to our father. Drew is the same way.

He's driven by his hatred of his dad. He wants to prove he can be richer and more powerful than Kent. Henry struggled to get Graham's respect, too." Trent shook his head. "You have no idea the kind of pressure our parents have put on us. Everyone thinks we're just entitled rich guys, and we are, but there's a dark side to it, as well."

She doubted any of their lives had been as dark as hers or as Landon's, but she didn't interrupt because keeping Trent talking was all that was important.

"I can't make any promises about your sister," Matt said. "After we talk to you, we'll speak to Jill. If she's willing to turn against her fellow conspirators, then she'll be in a better position to make a deal." Matt motioned to Andi, who got up from her seat and joined them at the table. "This is Agent Hart. Another agent is waiting outside. They'll escort you to our office," Matt said. "Haley and I will be right behind you."

Trent looked at them, then at Agent Hart. "This feels like I'm being arrested."

"You're not," Matt assured him. "You're helping us catch the people who killed Landon and who want to frame you for it. The sooner we get all the information you have, the sooner we can stop them."

"And the sooner you'll be safe, Trent," she added. "This is the right thing to do."

Trent nodded reluctantly, then stood up with Agent Hart. "My car—"

"We'll have someone bring it to you later," Matt said. "Right now, we need to move quickly. Your phone?"

Trent hesitated one last time, then turned over his phone and gave them his password. Then Agent Hart led him outside to the waiting vehicle. Haley felt both relief and anxiety. They finally had someone willing to talk, but did he know enough to make a difference?

———

Haley was surprised that Matt's office building looked like any other office complex in Santa Monica. She'd expected more official signage, but there was nothing out front. However, the entrance to the parking garage included a palm print scan and a security code, the same as the elevator that swept them up to the third floor. It was almost six, and there had been only a few cars in the garage, so she had the feeling the building was fairly empty.

She and Matt rode up in the elevator with the other two agents and Trent. The agents exited the elevator first, entering a large office suite with a dozen or so desks and cubicles in a large room, with offices around the perimeter. All the offices were dark, but the conference room was lit up, and that's where the agents took Trent.

Matt put a hand on her arm. "Haley, this is as far as you go."

"What?" she asked in surprise. "But I want to hear what he says."

"I understand that, but the interview has to be done according to protocol, in case we need to use it in court."

"I thought it was just an informal talk."

He shrugged. "I'm not sure where it's going to go. But I'm going to show you to the breakroom, where we have a TV, newspapers, snacks, drinks, and a couple of couches. You can wait there."

Through the glass walls of the conference room, she could see Trent sitting at a long table with Jason and Agent Hart. Even from a distance, she could see the tension in Trent's shoulders, the way he kept running his hands through his hair, as if he didn't know if he was doing the right thing or not.

"I should be in there," she argued. "I might catch something you miss. I've spent a lot of years learning about Trent and the others."

Matt shook his head. "You're too close to this, Haley. Your emotions about Landon could interfere with the questioning." He paused, giving her a sympathetic look. "I know this is frustrating, but you asked me to trust you when you set up the meeting with Trent, and I did. You got us this far, and we couldn't have gotten Trent here without you. Now you have to trust me to get the information we need."

She wanted to argue, but she knew he was right. Her anger at whoever had killed her brother could easily derail a delicate interrogation. "All right. But I want to know everything he says."

"You will," Matt promised. "Follow me."

He led her down a hallway to the breakroom, flipping on the lights as they entered. It was a very comfortable room, exactly as he'd described. "There's food in the fridge. Help yourself. When this is over, we'll get a late dinner."

"How long do you think it will take?"

"Judging by what he has said so far, probably not that long. Either I or one of the other agents will give you an update in an hour, if not before."

"Okay. Good luck."

She wandered around the breakroom, checking out the fridge, which was fully stocked, but she wasn't hungry. She grabbed a soda and sat down at the table, and spent the next twenty minutes perusing the newspaper, which happened to be her newspaper. It was amazing how little she had thought about work the past week. Everything in her life had flipped upside down last Thursday when Sabrina had shown up. She'd been forced back into the past and had learned so much more about the last days of her brother's life. But she needed to know it all. She needed to know who had killed him so she could make them pay.

Matt wanted that, too, but he was also focused on what the group was going to do with her brother's algorithm, which was probably even more important than her finally getting answers. She also wanted to stop whatever was coming, because she didn't want to see her brother's work used for an evil purpose, something that would hurt the very people he'd wanted to protect.

As her thoughts grew more frenetic and anxious, she got to

her feet and paced around the room, hoping someone would be in soon with an update. She hoped that the passing time meant that Trent was giving them valuable information. *But what if he didn't know enough?* He'd said he was on the outside. *What if they were running out of time, and the plan was already being put in motion? Were they making progress or wasting time?*

She paused by the window, looking out at the city lights, wondering what was happening outside this building. Were the co-conspirators at their own homes, enjoying their lives, or were they meeting somewhere, talking about Trent and the rumor that he might have been responsible for Landon's death? The real murderer would know that wasn't true. Would he or she feel more emboldened now with the finger pointing to Trent? Or would that person realize that the truth would eventually come out, that Trent would try to save himself, and they needed to move up their timeline?

With an endless line of questions running around her head, she left the breakroom and went down the hall to use the restroom. She killed a few more minutes in there, finally, splashing some cold water on her face before heading back. As soon as she stepped into the hallway, the lights went out, and she froze, panic shooting through her body. It was pitch black, with no windows illuminating anything.

She heard shouting. She thought Matt might have called her name. Then she felt a rush of cold air. It must have come from the stairwell. Before she could turn, she felt a figure behind her, and then something hard crashed down on her head.

Pain exploded through her skull, and she felt herself hit the ground as everything turned to black.

CHAPTER TWENTY-FIVE

Haley woke up slowly, her head pounding like someone was using a sledgehammer against her skull. The first thing she noticed was an industrial, metallic smell. The second thing was that she couldn't move her arms. She was tied to a chair, and as her gaze cleared, she realized she was in a warehouse. A high ceiling, concrete floors, and rows of empty shelving stretched into darkness. A few work lights provided harsh illumination in the immediate area, but everything beyond that circle was lost in shadows.

She wanted to scream for help, but she had the feeling there was no help nearby, only danger. Maybe it was better to remain quiet, to pretend to be unconscious.

As her brain cleared, she remembered what had happened. She'd used the restroom at Matt's office and had been in the hallway when the lights went out. Someone had come out of the stairwell, knocked her out, and obviously kidnapped her and brought her here.

What had happened to Matt?

Panic gripped her chest as terror raced through her. Trent and the agents had not been that far away. She'd heard shouting, but what else...*Had they been in trouble? Had someone been attacking them while she'd been grabbed? Was Matt okay?* Her anxiety escalated at the thought of Matt being stabbed or shot or worse...

She tried to move but then realized it wasn't just her hands tied behind the back of the chair; her ankles were also bound to the chair legs. She wasn't going anywhere. She couldn't help anyone, not even herself.

A door slammed, jolting her with new fear. Footsteps came from behind her. And then three men walked into view, one she didn't recognize, but the gun in his hands told her he was there to ensure she didn't get away. The second man was Viktor Danilovich, the man she'd seen at the hospital with Kyle, and the third man...

Her blood ran cold as she stared at Drew Sanderson, Landon's big brother in the fraternity, the guy who'd pretended to care about her brother, about her loss. In the last few days, things had been pointing to Drew, but she'd secretly been hoping it was Henry who was in charge, not Drew.

"You're the one in charge? The one who killed my brother?" she asked Drew.

"Well, look at you. You finally figured it out," he drawled, no sign of the easygoing, happy-go-lucky, didn't-care-much-about-anything man she'd thought he was.

"Landon was your little brother. He was supposedly one of your best friends. How could you kill him?"

"That was an accident," Drew said with an unapologetic shrug.

"I don't believe you."

He shrugged, his eyes stunningly cold. "I don't care what you believe. It's not going to matter. You're not going to tell anyone anything. This is the end of the road, Haley. Your unwillingness to let Landon's death go finally caught up to you."

She shuddered at the threat behind his words, but she wasn't going to give him the satisfaction of seeing her fear. "If it's not going to matter, tell me what happened to my brother."

He hesitated as if he wasn't sure what he wanted to tell her, but clearly, he wanted her to know. That's why he was here and not just Viktor. He wanted this conversation. And she needed to keep him talking as long as she possibly could.

"Landon was being uncooperative," he said finally. "Not as helpful as he was supposed to be as one of our brothers—as my little brother, the one who was supposed to have my back."

"You didn't have his."

He ignored her. "Landon didn't understand the concept of all for one, one for all."

"You wanted him to cheat. You wanted him to do illegal, immoral things. Of course, he'd say no. He knew what was right and what was wrong."

"Annoyingly so," Drew agreed.

"What did you do? How did it happen?" It was going to hurt like crazy to know about her brother's last moments, but she had to hear what he'd gone through. She had to finally know the truth.

"Landon came to the house that night. He was worked up about Professor Harrington going over his head and changing our grades after he'd already refused to do it. He felt betrayed by Harrington's willingness to use his access code in case the scandal ever leaked. The man he'd admired was a loser, and Landon finally saw that."

"But that wasn't all you wanted from Landon, was it? It was about more than getting your grades changed. Because you didn't really need Landon after Harrington agreed to bypass my brother."

"You're right. I wanted more. I wanted Landon to share his brilliant idea, something he'd told us a little about one night when we were drinking. I couldn't stop thinking about his plan, but I knew he wasn't looking at it the right way. He wanted to build a safeguard for smaller investors, but there's no money in safeguards. You don't change the world by lowering risk; you change it by increasing risk, by taking chances, thinking big."

She shook her head in disgust. "Landon wanted to save people; you wanted to destroy them."

"It's survival of the fittest, Haley. My father taught me that a long time ago."

"What did you do to him?"

"I had to make him see reason. But the anger and betrayal in his eyes made me realize that Henry was right. Landon was losing it. He was never going to go along with anything. He was going to go to the dean about Professor Harrington. He was going to take all of us down, unless we forced him to our side."

"How could he be on your side if he was dead?"

"That wasn't the plan," Drew snapped. "We were going to set him up. I poured him a drink, and when he wasn't looking, I put a drug into it. Just something to make him stay put and forget the whole night. When he woke up in the morning, he'd just think he'd gotten drunk. But there would be photos of him and an underage girl. It would look like he had sex with her and knocked her around. If he didn't do what we wanted, he'd be kicked out of school, arrested, embarrassed, and his life would be a shambles."

She shook her head in disbelief. "You are sickening. How could you do that to your friend?"

"He wasn't being a friend," Drew said in an uncaring tone.

She realized then that Drew had no real feelings, no heart, no emotions, except greed and desire. But she needed to hear the rest—every last horrifying detail. "If killing him wasn't the plan, how did he end up dead?"

"The drug made him crazy, not relaxed the way it was supposed to work. I left the room to talk to Henry, to get the girl, and when I got back, Landon was gone. We tried to find him, but we didn't see him in the woods, and he wasn't at his apartment. It turns out he stumbled and fell into the pond, just the way everyone said."

"That was convenient for you, which is why I don't believe it," she said hotly.

"It's what happened. It was an accident."

"You caused the accident. You drugged him. Why didn't that show up in the toxicology report?"

He waved his hand as if that was the stupidest question he'd ever heard. "Because evidence can be tampered with. People can be bought."

"Investigations can be shut down," she said heavily.

His evil smile sent a chill down her arms.

"Did you and Henry do it alone? Or did your fathers help?"

"Everyone helped. Every parent of a kid in that fraternity was concerned that their son would be in trouble. Many calls were made. I didn't have to do a thing. Only a few people knew what really happened."

"But Henry knew what you did. You two were in it together."

"We're brothers."

"Landon was your brother, too."

"Not when it counted," Drew said harshly.

She hated that Landon had run from the frat house, probably knowing something was terribly wrong, but not being able to escape. She just prayed that he'd been so out of it he hadn't really known what was happening, that his death had come quickly and not painfully.

She looked back at Drew. "He never did anything to hurt you."

"He was going to hurt me. He was going to destroy me. I couldn't let that happen. And it didn't have to be that way. We weren't going to cut him out. We could have all gotten rich together."

"You already had his notebooks. Why did he have to die? You had what you needed?"

"Not all of it. Some of it was on his laptop."

"Which you stole along with his phone."

"When he first passed out, yes, but that was because I was going to hold the information over his head. Once we had the notebooks and his computer, we could force him to finish building the algorithm."

"So, it wasn't done?" she asked in surprise.

"No. And some of the information was false. Some of his later notes changed the way it worked."

"He was trying to protect it from you," she said, realizing the truth. "He must have anticipated you were going to try to steal it, and he changed key points to prevent you from making it work. That's why he had the videos from his apartment and your room."

"Yeah, I found that camera the day after he died. He was spying on me."

"He didn't trust you, and he had good reason." She paused. "Is that why it's taken you six years to get to this point? You killed the brains behind the algorithm, and then you had no one to finish it."

His lips tightened. "Most of it was there. It just took a little longer than we thought to bring it to fruition. But it's ready now, and we are going to be very, very rich. Landon built the perfect weapon for financial warfare, and he didn't even realize it."

"He realized it; he just wasn't evil."

"Maybe not, but he's dead." Drew gave her a hard look. "I thought we were done with him a long time ago, until that stupid woman started digging up the past."

"How did you find out about Sabrina?"

"She was digging into one of our test company's stock drops, and we have had people in place to watch for that for a very long time. When she went to see Harrington, we knew she was putting the entire picture together."

"So you had her killed," she said flatly.

Drew's gaze shifted to Viktor, who stared at her with an inscrutable expression. Then Drew turned back to her. "I'm not a killer, Haley."

"You just have others do your dirty work."

"Why would I do it any other way? I am my father's son after all."

The mix of admiration and hatred in his voice startled her with its force. "Is this about your father? About being better than him?"

"Now you sound like Trent. Of course, it's not just about my father, but I will take great joy in watching his financial collapse."

"You're going after your dad's company?"

"I'm going after all of them. Because you and your FBI friends have been interfering, we had to move up the timeline, but it doesn't matter. We're ready. In less than three hours, we're going to trigger the largest financial collapse in history. It will take out the leading candidate for president. He'll lose all his money, and so will his donors. When the dust settles, the old guard will have lost everything," he said with smug and evil satisfaction. "It's time for change. My father, his precious alumni network, all these old men who think they rule the world—they've had their turn. Now it's ours."

"You're insane. You're going to destroy millions of lives because you want to take down your father?"

"He's just a piece of delightful collateral damage. He thinks I'm stupid, that I can't compete with him, that I would never be worthy of running his company. That's why I went out on my own, why I created a dozen shell companies, all of which are going to benefit tremendously while he watches his investments go to zero. And the beauty of it is that no one will ever know what happened. Your brother's algorithm will trigger cascading failures across multiple markets simultaneously. We'll profit from the chaos while everyone else scrambles to understand what went wrong. And in the end, they won't be able to prove anything."

"Someone will figure it out. The FBI is already on to you."

"I have people in place to make sure that investigation doesn't touch us. We own pieces of the system at every level,

Haley. You can't stop us. We're invincible. Haven't you figured that out yet?"

She felt sick to her stomach. "You and your friends are already rich. You already have so much. When will it be enough?"

"It will never be enough until we have everything." He paused. "You didn't have to end up here. All you had to do was look away, go on with your life."

"I could never look away from my brother. And you're wrong that there won't be evidence. Landon left something behind. The FBI has already decrypted it. They're going to stop you."

"They'll be too busy looking for you." Drew checked his watch. "This was fun, but it's almost time for your final performance." He gave Viktor a nod. "Once I get to Branson, I'll text you."

"What final performance?" she asked.

"You're going to call Agent Lawson and tell him where to find you."

"I don't know where I am, so how can I tell him?"

"We'll make sure you have enough information for him to find you. He and his FBI buddies will be desperate to do that, turning all their attention from me to you. At the right time, he'll come running to save you, and when he does, this warehouse will become his tomb along with yours and everyone who comes with him."

Terror ran through her as Drew and Viktor walked toward the door, leaving the third man behind to watch her. There was no way she would tell Matt where she was and lead him to his death. She would never do that. She cared about him too much. She couldn't imagine letting him get hurt. She wanted him to have a long life. She wanted him to have love and a family of his own. She wanted that so much, because she was falling in love with him.

Tears filled her eyes. She wished she'd told him that. Although maybe it was better that she hadn't. He would blame himself for whatever happened to her. She knew that, and she didn't want him to feel guilty, because she'd spent the past six years living in that kind of hell, and she wouldn't wish it on anyone.

So, she wouldn't call him. Maybe they'd put a bullet through her if she didn't. But at least, she wouldn't betray him. She'd save his life even if she couldn't save hers.

———

They'd gotten the lights back on an hour ago, but Matt's anger at himself for sending Haley into the breakroom alone had him impatiently raging on the inside as Derek and the others tried to figure out how someone had gotten past their security measures, accessed the building, and kidnapped Haley.

When the power had first gone out, he'd thought it was about Trent, that they were trying to get to him. But instead, they'd grabbed Haley. He still didn't quite understand it, although as time passed, and all their resources were focused on getting Haley back, he wondered if that wasn't the point. They'd needed a distraction to buy time, and what better way than to kidnap Haley?

He tried to convince himself that they would keep her alive, at least for a while. But how long did they have? It had already been an hour, and they were getting nowhere fast. Trent had been steadfast in saying he had no idea where she was or why they'd taken her. He'd even agreed to call his sister, to pretend to have slipped away from them, to be in hiding, so she would talk to him more freely, but Jill had said she couldn't talk, that he should stay quiet or something bad could happen to him. There had been real fear in her voice, as if she'd suddenly realized that she was in the middle of something very dangerous.

He sighed as he looked around the now much busier room. Jason had called in more agents to not only help find Haley but also to locate Henry, Drew, Jill, Kyle, and Viktor. It should have made him feel better to see more agents at work, but the deep pain in his gut for Haley was the only thing he could feel.

He'd let her down. He'd promised to keep her safe, and now... he couldn't even contemplate what she was going through. He felt so connected to her that her pain was his pain, her fear was his fear. His emotions were tying him up in knots. And he had to get off that agonizing rollercoaster. He had to compartmentalize, to stay focused. It was the only way he could save her.

A moment later, his phone rang. He'd reactivated it once they'd left the safehouse. "Agent Lawson."

"This is Julia Harper. I don't know if Haley told you about me."

"She did. What do you want?"

"I know where Haley is. She's in trouble."

"Where?" he asked sharply.

"It's a warehouse by the airport, fourteen Crane Way. It belongs to Viktor Danilovich."

"How do you know she's there?"

"Because I've been following Drew Sanderson, and he arrived shortly after a gray van pulled up at the loading dock. I saw them carry Haley inside."

"How many are there?"

"At least two men besides Viktor and Drew. I would have gone in after her, but I couldn't take them all down by myself."

"We're on our way. Hang tight. Call me back if there's any movement or action at the warehouse."

He was on his feet before he finished speaking, and within minutes, they were headed across town to the airport. He and Jason were in one car with Agents Andi Hart and Nick Caruso in another.

"Are you concerned this might be a trap?" Jason asked as he sped down the freeway.

"Yes," he said flatly. "It seems very convenient that Julia is telling us exactly where Haley is."

"What do you know about her?"

"Not much. Former LAPD detective who worked on Landon's case. Haley trusted her. She said Julia was the only one who was trying to solve Landon's murder, and she left the force about six months after that to become a private investigator because she was disgusted by what happened on Landon's investigation. She could still be trustworthy, or maybe she was just playing Haley all those years ago, trying to keep the desperate older sister at bay so they wouldn't have to come up with more proof that Landon's death wasn't an accident." He shot Jason a look. "I don't want the team to walk into a trap. You should all stay outside while I go in alone."

"That's not the way this works. We're a team. We're doing this together. And we'll figure out if it's a trap before we go inside."

"If we have that kind of time. I have a bad feeling, Jason."

Jason gave him a knowing look. "I know. This case has become personal to you, and I've been in your shoes, worrying that someone might die because I can't get there in time. Hopefully, we will get there in time."

Hopefully...the word echoed through his head like a constant silent prayer.

————

The buzzing of a phone sent the man who'd been left to watch over her out of the room and while he was gone, Haley desperately tried to free herself.

This was her chance. Maybe her only chance.

She was zip-tied to a wooden chair in the middle of the main warehouse floor, surrounded by rows of tall metal shelving units that stretched toward the ceiling. Most were empty, casting long shadows under the harsh industrial lighting. Stacks of wooden pallets and abandoned equipment created a maze of hiding spots toward the back of the building.

She tested the zip ties again. The ones around her wrists

were tight enough to cut off circulation, but the tie around her left ankle had some give to it. She kicked off her sneaker and began working her bare foot, twisting and pulling despite the plastic edges cutting into her skin.

In the upstairs office, behind frosted glass, she could see shadows, at least three people. Their voices grew louder as there appeared to be some sort of argument going on, which was a good opportunity for her to try to escape while they were distracted.

Her left foot was almost free. Blood trickled down her ankle where the zip tie had torn the skin, but she kept pulling, biting back a cry of pain as the plastic finally slipped over her heel.

One foot free.

The voices upstairs grew louder. Someone's voice rose above the others. "Should just finish her now. Too risky to wait..."

Then Viktor's voice rang out loud and clear. "Enough! I give the orders. When I get to Branson, I'll send you a text. Only then will you act."

Sensing their conversation was ending and that one of the guards might be returning soon, she struggled to her feet, the chair still attached to her right leg and weighing her down. She tried to hop toward the back of the warehouse, but the chair was heavier than she'd expected, and the scraping sound it made against the concrete was too loud.

She needed a different plan. Looking around, she spotted several concrete support pillars hidden behind the shelves. If she could get the chair to one of those posts and break the leg...

She hopped forward, happy to be a little further away, even if she wasn't yet free. When she reached the pillar, she began ramming the wooden chair leg against the concrete, over and over, trying to break it. Each impact echoed through the warehouse, but she couldn't hear or see anyone from this vantage point. Maybe they'd left. Maybe the guard had gone outside. Or maybe they were about to discover what she was doing and put an end to her escape and her life.

She had no idea, but she had to keep trying.

On the fourth impact, she felt the chair leg splinter. Three more hits and it cracked completely, freeing her right foot.

Now she had to get her arms free. The zip ties around her wrists were still secure, but with both feet free and the chair broken, she was able to slip her arms over the back of the chair, her shoulders screaming in protest, but finally, she was away from the chair. Her hands were still tied behind her back, but she could run.

As she started toward the back of the warehouse, she heard a shout. Someone had realized she was gone.

She looked around for cover. The shelving units were too exposed, but there was a cluster of equipment and pallets near the far wall that might hide her.

She moved as quietly as she could, staying low and using the shadows between the overhead lights. Her bare feet made almost no sound on the concrete, but every breath seemed impossibly loud.

She'd just reached the pallets when she heard another man yell, "Viktor said to forget her. They're here. It's time."

His footsteps moved away, and she let out a breath in relief, which was short-lived. If Matt was here and the warehouse was wired to explode, she had to warn him. She emerged from her hiding place and ran toward the back of the building. There was a rolling door by what appeared to be a loading dock. It was thirty yards away and probably locked, but it was her only way out, as any guards would probably be in front. She ran for her life, praying she would be fast enough...

CHAPTER TWENTY-SIX

Matt met Julia just outside the warehouse parking lot. There were no cars in the lot, but lights were visible from one of the windows.

Julia Harper got out of her car. She was in her fifties, a tall woman with brown hair and eyes that were tense and worried. "Drew Sanderson left fifteen minutes ago. Viktor departed five minutes ago, and two men just drove out of the parking lot."

"Haley?" he demanded.

"Haven't seen her leave. I think she's still in there."

"We're going in," he decided. They were all wearing protective gear, weapons at the ready. "Jason and I will take the front. Andi, you and Nick take the back."

"Be careful," Julia warned. "I can't think why they'd leave her alone, unless they've wired the building. If you try to breach, this could go badly."

"Understood." They needed to be careful, but careful was the last thing he wanted to be. He wanted to rush inside and get to Haley before she was hurt, but Julia was right. The building could be a trap, a way to take out the entire team. "No one goes inside until we check for explosives."

As they entered the parking lot, they split apart. They hadn't taken more than ten steps toward the building when the explosion hit, sending them all flying as debris rained down upon them.

Heart pounding, ears ringing, he stumbled to his feet, horror running through him as he realized the entire warehouse was engulfed in flames. "No," he shouted. "Haley!"

He heard Jason call him back, telling him there could be more explosions to come, but he didn't care. If he could still save her, he had to try.

He ran toward the back of the building, which wasn't as heavily ablaze as the front. A huge portion of the wall had broken apart, and he plunged into the smoke-filled building. The heat was intense, and he could barely see three feet in front of him. The air was thick with smoke and chemical fumes from whatever had been stored in the warehouse.

He looked over his shoulder, shocked to see Jason right behind him.

"I'll go to the right, you take the left," Jason said.

He nodded, moving toward his left. "Haley!" he shouted. "Haley, where are you?" There was no answer. He probably had only minutes before the fire consumed the rest of the warehouse. "Haley," he shouted again in desperation, hearing Jason also yelling her name.

Finally, he heard a weak voice. "Here! I'm here!"

"Keep talking," he yelled, following her voice through a maze of burning debris. He found her crawling along the floor, hands tied behind her back, her clothes singed, her face streaked with blood and soot. "I've got you," he said, pulling her to her knees and putting his arms around her so he could finally believe she was all right. He hugged her tightly, then gave her a hard look. "Are you hurt? Can you walk?"

"I'm okay," she gasped. "We have to get out of here."

He helped her to her feet and shouted for Jason. The smoke was getting thicker, making it difficult to see, but as the air grew cooler, he knew they were close to the door. Then Jason appeared like a beacon in the night, and they made their way into the fresh air.

The fire engines were pulling up at the scene, the captain asking if anyone else was still inside. Haley shook her head, and Matt ushered her across the parking lot to where their group was waiting. Andi cut Haley free from her ties, and she gratefully pulled her arms to her sides, then rubbed her fingers together.

"I need to get you to the hospital," he said, seeing small cuts on her forehead and not knowing how much smoke she had inhaled or what else they'd done to her.

"I'm fine," she said, sending him a reassuring look. "We need to stop Drew. It's happening tonight. They're launching the algorithm."

"We don't know where he is," he said heavily.

"I heard Viktor say Branson. I don't know if it's a street or a building, but it's where they were meeting," she added.

He turned to Jason, who was already on the phone, then he looked back at Haley. "I'm going to have someone take you to the hospital while we look for Drew."

"No way. I'm staying with you," she said forcefully.

He couldn't argue with her because he wasn't sure he could let her out of his sight, either.

"How did you find me?" she asked. "They were going to make me call and tell you where I was. Then, once you came, they would blow up the building with all of us inside. I wasn't going to do it. I would never lure you into a trap. But then something changed. They said you were already here, and they left. Then the building blew up." She paused. "I was so worried you were already inside."

"I wasn't. And I'm here because of Julia." He stepped back as Julia came forward.

"You knew where I was, Julia?" Haley asked in bemusement. "How?"

"I've been following Drew and some of the others since the

attack on Professor Harrington. I always had a bad feeling about Drew, and it looks like I was right. I never thought he was as dumb as everyone thought he was. I would have come in after you, but I thought the FBI would have more manpower. I didn't want to get you hurt, Haley, by acting impulsively. That's the last thing I would want. But when the building exploded..." Her voice drifted away as her face tensed. "I was afraid I'd waited too long."

"I'm okay. And thank you for reaching out to Matt, to the FBI." Haley paused. "But why didn't you tell me you were following Drew?"

"I wasn't sure I'd find anything. I didn't want to raise your hopes and then let you down again. You've been disappointed too many times."

"Got it," Jason said, interrupting their conversation. "Viktor Danilovich owns a shell company, whose building is located at two-ten Branson Street. It's only two miles from here. Derek said it looks like a data center."

"That has to be where they're launching the algorithm," he said. "Let's go."

As Haley got into the backseat, he jumped in beside Jason, while Andi and Nick, as well as Julia, followed behind.

"Derek told me someone started running automated trades through multiple offshore accounts ten minutes ago," Jason said as he raced down the street. "It looks like pre-launch action for the algorithm. Derek will meet us at the site. We may need him to shut everything down."

"Good idea." Matt glanced back at Haley, hoping she was as okay as she'd said she was. "This is almost over," he told her.

"It has to be," she said. "Drew was responsible for Landon's death. He told me everything. He wanted me to know how smart and brilliant he really was and also how evil."

"Drew killed your brother?"

"He drugged him. He and Henry were going to set Landon up with some underage girl and blackmail him, but when they left him alone, he came to, and he stumbled out of the house and fell into the pond." Her voice broke. "Drew might not have pushed Landon into that pond, but he's responsible."

"He might have pushed him in and just didn't want to tell you."

"Either way, we have to get him."

"We will," he said, even more motivated to take Drew down. Haley deserved justice, and so did her brother. He wanted to ask more questions, but they were almost there, and the focus had to be on taking Drew and his team down and stopping the launch of the algorithm.

They went back and forth on comms with Nick, Andi, and Derek, setting their plan of attack, and when they pulled into an office park ten minutes later, the team was ready to go.

Wanting to use the element of surprise, they parked around the corner from the address registered to the shell company. Derek got out of a van when they arrived, wearing safety gear. Matt was somewhat surprised to see him in field agent mode, but he was as well-trained as they were.

"Two guards at the front entrance," Derek said. "No idea how many people are inside."

He turned to Haley, who was still in the car, but with the door open. Julia had parked and was now walking toward them. "You two stay out here," he said. "Julia, I'm counting on you to keep Haley safe."

"I will," Julia promised.

He gave Haley a pointed look. "No matter what you hear, do not follow us inside."

"All right. Be careful, Matt."

He wasn't going to be careful; he was going to take down Drew and his entire operation. But he gave her a nod and then led the team forward. Andi and Nick headed to the back of the building, while he and Jason took the front, with Derek staying a few feet behind them.

He approached the front guard from his blind spot. The man

was focused on the parking lot entrance. He moved quickly behind him, snaking his arm around the guard's throat, cutting off blood flow to the brain. The guard struggled for maybe ten seconds before going limp. Matt lowered him quietly to the pavement. A moment later, Andi's voice came through his earpiece: "Rear clear."

He and Jason entered the building, guns drawn. They met up with Andi and Nick in the hallway, who would clear the first floor while he and Jason moved up the stairs, with Derek following. He cracked the door open, seeing another guard in the hallway outside a glass-walled data center that was buzzing with activity.

Drew stood next to Henry and Viktor while a young man worked on a computer terminal.

Andi's voice rang through his ear, telling him the first floor was clear, and they were on their way up the stairs. As Andi, Nick and Derek reached them, he saw another guard had joined the one in the hallway. They were talking to each other, then one reached for his phone, asking someone to check in. They would soon realize the security was compromised.

He pushed open the door, gun drawn. "Federal agents, drop your weapons," he shouted.

The guards lifted their weapons, but they were faster. He took the first one down, and Jason, the second. Then they moved down the corridor and into the data center.

Viktor turned and started shooting along with the man who had been sitting at the computer.

Glass exploded as bullets flew across the room. Henry dropped to his knees as a bullet caught him in the leg, and he screamed with pain as he pressed himself under a desk.

His team advanced into the room, dodging gunfire, hitting Viktor in the chest and shoulder, the other man in the arm. When all the combatants were finally down and the shooting had stopped, Derek ran to the computer terminal, to the screen that was scrolling with data.

"You're too late," Henry gasped. "It's already happening."

He gave Henry a hard look. "It's not too late for you to go to jail."

"Need help. Need a doctor," Henry begged.

"Don't worry. You'll live." He looked around the room. The team had secured the other men with zip ties and removed their weapons, but there was one person missing—Drew.

He swore. "Where the hell is Drew?" he demanded, his gut tightening as he saw an open door behind the bank of computer terminals.

———

Every gunshot made her flinch. Haley sat in the back seat of the vehicle next to Julia, her hands clenched so tightly her knuckles were white.

"It's okay," Julia said, but her own voice was tight with worry. "They know what they're doing."

"But we don't know how many people are inside. They could be outnumbered. We have to help."

"I promised to stay here with you," Julia said, but Haley could see the frustration in her eyes. Julia wanted to be in the battle, too.

She suddenly saw movement to the side of the building—a figure running toward the back of the complex.

"There," she pointed. "Someone's running away. We have to stop him."

"You're not going anywhere," Julia said firmly. "I'll check it out. Stay here."

"They went behind that building," she said, pointing to the building to the right.

After Julia left, Haley opened the car door and got out. She was parked out of sight of the main building, but she could hear more shots being fired, and then she heard a woman scream. Julia was in trouble.

She had to help. She ran around one building and then another, until she saw Julia struggling with a man in the shadows. They were fighting over her gun. It suddenly went off, flying out of Julia's hands and down the pavement toward Haley.

She rushed forward and grabbed the weapon as Julia sank to the ground, and the other man turned to face her.

"Drew," she breathed, pointing the weapon at him. "Stop right there."

"You're not going to shoot me," he said, but there wasn't as much confidence in his voice now.

"You killed my brother. Why wouldn't I shoot you?"

"Because you're not a murderer."

"I could be," she said, thinking how much she would like to wipe that smug look off his face. Her finger tightened on the trigger. Six years of grief and rage and sleepless nights merged into this moment.

This man had drugged Landon and had caused his death. He was responsible for Sabrina's death, for Brooke's stabbing, for Harrington getting shot. Maybe it hadn't been him alone, but he'd been at the center of all of it, especially what had happened to Landon.

"You betrayed my brother. You stole his life. Why shouldn't I take yours? Why shouldn't I make sure you can't pay off a judge or an FBI agent or whoever you'll use to get yourself out of this when I can end it right now?"

Her arm was starting to shake with tension, but her finger was still on the trigger, ready to squeeze off a shot.

Drew put up a hand. "I told you I didn't kill Landon. I was just going to set him up. Put down the gun, Haley."

"No," she said flatly, shaking her head. "You're not getting out of this. I'm not going to let you."

"Haley!" Matt's voice rang out behind her as he came running toward her.

"Stop," she said, without looking at him. "Go away, Matt. You don't need to be here."

"You can't shoot him," Matt said, keeping a few feet between them as he came around to her side.

She flung him a quick glance. "If I don't, he'll get away. He'll buy his way out of this."

"He won't. He's going to prison for a long time," Matt said. "Think about how his life will be there, this rich, privileged kid in general population. He'll be a target every day for the rest of his life."

"He'll buy off the guards. Buy off the warden. He always gets away." Her voice cracked. "Not this time."

"Look at me," Matt said softly. "Look at me, not him."

She glanced over, seeing the understanding in his eyes.

"This isn't who you are," he said. "Would Landon want you to do this?"

And suddenly, she could hear her brother's voice in her head, as clear as if he were standing beside her: *This isn't who we are, Haley. It's who they are.*

He was right. Her brother was always right.

Slowly, carefully, she lowered the weapon.

Matt took it out of her hands as Jason took Drew into custody, and Andi attended to Julia, who was slowly getting to her feet.

Matt handed the weapon to Nick, and then he put his arms around her shaking body. "Thanks for stopping Drew from getting away," he said.

"Julia did it. I stayed in the car until I heard her scream. I couldn't stay after that."

"I know," he said, gazing into her eyes with admiration. "You are definitely not short on courage."

"What happened inside? I heard so many gunshots. I was really worried about you." She paused, hearing a flood of sirens. "Are people dead?"

"Viktor is deceased. He wasn't going down any other way. Henry is injured, but he'll live. There are some other injuries, not sure if any others will be fatal, but we stopped the launch of the algorithm. Derek was able to minimize the damage. It's over, Haley. It's finally over."

CHAPTER TWENTY-SEVEN

Three hours later, at a little past midnight, Matt came into the breakroom of his office, where he'd put Haley under the watchful eye of another agent this time. He'd been in and out to check on her every twenty minutes, not willing to let her out of his sight for very long, but there had been a lot to do. He knew she was probably exhausted and wanted nothing more than to go home and go to sleep, but he'd had to make sure they had everyone in custody before letting her go anywhere else.

She gave him a weary smile. "Are you done?"

"Just about. You can go," he told the other agent. "Thanks."

"What's happened?" Haley asked when they were alone.

He sat down on the couch next to her. "Henry Adler is in the hospital, undergoing surgery. He's expected to survive. His father, Graham Adler, has hired the best defense attorney in town for his son."

"I'm sure," she said cynically. "Those fathers are going to protect their sons, just like they did before."

"Not all of them. Kent Sanderson was stunned to realize that his son, Drew, was plotting his downfall. The early moves that we were unable to stop hit Kent's holdings hard. He lost a lot of money even before the algorithm launched. He's not offering to pay for Drew's defense. In fact, he's disavowing all knowledge of anything."

"He turns on his own. Those families are sick," she said.

"Speaking of families...we picked up Jill Adler. She was eager to make a deal. She's rolling on everyone, giving us all the details, all the players, including the moles in the FBI: Shari and Director Markham. Because of the complicity of those agents and the LA field office, we're handling all the interrogations here, but we'll be getting some help from agents in our San Diego office. They just arrived a short time ago."

"What about Charles Adler?"

"Jill said her father knew about the algorithm and was positioned to make money when it launched. She also stated that Trent had nothing to do with it and wanted no part of it. She claimed she had no idea things were going to get so violent, that Brooke would be hurt, almost killed. She also started to panic then, but it was too late to get out."

"I don't feel sorry for her."

"I don't, either," he agreed.

"And Kyle Vance? Did he know his girlfriend was on the hit list?"

"No. He was terrified to talk after what happened to Brooke, but once we told him Viktor was dead, he opened up. Drew and Henry were the leaders. Viktor was the muscle and was in charge of hiring mercenaries on the dark web, the gunman who shot Sabrina Lin, and the men who attacked Brooke Mercer and Justin Harrington. We arrested Viktor's men at the warehouse, and some of them are giving us information on Viktor's operation as well. We will take down every last one of his cohorts, but he's dead, so he's done."

"Do you think you have everyone that matters now?"

"We have everyone connected to the algorithm, but, no, we don't have everyone from the Westbridge alumni system, who have been buying and selling favors with judges, politicians, FBI agents..." He saw the disheartened look in her eyes. "But we have a lot to go on. And people like this are always looking to sell someone else out to save themselves."

"I hate the idea of any of them getting a deal."

"I know. But we want to arrest as many people as possible, and sometimes that information is worth a deal."

She let out a sigh. "I can't believe this is over, Matt. I wasn't sure we'd ever get to them. That we'd ever get justice for Landon."

"You're a big reason why we did," he said, meeting her gaze. "I haven't forgotten your brother in all of this, Haley."

She gave him an emotional smile. "I know, and I appreciate that, Matt."

"I don't know if we'll ever find out more than what we already know about the night he died, but I'll do everything I can to get the complete story and to make sure they all pay."

Her chest rose as she drew in a deep breath. "I'm sure you will. You've been amazing through all of this."

"So have you. Why don't we call it a night? This investigation is going to take weeks, not days. We need to pace ourselves."

"Okay," she said as he helped her to her feet. "But I don't want to go home. My place is still a mess from the break-in."

"How about my apartment? You have some clothes there."

She gave him a tired smile. "That sounds good."

He led her out of the office, keeping her hand in his as they made their way down to the garage and into the car. He knew they were safe, but he still didn't want to let her go.

———

As Matt let her into his apartment, Haley felt like she was coming home. It was such a strange feeling, because she'd only spent two nights here before they'd had to go to the safehouse. But it wasn't really the apartment that made her feel safe and warm and protected; it was the man in front of her.

"Do you want something?" he asked. "Water, food? I can't remember when we last ate."

"I'm not hungry, and I drank a gallon of water in the break-room to get rid of the smoke in my throat."

His gaze moved to the bandage on her head. While he had been interviewing the suspects, a medic had come into his office to clean her cuts and make sure she wasn't suffering any damage from smoke inhalation.

"If I hadn't gotten to you in time..." He shook his head, his lips tight. "I never would have forgiven myself. It was my fault you got kidnapped. I shouldn't have left you alone for even a second."

"You had no idea they could find a way into your security system."

"Which needs to be better," he said with annoyance. "You should have been safe there. Apparently, someone in the LA field office who had worked with Flynn had the security code, and Rebecca Markham was able to get it from him."

"Are those FBI agents really going to be held accountable?"

"They've already been suspended pending further investigation. Replacements are being sent to review all the employees in that office. Apparently, the regional director has a personal grudge against the Westbridge alumni network. He went to USC."

She gave a faint smile. "Thank God! Someone who didn't drink the Westbridge Kool-Aid." She walked over to the couch and sat down, with Matt sliding in next to her.

She slipped off the flip-flops that Julia had given her while they'd been waiting outside the data center, having realized she'd left her shoes in the warehouse. Fortunately, Julia had had the sandals in her car. Which reminded her...

"Have you heard anything about Julia's condition?"

"The bullet didn't hit any vital organs. They stitched her up and sent her home."

"Thank goodness. I'm glad Julia turned out to be the person

I thought she was, and that she wasn't part of Landon's case being shut down or anything that happened to me now," she said, turning to Matt. "You did make me doubt her motives."

"I was wrong."

"You were right to be cautious, but I am glad you were wrong about her. In the end, she saved my life when she called you. I'm just glad you didn't come through the front door a few minutes earlier."

"I wish you hadn't had to go through that." He put a comforting hand on her leg. "We haven't talked about what happened there. And we don't have to do that now. But whenever you're ready, I'll listen."

She turned sideways on the couch so she could look into his eyes. "I told you what Drew said about drugging Landon so he and Henry could set him up with an underage girl and then blackmail him."

"Yes. But the drug didn't render Landon unconscious."

"No. But it was disorienting. He stumbled out of the room, the fraternity house, and down the hill. I guess he fell into the pond. I'm not sure if I'll ever really know if that's exactly what happened, or if Drew or Henry followed him and pushed him in. The bottom line is that Drew caused Landon's death when he put that drug in his drink, but I'm not sure we can prove it. Although, when I asked why the drug didn't show up in the toxicology report, Drew laughed at me and said reports can always be changed. So maybe there's a trail we can find leading to that bit of bribery. I really want Drew to pay for my brother's murder, not just everything else."

"I know. We'll try to make that happen. It's not as clear-cut as I wish it were."

She nodded. "I understand. Drew also said that Landon had planted false information in his notebooks, that he'd made it harder for them to use the algorithm. That's why it took so long for them to make it work. Landon slowed them down, so we had enough time to catch them."

"Your brother was very smart."

She nodded, thinking about everything that had happened, especially one pivotal moment. "I really wanted to shoot Drew today, and I've never shot anyone. But I wanted him to die. I know that's not good."

"It's a very human emotion. You loved your brother, and Drew took him away from you."

"But it would have been wrong. I heard Landon's voice in my head: *'This is who they are, Haley. It's not who we are.'* And I realized he was right. I didn't want to be the same as them. I wanted to be better."

"You are a hell of a lot better, Haley. They're scum. And when we're done with them, their lives are going to be worth nothing." He reached out and brushed a strand of hair away from her eyes. "You look exhausted. You should go to sleep. We can talk about everything tomorrow."

"Are we going to keep talking? Not just about the case or my brother... " She licked her lips. "But about other stuff. Or is *this* over, too?"

A wary gleam entered his brown eyes. "Do you want it to be over?"

"No. And it feels a little scary to say that. It hurt so badly when I lost Landon, I never wanted to get that close to anyone else, until now, until you. But I know that this relationship, or whatever it is, has been forged in danger and adrenaline-fueled nights. Maybe it was never meant to last longer than the case."

"I have never wanted to get that close to anyone, either," he said. "Watching my parents' marriage fall apart, feeling split between people who had gone from love to hate in what seemed like such a short time, made me cautious. Love seemed like too big of a risk. It was safer to keep everything casual."

"So, this is casual?"

He immediately shook his head. "That's not what I meant. That's how I felt before I met you. But you are a force of nature, Haley Kenton, and you have broken down every one of my walls.

I have never met anyone who loves so loyally, so fiercely, who would literally die not just for the person she loved but for their memory. I had lost faith in people over the past few years, but you made me see I was just not spending time with the right people." He paused. "I think we should see what could happen between us."

Relief ran through her. "I think we should, too. Frankly, I can't imagine not seeing you when I wake up in the morning or talking to you before I go to bed at night. But maybe after everything calms down, we'll be bored with each other."

He laughed. "Not a chance. You and I will never be boring."

She grinned back. "That's probably true. Because you're going to keep working for the FBI, and I'm going to keep trying to put a spotlight on corruption."

"Seems like we have a whole lot more trouble to get into."

"And a whole lot more excitement. I think we should start now."

"You're exhausted."

"I'm..." She shrugged. "I actually don't know what I am. So many feelings are running through me. Relief, a sense of freedom, and satisfaction that people are going to pay for what they did to me and my brother, and what they were going to do to hurt so many more people. But I also feel happy because we're together. We're alive." She paused, then decided to put it all on the table. "And because I'm falling in love with you, Matt."

He sucked in a quick breath. "I'm falling in love with you, too."

"Then we don't need to wait for anything, do we?"

"Not even for a second." He covered her mouth with his, and the warmth of their embrace, their kiss, their love, filled her to the brim. All her lonely feelings evaporated in Matt's arms. And as she kissed him back, she wanted to fill those hollow spaces inside him. Apart, they'd been a little broken, but together they were finally whole.

EPILOGUE

Three months later...

The Library Café near the Westbridge campus was busy for a Tuesday morning, filled with students hunched over laptops and professors grading papers. Haley sat at a corner table, her laptop open, putting the final touches on her investigative series exposing corruption in elite academic institutions. It was a three-part series, and the first part, focusing on Westbridge, had already garnered widespread attention, especially with the media avid for information to enhance their reporting on the upcoming trials of the key players.

Drew Sanderson and Henry Adler had been charged with multiple crimes and denied bail. She loved that they were still sitting in prison, away from their fancy lives, designer suits, and expensive homes. The rich boys had finally been brought down to earth.

Jill, Trent, and Brooke had all made deals for immunity while revealing evidence about the conspiracy network. Kyle Vance, Charles Adler, and Graham Adler were in the midst of making plea deals, and the individuals responsible for Brooke's stabbing and Justin Harrington's attack had also been arrested and charged with multiple crimes, including attempted murder.

The LA field office of the FBI had undergone a thorough audit with the director, Rebecca Markham, and Matt's former partner, Shari Drummond, now awaiting trials for fraud, obstruction of justice, and other charges. Two other individuals at the FBI were also being investigated.

Senator Matson was under investigation as well but had yet to be officially charged as they continued to build a case against him.

The entire Westbridge alumni network had come under a great deal of scrutiny, and there were now other journalists, as well as the FBI and the police, who were working on uncovering crimes, bribes, and payoffs committed by other individuals tied to the university. It would take a while to catch everyone, and there would probably be people who slipped through the cracks, but the school's reputation and alumni network had been severely damaged.

As for the launch of the algorithm, the market had bounced back after the warm-up fall, and thankfully, fully recovered without the chaos and mayhem that Drew and Henry had desired.

Kent Sanderson's company had lost a lot of money, and while he'd been oblivious to his son's dangerous intent, his reputation had taken a hit, and his investors were leaving him in droves, lowering his net worth by a great deal.

Also, in the plus column, Anthony Devray's complaints against Meridien Developments were now being reinvestigated, and Matt was determined to make sure the players responsible for the fraud at Meridien went down, and Anthony could finally be free.

But the most satisfying result for her personally was that Landon's algorithm was now being used by the SEC to detect and prevent exactly the kind of financial crimes that had killed him. Her brother's work was finally going to help protect investors, the way he'd wanted.

"Mind if I join you?"

She looked up to see Matt standing beside her table, holding two cups of coffee. He looked good—rested, happy, more relaxed than she'd seen him in months.

"I was wondering when you'd show up," she said, closing her laptop. "You said you'd be here by ten."

"I got caught at work. Looks like we're about to take down another Westbridge alum for corporate fraud."

"That seems to be never-ending. But I love it."

"So do I. That school will never be the same."

"Good."

He sat down across from her and sipped his coffee. "How are the last two parts of your series coming?"

"The second one is done and being published tomorrow. The third will go out next week. I have to say the series is opening more doors than I ever imagined. I got a call from two major news networks that want to interview me about my investigation that helped expose the biggest financial conspiracy in American history." She smiled. "It's the best story I've ever written. I just wish it hadn't come at such a high personal cost."

"Landon would be proud of you."

"He would be. And now that I know the truth, it's getting easier to remember happy times with my brother and not the way his life ended. I want to honor the good he did."

"You are doing that every day."

"I'm trying. What's happening with you?"

"I got a call today about a job in DC, a promotion, actually, if I want it."

Her eyes widened. "Really? That sounds big. But I thought you loved working for Flynn."

"I do. My life is here. I love my work, my team, and I love you. How could I leave?"

"But if it's a big promotion..."

"I don't need a promotion to be happy. I have what I want. I turned them down."

She gave him a searching look. "Are you sure you don't want to think about it?"

"Do you want me to think about it?" he challenged.

"I just don't want you to turn something down for me. I love living here and working at the *Sentinel*, but if you have a better opportunity elsewhere, Matt, I'll go with you. I can write anywhere. I want you to know that."

"That's very generous, Haley. But I'm good. I'm happy."

"Me, too," she said with a smile. She'd given up her apartment and moved into Matt's place two months earlier and was in the process of warming up his life in every possible way, including his décor.

They'd bickered about a few items, like an orange and red rug she'd wanted to put in the office, and the purple pillows for the bed, but those silly little arguments had ended in compromise and a passionate tumble in their beautiful bed.

"I never thought I'd feel so perfectly safe with someone, and I'm not talking about outside danger," she added. "You give me a sense of security that allows me to be myself, to let go of constantly trying to control everything, and just live in the moment."

"And you have not only brought the color back into my life in every possible way," he said with a teasing smile. "Every day you remind me that there is at least one good person in the world."

"There's more than one. You have to stop being cynical."

"You make that a lot easier." His gaze turned serious. "I mean that, Haley. You light up every room you're in, and I do not ever want to be out of your light."

Her eyes filled with moisture. "That's the sweetest thing anyone has ever said to me."

"It's the way I feel. I never wanted to risk everything I had on love, but you made me realize it's not a risk, but it's you."

"I feel that way, too. So, we're staying in LA?"

"We're staying together," he corrected, reaching across the table to take her hand. "Wherever you go, I go."

"And wherever you go, I go," she promised.

"I love you, Haley."

"I love you, too, Matt." She couldn't stop the smile from spreading across her face. "I feel so free now. I'm looking ahead instead of back. I'm not trapped in the past, not stuck on the worst night of my life. I can see the future, and it's amazing."

"It's going to be."

"I feel like Landon is free, too. His work will do the good he wanted, and the people who caused his death will suffer in a prison of their own making. He finally got justice."

"He always deserved it, and so did you." He squeezed her hand. "I think we should get married."

Her jaw dropped. "Are you seriously proposing to me in the middle of a coffee shop?"

He laughed and gave her a helpless shrug. "I'm sorry about the venue and the spontaneity. I'm not the most romantic person on the planet. But I do want to marry you, and I want you to know that. But I'll ask you again with dinner and candlelight and a ring," he said, shaking his head in disgust. "I can't believe I asked you to marry me without a ring."

"I don't want you to do it again. I love this moment because it's real. It's us. I don't need the other stuff. Every day with you is the best day of my life, and I will marry you." She leaned forward and gave him a kiss. "Thanks for believing in me, Matt. For always having my back. I hope you know I have yours, too."

"I do," he said, then laughed. "Oops, I said the words already. I am really jumping the gun today."

She grinned back at him, then leaned across the table to kiss him, knowing that they were already married to each other in their hearts, but one day soon they'd have a party to celebrate.

WHAT TO READ NEXT...

Want more thrilling romantic suspense? Check out my **LIGHTNING STRIKES TRILOGY** *that begins with:* **BEAUTIFUL STORM**

In these connected novels, lightning leads to love, danger, and the unraveling of long-buried secrets that will change not only the past but also the future...From #1 NY Times Bestselling Author Barbara Freethy comes the first book in a new romantic suspense trilogy: Lightning Strikes.

When her father's plane mysteriously disappeared in the middle of an electrical storm, Alicia Monroe became obsessed with lightning. Now a news photographer in Miami, Alicia covers local stories by day and chases storms at night. In a flash of lightning, she sees what appears to be a murder, but when she gets to the scene, there is no body, only a military tag belonging to Liliana Valdez, a woman who has been missing for two months.

While the police use the tag to jump-start their stalled investigation, Alicia sets off on her own to find the missing woman. Her search takes her into the heart of Miami's Cuban-American community, where she meets the attractive but brooding Michael Cordero, who has his own demons to vanquish.

Soon Alicia and Michael are not just trying to save Liliana's life but also their own, as someone will do anything to protect a dark secret...

The complete trilogy is now available! Grab it today!

ABOUT THE AUTHOR

Barbara Freethy is a #1 New York Times Bestselling Author of 85 novels ranging from mystery thrillers to romantic suspense, contemporary romance, and women's fiction. With over 15 million copies sold, twenty-eight of Barbara's books have appeared on the New York Times and USA Today Bestseller Lists.

Barbara is known for her twisty thrillers and emotionally riveting romance where ordinary people end up having extraordinary adventures.

For further information, visit www.barbarafreethy.com